I0576310

Murder at Heartbreak Ranch

Murder at Heartbreak Ranch

By S. M. Arthur

Shalako Press
P.O. Box 371
Oakdale, CA 95361

© 2020 S. M. Arthur. All rights reserved.

No part of this book may be reproduced, stored in a retrieval system, or transmitted by any means without the written permission of the author.

ISBN: 978-1-7340795-8-6

This is a work of fiction. All characters and events portrayed in this book are fictional, and any resemblance to real people is purely coincidental.

For information contact: Shalako Press
P.O. Box 371, Oakdale, CA 95361-0371
http://www.shalakopress.com

Cover design: Karen Borrelli

PRINTED IN THE UNITED STATES OF AMERICA

Author Acknowledgments

This novel is situated in western Colorado, more specifically the fictional city of Hawk, Colorado in the fictional County of Hawk (loosely based on Eagle County, Colorado). I grew up on a ranch in western Colorado and have fond memories of country life and the farm and ranch communities in that part of the state.

I'd like to thank Sisters in Crime and Rocky Mountain Fiction Writers for support, editing and critique services and general support.

My husband Jay Arthur, a writer himself and an avid reader, was the first to read this book, and I thank him for his encouragement, criticism and love. I'd also like to thank daughters Kristina and Kelly, who are always there for me.

I'd like to thank Major Mitchell of Shalako Press for his care and professionalism in publishing this book.

Dedication

For my husband Jay

Chapter 1

Friday at Heartbreak Ranch

Mona Morgan first knew something was wrong when her cattle dog, Bo, came back without Brian, panting and circling, the dog's crazy eyes looking crazier than usual. Mona took a deep breath and calmed her alarm. It wasn't like Bo to leave Brian. Wild horses couldn't drag the Border Collie away from the job. Bo hardly ever left Brian's side. She glanced at his cell phone, which lay next to hers on the table by the door. She felt her heart beating fast beneath her sweater. What if he'd broken an ankle? A leg?

Bo paced in a frantic wide circle.

"What is it Bo? Where's Brian? Do I need to go get him?"

The dog looked at her like he'd been waiting all this time, and what took her so long. She swallowed the panic that threatened to take over and render her useless. She slid her winter gloves over her long thin fingers, over the fingernails that hadn't been manicured since they left Denver. She pulled on the tall Hunter black rubber boots that she kept by the door and grabbed the emerald green cashmere cardigan that Brian had bought for her because he said the green brought up the green in her blue-green eyes. Blonds and red-heads should wear green, he'd always said. As if he was an expert. As she started out, she wrapped the belt of the sweater around her thin frame twice, thinking briefly with satisfaction how it had only wrapped around once when she had a desk job.

Guilty now for not moving faster, she told Bo she was sorry for not listening. Brian's beloved dog looked at her with the typical haunting eyes of the Border Collie, one icy blue and one brown. Bo let out a pathetic whine.

"I'm coming Bo," Mona said. She could almost hear Brian's admonition not to talk to the dog like he was a person.

She walked faster and followed Bo, her heart racing, hands shaking. She felt her legs begin to run, almost a sprint, although it was as if she were disconnected from her legs and they were doing it all on their own. Running. Out of breath. Walking. She'd forgotten her phone and her stomach sank at the thought of the two cell phones now, two missed opportunities lying side-by-side on the table. Hers and Brian's.

Mona got to the pasture in about seven minutes by her estimation, which was a rough uneven sprint down a furrowed alfalfa field. She had more than once turned an ankle walking the furrows. She pictured herself icing his ankle later. They'd drink scotch by the fire and ice each other's ankles. They'd laugh about this as they relaxed. She'd feel guilty about feeling sad earlier.

She tried to turn her fear into irritation. Brian should know better than to make her worry. Bo barked nervously and ran circles around her as she walked. He appeared to know the direction so she followed him. "You'd better be right." Bo stopped and looked back at her before continuing his mission.

Bo led her right to Brian as if he had a GPS in his brain, and looked up at her with those two odd eyes, one blue and one brown, like she was some kind of genie that could help his best friend.

"I don't have time for this Brian Morgan," she said.

She saw Brian's brown work boots first—the soles of them.

Brian lay face down in the ditch, his face resting between two clay furrows. Mona struggled to turn him over, her cold-numbed hands shaking violently. His Denver Bronco blue and orange ball cap lay by his side in the water. His full head of soft brown hair stood out like a long crew cut, exposing the red, leathered neck skin as furrowed as the field he lay in.

She knew she had wasted too much time. She should be doing CPR or something, but in her heart she knew he was too far gone already. He was—dead. She saw the same vacancy in his eyes as last year's stillborn lamb. Still, she had waves of hope. Maybe he was alive. Maybe she was mistaken and should keep trying CPR.

She knelt beside him, Bo right there with her, and began CPR. Brian's body, unyielding and cold, resisted.

Brian's face glistened purple and his chest stayed rigid as the arms flung to each side. His eyelids were open and his eyeballs pushed against the lids. Bloody foam bubbled from his mouth and nose now that he was out of the water. One of his leather gloves was off and had fallen onto the ground. She could feel the little jolts from the electric fence that he had fallen against. She pulled him away from it, amazed that her hundred and twenty pound frame could manage it. He looked every inch his six feet lying there motionless on the cold wet ground.

She desperately tried to force her air into his lungs and only getting resistance. Why hadn't she paid more attention in CPR class? She remembered snippets. Clear the airway. Tip the head back. Or, is it tilt and clear? She went back to step one, tilted Brian's head back and stuck her finger down his throat. It felt clear to her. She pumped up and down on his chest madly while Bo circled and barked around him. Still, Brian lay lifeless and gray and Mona could see no sign that he would start breathing again.

Bo lay down, panting, watching her every move

She had even tried to get Bo to go get help, wished she had taught him some handy trick, like fetching her cell phone.

Who would he get? Her two daughters were away at college, one at CU and the other at CSU. The ranch hand?

"John would pick now to be at the cattle auction," she said aloud. "We cannot even afford new livestock right now."

She screamed at the top of her lungs, her voice thin and shaky, and on a good day would only carry a hundred feet or so. Her screams served only to set Bo howling, so she stopped. She turned again to the CPR, which she continued for another ten minutes by her estimation until her thin arms ached and shook with the effort. Her slight size had betrayed her.

Icy panic ran through her body. What should she do? She had no choice but to run back to the farmhouse.

"Stay, Bo. Stay," she yelled.

At least Brian isn't alone. Bo lay down next to Brian.

Regret flooded Mona as she ran all the way back to the house to dial 9-1-1. Brian rarely took his cell out because half the time it didn't work. No cell tower. She tried to remember the exact location. She wouldn't have Bo to direct her on the way back. If only he'd taken his cell. If only she'd taken hers.

"9-1-1, what is your emergency?"

"It's Mona Morgan. Please send an ambulance, something's wrong with my husband."

"What is the problem?" asked the male voice.

His question roused panic in Mona. Why didn't they just listen to her? Then she remembered that they probably already had dispatched an ambulance. At least, she hoped they had.

"Please hurry. He's in the field."

"Address please."

"20 G ½ road in Hawk. Hurry." Mona knew that since Hawk didn't have its own dispatch center, the ambulance would be dispatched from Vail or Glenwood Springs.

"It's Heartbreak Ranch. There's a big sign at the beginning of the driveway."

"Is your husband with you right now?"

"No. I had to leave in in the field to get to a phone." Mona wondered if they had listened to her or if they were simply reading questions from a piece of paper.

"Where did you leave him?"

"In the pasture. He was irrigating."

"Was he breathing when you left him?"

"No."

"Okay, Miss. We've dispatched an ambulance. Is that the old Stewart ranch?"

"It's Heartbreak Ranch," Mona said. "Yes, the old Stewart ranch. They were my parents."

"Sure," said the voice. "Will you stay on the line with me?"

"No. I've got to get back to Brian. I'll take my cell, but there's no guarantee it'll work. Cell coverage is spotty out here." Mona hung up the phone.

She scribbled a quick note on a yellow sticky pad approximating Brian's location on the property and slapped it on the front door as she left to go back to Brian. All the way back to him, running until her lungs hurt to bursting point, she thought that maybe she'd made a mistake, that she had not seen what she thought she had, that Brian and the girls would all be teasing her later. They'd tease her about the time she thought their dad was dead in the field. She remembered the Ambien she'd taken last week. Maybe it was still in her system. The cell phone felt like a lifeline in her hand. Why hadn't she left the number on the note? She had called 9-1-1 on the landline, which meant that although it meant they probably could verify her address, the cell would add the advantage of GPS.

Mona heard Bo barking in the field. As she approached the two of them, she dialed the cell again.

"9-1-1, what is your emergency?" The voice was the same, much to Mona's relief. Only in a small town would that happen, she thought.

"Yes, this is Mona Morgan again. I wanted to give you my cell phone so they could track us if they need to." Time slowed, and Mona noticed the owl that Brian had talked about yesterday, hanging around in the old cottonwood

"We have it. I've dispatched the ambulance. Are you with him now?"

"Yes. Where is the ambulance?" Mona's hand shook against the phone and she used her other hand to steady it.

"They are on their way. Now, can you tell me if he is breathing?"

"No. He's not breathing."

"I'm going to guide you through CPR." He sounded as if he were reading from a list.

With a heavy sigh, Mona put the dispatcher on speaker and put the phone down, started the process again. This time she'd do it right. She kept it up until she saw the ambulance coming right at her, kicking up mud and leaving deep scars in the furrowed field.

After what seemed like both an eternity and just a few moments, she and the paramedics stood over Brian's body.

"Damn, it's muddy out here," one of the two EMTs said. He flicked a chocolate splat off his sleeve onto the ground as he got out of the ambulance. "We'll be lucky not to get stuck out here."

They had stopped a few hundred feet back to turn off the electric fence at the switch-box, something that Mona hadn't thought to do, even though she could feel its currents run through her occasionally, even though she'd moved Brian out of the water. There were two EMTs and they took a lot of time making sure the fence would not electrocute either of them. Their apparent lack of urgency with Brian made Mona queasy.

"Please hurry," she pleaded. The strobing light of the ambulance threatened to give her a headache, but at least they had turned off the ear-splitting siren.

"Hold on miss," they said. Hoped ebbed and waned. Denial and reality.

One of them shouted questions to her, which she answered as quickly as she could, irritated that she had answered them before to the dispatcher.

They listened for Brian's airway, giving Mona some hope that she had missed something. They tried to put in an airway, but Mona saw one shake his head to the other. They brought out the paddles and tried three times to get Brian's heart started. Then one said, "Patient found not breathing, no audible heartbeat, no detectible blood pressure. Will notify coroner." He sighed. "That's what I'm writing if anybody cares." Mona had the feeling that he'd been chastised before for not following their protocol.

"There wasn't nothin' you could do," said the paramedic. Mona wondered about his qualifications, but it hardly mattered so she didn't ask. Panic flooded her and she wanted to turn and run and not stop.

"Isn't that what they always say, that there wasn't anything I could have done?" asked Mona. "I just want to..."

"We're sorry ma'am. Looks like he just had himself a heart attack or got himself electrocuted, that's all," he said. "If I was you, I'd have that fence looked at before you turn it back on."

"God damn it," she said to the paramedic "Couldn't you have tried harder?" But, she knew he was dead when she left him to go call 9-1-1. It just wasn't fair. Could she have tried harder? She started adding up the mistakes in her mind.

The young EMT made a note on his pad. "Sorry, ma'am. This ain't television. Ain't no Hollywood movie. Things don't happen that way. Your husband's already met his maker more than an hour ago. That's in my opinion. Nothing official. I'm making a note of unsuccessful resuscitation and no vital signs after repeated attempts to revive. Since this is an unexplained traumatic death, I'm going to call the sheriff and let him deal with this. I'm truly sorry for your loss ma'am."

As soon as he said it, the sheriff's car appeared. He had followed the same ruts the ambulance had chiseled into the field, but that hadn't saved the car from being coated in Colorado clay and mud.

"Hey Deputy McClain," said one of the EMTs. "We got a possible unexplained death here. Not sure if it was electrocution or heart. Thought we'd better call you. Where's the sheriff?"

"He sent me. He's not working today."

"Travis McClain." The tall lanky man thrust out his uniform-sleeved arm toward Mona.

She took it automatically and shook the big hand attached to the end of the sleeve.

"Mona Morgan."

"Sure. Used to be Stewart? I went to school with you. Couple years later of course."

"Sure. I think I recognize you." The muscles bulging through Travis' western-style shirt belied the fact that he'd once been the skinny kid that she had begun to remember.

"This the husband?" asked Travis. "Oh yeah. I recognize Brian. Course he's a little older than I remember."

Mona started to speak and to her surprise a choking sobbing sound came out instead. She listened to the sound and couldn't get it to stop.

One of the EMTs sat her down, took her blood pressure and offered her what he called a mild sedative.

"Don't take it until you get back to the house," he told her. "You're not allergic to anything?"

"No allergies. I'll take it in case I need it for later," she said. She was sure the little blue pill wouldn't make a dent in her situation.

The deputy began walking around Brian's lifeless body and taking notes, asking the EMTs questions and examining the fence. After about fifteen minutes he came back to the back of the ambulance to talk to Mona.

"Well, of course, I can't tell what caused his death. An autopsy is warranted. I'm going to call the coroner and he'll probably have an autopsy done."

"I'm not sure Brian would like that." The thought of an autopsy sent panic through Mona.

"I understand, but in a case of unexplained death like this, I think it's warranted."

It wasn't a question and so Mona nodded her agreement.

"Do you want to wait with the body, or should we take you back to the farmhouse?" She cringed at Brian being called a *body*.

"I think I'll go home and call my girls," she said.

Travis offered to drive her to the house, but she refused, wanted to walk back with Bo. She knew she'd never get Bo in Travis' truck. Travis left his truck in the field and made the trek with Mona to the house, saying he'd get his truck later. Mona could barely hear his questions, although she heard herself answer them accurately. Travis chattered on the way back.

"How much acreage you got?" he asked.

"About thirty-five hundred acres." Mona looked over the expanse of the ranch that dwarfed the eight thousand square foot lot they'd had in Denver. If they were still in Denver, this wouldn't have happened. Mona shook off the thought.

As they walked, Mona looked across the field to the ghostly stand of aspen to the west. This place was beautiful but harsh. If you turned east, you'd be looking toward Vail and the Rockies; west and you'd be looking at Glenwood Springs and toward Utah.

"Heard you folks moved away. How could anyone move away from Hawk, Colorado?" Travis laughed and winked a sky-blue eye her way.

"Quiet place nested down-valley from Vail about twenty miles and twenty years of progress," he continued.

"Your folks owned this ranch for a hundred years, I suspect. I'm glad you decided to keep it. You were the talk

9

of the town when it was up for sale. And again when you came back."

"The time seemed right. We'd both been 'down-sized anyway."

"Sounds painful."

"Yeah. It was. And looking back, I'm not sure we should have moved here."

"Don't say that," Travis said. "You know what they say about things happening for a reason. I know it doesn't seem like it now."

Finally they arrived at the house.

"I like what you've done to the place," he said. "I haven't been inside this place since it had that old flower wallpaper. Your mother had me here a couple of times when we helped your dad with the hay."

"Brian insisted on all the most expensive stuff when we renovated. He even made us renovate the bunk-house and barn."

"We used to go hunting up in your South acreage. Never told your dad, but it was crawling with elk and deer come September. Some of those Lodge Poles have got the pine beetle disease though. You might have John go cut them down before they fall. You ever use that cabin up there?"

Mona heard herself let out a loud sigh.

"I'm so sorry, Mona. I'm babbling and you must be in shock," Travis said as they stood in her kitchen. "I think I need to go back out and work with the coroner. Can I call anybody for you?"

"Yes, call my daughters? I don't think I can talk. I don't want to frighten them. My God. They'll be devastated." Part of her wanted to wait to tell them. Give them another day of blissful ignorance.

"How old are they?"

"Two girls. Skye is a junior at University of Colorado and Miranda is a freshman at Colorado State. Miranda wants to be a vet and work with animals. They're eighteen and twenty years old now."

"Oh yeah, I remember now," Travis said.

"Oh, that I got pregnant in high school?"

"You finished though." His face reddened. "And went on to get a college degree. That's why it's so important to me that the girls are in college."

"Brian was a bit older than you, right? If I remember right, he was already out of high school?"

"Yeah. He's six years older than I am," she said. The mention of Brian brought a suffocating feeling to Mona and she gulped for air. Brian would never get any older.

Travis made the calls on the landline while Mona sat numbly in a kitchen chair staring out the window at the skeletal gray peach and apple trees that Brian had planted in the back yard only a year earlier.

"The girls are on their way home," Travis said. "It'll be a few hours, you know. That drive from Boulder is a killer. Fort Collins, even farther. Vail Pass is clear though. Both girls said they'd have a friend drive with them. You want me to call someone to sit with you? Wanda down the road, maybe?"

"No, I will wait for the girls."

"The EMT said he gave you a sedative for later, but maybe you should wait 'til someone is here with you before you take it," he advised. "You never know about allergic reactions. I'll come back and check on you tomorrow."

Mona nodded at him, willing him to leave her alone. Once alone, she sobbed at the top of her lungs, with Bo staring at her with those strange sympathetic eyes.

It took the girls four hours to get home from their respective colleges on the other side of the mountains, and the entire time Mona sat in the same spot. The two girls that came with them had relatives in the area and so didn't stay.

She had taken the sedative, which didn't seem to numb her pain much, but at least it calmed her enough she could sit. Even through the sedative she could feel the panic well up in her.

***

"Mom?" Mona heard Miranda's voice first, and Skye's followed soon after.

Both girls looked even more tall and thin than when they had left for college just over a month ago. Soon Mona found herself looking into Miranda's tear-filled brown eyes and Skye's red-rimmed blues. Skye's blond hair was pulled back in a ponytail, while Miranda's chestnut brown hair hung loosely to her shoulders. Both girls cried non-stop once they found out and Mona found it took her own pain away to comfort them and it took some of her pain away to keep busy.

"How could it have happened?" Miranda kept saying. "He was smarter than that, to get electrocuted. I think he was too healthy to have a heart attack."

"I don't see how an electric fence could have killed him," Skye said. "I used to grab it all the time just for fun."

"After all the times I told you to stay away from that fence?" Mona asked. She wondered exactly how much detail Travis had given them. Certainly more than she wanted him to. Why had Travis decided that Brian was electrocuted? It was the first she'd heard any such opinion.

"Mom, you know me," Miranda said. Her chin trembled and tears spilled from her eyes again.

The coroner called Mona to say they'd be doing an autopsy to determine cause of death.

"He's at the mortuary in Glenwood Springs. They didn't want him at Vail. I can give you a definite answer after the autopsy. Maybe he had a coronary or aneurysm or something like that."

His statement about Brian not being wanted at Vail dug at her in the way only a native Coloradoan could be bothered. Vail and Aspen had their own set of values, their own way of looking at people. Anyone "down valley" from Aspen or Vail was considered of lessor class. At least that's the way they were made to feel.

"It'll take a couple of days to get the autopsy done. This isn't the big city and it takes a little longer," he said.

That is good, thought Mona. She'd need a couple days to plan a funeral. My God—a funeral.

Chapter 2

Saturday, Heartbreak Ranch

Brian had been dead for only one day and it seemed like weeks. Mona hadn't slept and had hardly eaten. She wanted to be alone and not "hovered" over by her girls and neighbors; and yet she feared being alone. Her stomach was constantly queasy in a way it hadn't been since her pregnancies. Mona and her two adult daughters sat on the front porch most of the day, swung together on the porch swing or paced back and forth on the gray painted wood porch floor. There was no normal in this new life. Their lives had changed in a seeming blink of the eye.

The news of Brian's demise swept through Hawk County like the wildfires that had taken over much of the pine forest in Colorado the previous summer. Neighbors came and went, carrying dishes of macaroni and cheese, baked dishes made with tater tots and canned cream of mushroom soup, fried chicken, chocolate cake, apple pie and more delicious, caloric and heavy food than three grieving women could ever eat. Turns out there were so many visitors the Morgans didn't need to eat it themselves.

Wanda, the old woman who owned a neighboring ranch, arrived with a gigantic chicken potpie, the crust shiny and golden, and a true pastry masterpiece. If only Mona had any kind of appetite. The nausea that clenched her stomach would not let up. On a normal day the girls would have devoured it right from its ceramic container. On a normal day Mona would have admired the pie and would have asked how to make it.

"Didn't want you to have to cook," Wanda said. "I remember how it was when my Harold died. Couldn't bear to do anything in the kitchen for the longest time. Lost my appetite. Both cooking and eating."

Wanda also had the foresight to bring paper plates and plastic spoons and forks so that the cleanup would be easy.

A spry old woman of about eighty, Wanda floated around on a deceptively frail frame carrying tea and little tidbits of food to the grieving women. She was probably the physically strongest woman Mona knew. The slight woman wore heavy turquoise jewelry every time Mona saw her; large silver and turquoise rings, bracelets and even a squash blossom necklace. Jewelry likely collected over a lifetime. Wanda wasn't a pretty woman, but somehow the silver and turquoise made her seem attractive, at least for someone in her eighties. She'd bring Mona a cup of tea and put her cold bony hand on Mona's and just hold it for a few seconds and disappear back into the house where neighbors and friends were murmuring in soft tones. Sometimes a guilty laugh would steal out from the drone and low-tones. The laugh signaled to Mona that it would be okay if she wanted to laugh. If only she wanted to. If only something was funny.

The ranch-hand, John Davis, came back from Denver the day after Brian died. She'd tried to call him on his cell and asked him to come back the day before, but couldn't get him and he hadn't bothered to put a message service on his cell. He must've heard through the "Rocky Mountain Grapevine."

"Mona. My God," he said.

The three of them, Mona and the girls, waited outside for him to pull up. The breeze, soft and gentle as it rustled the gold aspen leaves, the sun, the sound of the Steller's Jays and robins comforted Mona. When John arrived they walked to his old pickup, not waiting for it to come to a stop. He was comfort. He had always been around since Mona remembered. The girls loved him, even as he always pulled away, not wanting anyone too close to him. People became

15

like cats around him, wanting him to acknowledge them, wanting them to like them, and all the while knowing he wouldn't take too much. Like a cat, he'd back off if you tried to get too close.

He pulled his chew out from his back pocket and pinched a little and put it under his lower front lip. He was a ruggedly handsome man, even more so at forty-five than he had been as a younger man. He usually covered his full head of brown hair with a cowboy hat, sweat-stained near the crown. The sun had tanned his hide, making Mona always looking on his hands and arms for signs of the skin cancer that plagued the locals who were made up of largely Scot and Irish ancestry. He was like a brother to Mona; an uncle to the girls.

"You're gonna get lip cancer," said Miranda, as she noticed the chew in John's mouth. She said it every time and every time John answered that you had to die of something. This time, there was no such retort. Miranda looked disappointed.

"Sorry 'bout your Dad," said John to the two crying girls. He looked down at his worn Tony Lama boots and took off his Stetson hat, held it over his chest.

That bit of sympathy sent all three women into a crying fit.

"Sorry ladies. I heard on the way over. Mr. Gilkinsen radioed me. Didn't even decide on the livestock. I'll have to go back to Denver soon as this is all over."

John had been with the family since his early twenties, having been "put out" by his family at seventeen, which wasn't unusual in the area. Few parents sent their children to college and many expected them to leave home at eighteen. There were rumors he had done a stint in a juvenile facility, but Mona's parents never seemed to mind.

Mona's brother, Andrew, had died in a car accident when he was seventeen and so there was no son in the family. Every rancher needed a son, it seemed. So, Mona's parents had taken him in a few years after their only son had died. They even built a bunkhouse for him on part of the ranch, with a bathroom, fireplace and stove to make coffee and simple meals.

They spent the day pacing and trying to plan the funeral, trying to avoid the dreaded experience. The three of them pushed food on John until he gave up and went back to his bunkhouse carrying bags of food with him.

Mona cried all night. The tears hurt her swollen eyes. Every time she cried in front of the girls, they started crying. She'd struggled to pull herself together. The girls kept commenting she looked pale. She felt pale, what could she say? Her normally clear skin felt sore and dry. She slathered on some lotion; put eye drops in her sore eyes. Her fine blond hair clung for dear life to her head. She knew she'd have to pull herself together.

The next night, she still hadn't slept. She looked in on the girls, wandered the house, paced the floor downstairs where there were no creaky boards. She wished she had gotten more of the little blue pills from the EMT. Valium. At least the pill had numbed her a little.

Mona wondered about fate and destiny and whether the move back to her childhood ranch had led up to this disaster. She had wanted to move away so badly as a teenager. She sat and thought of the local lore that if you never wanted to end back in Colorado, you had to take a mason jar full of dirt from the Book Cliffs with you. The Book Cliffs, made mostly of sandstone and bentonite clay and shaped like books stacked spine-up in a library, stretched barren for miles across Utah and western Colorado. The Book Cliffs were as bald as her grandfather had been, with a few straggly sprouts here and there. She never took her jar of dirt. What if they'd never moved back here? What if she hadn't listened to Brian, who had urged her to keep the childhood home her parents left her?

***

17

Wanda helped her make funeral arrangements. There were not too many decisions since the choices in Hawk were limited. The nearest florists and mortuary were in Glenwood and Wanda accompanied her there. She didn't want the girls to have to make those kinds of decisions.

The stream of visitors slowed. Due to the autopsy, the funeral wouldn't be until Friday.

Wednesday night, after Mona still hadn't slept more than an hour or so, she became frantic. Little electric bolts were shot through her. She now knew what "restless legs" were. The girls slept non-stop, waking only to cry, eat, and sleep again. People called with offer to help, but they could only wait. The service would be simple.

Wanda Watkins came over that night. "I want to make you some tea," she said.

"Tea won't help," she told Wanda. "I can't sleep. The last thing I need is caffeine. Every time I think I'm ready to fall asleep standing up, I lay down, and panic wells up."

"I know dear," she said. "When I lost my husband. That thyroid cancer took him in the worst way."

Wanda had disappeared into the kitchen. Mona hoped she hadn't stirred up painful memories. When Wanda came back she carried a big steaming mug. Mona reluctantly took a sip and nearly choked on the strong liquor that laced the drink.

Wanda patted Mona's back and Mona knew she didn't do that often. "Grief without a little medication is like going through childbirth all on your own. A person needs a little help sometimes."

Mona drank the tea, all of it, went to bed and finally slept.

Chapter 3

Thursday, Heartbreak Ranch

She looked from her bed, outside her bedroom window at the aspen and apple trees in the large backyard; they rustled as they hung onto the last of their quaking leaves, reminding Mona that it was September. She waited for the grief and nausea to subside and shook off the desire to go downstairs and drink a glass of whiskey. She wanted a clear head today.

Her dream that night had brought some relief; Brian, alive and talkative, speaking of the owl that Mona had seen, chatting away with her. He told her how beautiful she was, stroked her shoulder length hair, and told her that her blue-green eyes were glowing. The transition from dream to wakefulness felt like a cruel reverse nightmare.

She lay on her side, clothes from the previous day still on, and shivered with a cold that started from inside her; the kind of cold that no amount of clothing or blankets would warm. Her hands shook and her heart thumped wildly. Panic welled in her as she struggled with reality. Brian had died. *Died.* Even the thought of the word brought on the nausea and disbelief. The dark amplified her fear. She switched the light on with trembling fingers. She stumbled up off the bed and looked at the clock.

Two in the morning. Hours to go before dawn. Mona remembered dreaming good dreams with Brian alive and well. No nightmares. The dream had been a blessing.

Resigned that sleep would not visit her again that night, Mona looked into the girls' bedrooms. She peered into the first room and found the girlish bed that her daughter had long outgrown, still made and without indentations where a person might have lain. Skye's bed too had not been slept in and Mona felt a rise of anger and panic, harking back to her those frightening and wonderful days of being a parent to a teenager. She'd find them downstairs by the fireplace, but she hoped they had gotten some sleep.

Mona went down the stairs, cautious not to step on the creaky stair the third from the bottom. Bo lay at the bottom of the stairs between the stairway and the front door as if waiting for Brian to come home. What did dogs understand about death?

Mona peeked into the living room. No sign of Wanda in the house, so she hadn't stayed over. Wanda had said something about feeding her dogs. Tears filled Mona's eyes. She felt a light stab of headache; likely and hangover from the whiskey Wanda had given her.

Embers glowed red in the fireplace and girls had fallen asleep on the living room sofas. She and Brian had spent so much time picking out those two sofas, arguing over fabrics, one too masculine and another to frilly, as if deciding on fabric and style of a sofa would decide their futures.

The girls had their clothes on and had pulled wool blankets over themselves, annoyingly toned legs sticking out from underneath. Relief washed over Mona. They lay blissfully asleep in the warm room. An empty bottle of wine lay on its side on the coffee table. Wine glasses on the floor stood beside their respective sofas. Obviously, they were not afraid of Mona knowing about their underage transgressions. She supposed they could be excused during this horrendous time. Later, Mona would pretend not to have noticed. They had most likely built a fire and stayed up late talking. She has so far been able to pretend that she didn't know that her two daughters sometimes drank, and perhaps imbibed in marijuana—she didn't want to know. Now, especially.

Shamelessly, Mona picked up the bottles and glasses, sucked the remnants from them before taking them to the kitchen. Bo looked up at her, but didn't seem to judge, lay his head back down.

She put the teakettle on; the new red Le Creuset kettle that she and Brian had fought about. Too expensive. Not necessary. She'd regretted telling him the cost.

"I want everything perfect," she had told him. "I feel such satisfaction every time I walk into my new French style farmhouse kitchen."

"But so much for a damned teapot?"

"It'll last forever."

"You know I have to make this house mine," she told him. "I hated that old-fashioned flower wallpaper my mother had. The cheap countertops and old linoleum floor that screamed "poor." Actually it had screamed of "farm poor." The kind of poor where you had enough food but not enough for shoes and not enough to fix up the house. Not enough to go to school and have your clothes stack up to the "city girls."

Mona gleamed with pride, through her grief, at the sturdy oak plank floor that the linoleum had been hiding all these decades. Warmth. History. Rebirth.

She quickly grabbed the now screaming teapot off the expensive gourmet stove and set it onto the marble countertop.

She wished her mother could see the house after she and Brian put so much of their savings and time into renovating it. She wouldn't have appreciated it; would have shamed Mona for spending so much, for wanting so much. Mona broke into sobs as her mother's image and Brian's entered her mind.

Mona walked into the living room and looked out the French doors that looked onto the back yard through the back porch. Brian had insisted on wrapping the porch around the entire house so they could see the ranch from all directions out there. The fruit trees her father had optimistically planted still hung onto some apples and peaches. It wasn't easy growing fruit at almost seven thousand feet above sea level. Her dad always said that Hawk was "on the right side of the Rocky Mountains to grow fruit."

He'd tell her that Hawk was in that area that divided the mountains and all that entailed and the desert. The Continental Divide where the rivers choose between the Pacific and Atlantic oceans. He'd tell her about the "sweep spot" between The Rockies and the desert where grape vines and fruit trees grow, where the weather is warm enough and cool enough, where the water is plentiful enough and drought comes just often enough.

Mona drifted back to the kitchen and sat in the breakfast nook where she could watch the sun come up over the fruit trees. She drank her tea and tried to choke down a piece of toast to calm her stomach. Her swollen eyes stung with the tears that Mona couldn't stop. Her hand shook as she brought the toast to her mouth. Her heart literally hurt with each breath and she wondered if she could have a heart attack. She wondered if a person could die literally of a broken heart. It hurt to breathe.

Up for hours now, she watched the sun rise over the Rockies to the east as if it were an ordinary day. She decided to put some peppered bacon on and some potatoes. After another hour of sipping tea, she scrambled some eggs into the potatoes. The motions of cooking helped to calm her even if she couldn't eat a bite. She heard a knock at the back door. The knock sent Bo running into the kitchen.

"Come in." Her voice sounded high and strained to her.

She knew it would be John. The Heartbreak Ranch resident cowboy was tall and aged and sinewy. He was an early riser and had probably seen the light in the kitchen from his bunkhouse. His western pearl-snap shirts were always annoyingly tight, as if his farm-honed muscles were struggling to get out of them. He normally had his coffee in his bunkhouse and came up for breakfast.

Bo whined at the door for John.

"Hey Buddy." John reached down with the hand that didn't hold his hat and scratched Bo's ears. Bo, in typical Border Collie manner, crouched down and looked up at John.

"He's been keeping his distance from me," Mona said. "I guess he slept downstairs with the girls."

"Mornin' ma'am," he said. The way he looked at her she knew she looked horrible. Pity. How she hated it. The last time she'd seen that look was when she was fired from her job. Her eyes felt swollen and sore. No trace of the makeup she'd always slapped on when they lived in Denver. She blinked, each blink feeling like sand paper.

"I know I look like hell," she said. "And, I don't care."

The weathered ranch-hand looked politely away, as if looking at a terrible thing or a naked thing, his hat in his hand now. The sun may have destroyed his skin, but hadn't ruined his chiseled features. The angled heels of John's old Tony Lamas created a low thud on the red slate floor. He sat at the breakfast nook and she brought him a cup of coffee and a plate of bacon and scrambled hash. He hardly looked at her.

"Toast or pancakes?"

"Toast is fine," he said. "You felt like cookin' this morning, did you?" he asked. "I was going to come and get a little bacon to cook. Haven't been able to make it to the store. Then I smelled the coffee and bacon all the way from the bunk house."

He looked at her with large brown eyes that perfectly matched the brown of his hair. Only now, she noticed some gray at the temples of his still-thick hair. What was he now, she wondered, about forty-three? Forty-four?

"I haven't felt this way since your brother died and your parents took me in," he said. "Your Dad dyin' dealt a blow, but not quite like a young man dyin' before his time."

Mona knew that the long-time friend had just delivered his best condolences. The best he could do. And, it *would* do. She nodded her head in agreement and continued with making breakfast.

"It's good you and Brian kept the ranch after your parents died," he said. "Couldn't be a cake-walk leaving those cushy jobs the two of you had."

"They weren't so cushy. Besides, I was laid-off and Brian hated his job. It wasn't so much a huge decision."

"If I recall, those two girls didn't want to come," he said.

"Now they love it most of the time," she said. "Still, it makes me wonder if Brian would still be alive if I had done something different."

"Don't help much to wonder," he said. "Life such as it is."

He hunkered down over his food, scooping it in like he hadn't had a meal in days. One jeaned leg stretched to nearly her side of the table and the tapered end of his boot rested on the floor. A hole in the boot sole threatened to expose John's sock. Bo lay at John's side and Mona saw John hand him a piece of bacon.

Mona sat on the other side of the table and sipped her tea and nibbled on a burnt piece of toast. She looked at the sun peeking over the fruit trees outside the bay window. John stared at her like he wanted to say something. Always with John, it was as if the words were in there, deep inside and sometimes he'd get them as far as his throat and they never quite came out.

"Something wrong?" she asked. "Besides Brian, I mean?"

"No ma'am," he said. "This might not be the right time, but who knows when that might be. I was just wonderin' if you'd still be needing me now that this thing has happened."

She'd never considered that John would think of leaving. She'd be lost without him.

"John, we need you more than ever now. You know that, don't you? You know I've felt bad about the small salary we pay you, but right now it's all I can do." Who would help with lambing season? With sheep shearing? With getting the cattle vaccinated and bred with the roaming bull? Not to mention the daily chores that John did.

"Don't need more money," he said. "This is my home. I've been here for twenty years."

"That's right," she said. "For God's sake, you were here for my parents when my brother died."

"They were here for me," he said. He got quiet again and looked at his plate. Unasked questions from John hung in the air.

"We don't know yet how Brian died," she said. "I think they will do an autopsy to find out. It looked like he was electrocuted."

"That's what I heard, Mona. But, I don't know how that's possible. I grab that fence all the time to go under it."

"I didn't even turn it off yesterday. I felt a couple tingles from it, but nothing to knock me down. I just don't know, unless he had some heart condition or something."

"He had a heart attack?"

"Maybe," she said. Just the thought of it made her feel faint and she held her head. The bacon. The steaks that he loved. The stress of their old jobs, of their move.

"Sorry, ma'am."

"Don't worry. It helps me to talk," she said. Who would think that she'd be opening up to the quietest man on earth. She'd been wrong all these years about not mentioning the dead to recently bereaved loved ones; they wanted to talk, to say their name.

Still, John seemed unsettled, as if something else were hanging over them unsaid. Talking to him had always been a chore, like mining gold dust out of a played-out mountain.

"There's something else you need to talk about?" she asked. It was like pulling teeth.

He wore his feelings on his face and in his body language. She wasn't in the mood for trying to figure him out. She sighed and hoped he hadn't noticed.

John reached a lean hand into his front shirt pocket and pulled out a piece of paper that had been folded and unfolded maybe a thousand times. The creases threatened to tear through and had been taped in a couple of places. John unfolded the paper and pressed it into the table in front of her. His head went back down toward his plate.

He reached in his hip pocket and handed her the note that had been folded up there.

Chapter 4

Thursday, Heartbreak Ranch

The note John handed her looked like something out of the fifties, written on an ancient typewriter. Some of the letters stood higher than others. In particular, all the O and K letters. A twang of a memory stabbed at her. Her parents, maybe her mother, had probably used her high-school typewriter, an antique passed down from her grandmother, to type the note. Mona held little hope that John would explain the note to her, so she got up and pulled her reading glasses out of the cupboard.

She tried again to read the note. It was a crude contract signed by her parents. Mary and Walter Stewart. It was notarized and dated for around the time that John would have still been a teenager. "God, you've carried this around a long time."

"Yes," John said. He looked up at her and then the head went right back down. He looked relieved though, like he'd needed to show her this for a while.

She continued reading, "We, Mary and Walter Stewart upon our deaths . . ."

"It's a will!" Mona said. "We always thought they'd died without one."

The paper left John forty acres of land. It didn't specify anything else. The note mentioned nothing about the house, the belongings, or anything else. There was no mention of Mona or anyone else. The note didn't specify which forty acres John would get. Did that mean he could choose any forty?

"Why didn't you show this to us before?" asked Mona. She looked at him to get some kind of reading. Was it possible he wanted the house? She didn't need this on top of everything else.

"Brian knew about it. I showed him last year. Walter always said the north forty was mine. I'd like to build a little house there. Some kind of log house. That piece has part of the creek running through it. That would give me some irrigating water and a little fishing spot. I'd like to carve a road to it." John pulled out another piece of paper from his pocket. It was slick paper, like catalog paper. He put it on the table.

"It's a log house, alright." Mona couldn't recall seeing John so animated. He'd obviously thought about this for a while.

He looked worried. Maybe he thought she and Brian would fight it.

"I got started on some drawings. I was pretty good at drafting in school. I figured I could start slow and in a couple of years I could have it built."

Mona had to admit that the drawings were pretty good. The house was designed as a two-story, with a two-sided rock fireplace downstairs that connected the living room with the kitchen. She wondered if John had a girlfriend. This looked like a home he'd share with someone. She had always assumed that John had no dreams but she knew now that he just kept them to himself most of the time.

"Sure, John," she said. "You know I'm going to honor my parents' wishes. In fact, I'm going to sign over a hundred acres to you. We can do a quitclaim deed. You deserve that much. We're going to have to work out the details, get it surveyed to make sure Heartbreak Ranch doesn't lose any water rights or anything. The parcel you want is right by the creek. Go ahead and map out your hundred acres and it's yours to do whatever you wish. I'll continue to pay the property tax on it just to keep things simple, but you'll be responsible for upkeep and other expenses."

John nodded at her and continued to drink his coffee.

Mona's mood changed to worry, not about John and his integrity, but about her own mother's wishes. Had she been too quick to give in to John's claim? Maybe she needed a lawyer to look at it. Brian always chastised her for being too easy-going. Still, she wanted to honor John's claim if it was legitimate. She had no way of knowing what her parents had been thinking. She wasn't sure she wanted to contest it. She and Brian had paid John minimum wage and lodging in the bunkhouse and some food. It was hardly anything he could retire on.

"John. We thought my parents died without a will. I really don't want to go back through probate. So, I'll have a written agreement drawn up."

John looked physically more relaxed now; he had stretched a second cowboy-booted foot across the slate and had leaned back in his chair. He had finally gotten it off his chest.

"You got to know I'd never do anything to hurt Brian," John said. "Or you."

"I believe you," she said. Still, the comment bothered her. She had not had a thought about Brian and John not getting along. Mona remembered some awkwardness between the two of them, but had stacked it up to male posturing. She'd never really talked to Brian about John, because he seemed to bristle at his name. She sometimes wondered if John had looked at one of the girls, but she'd asked them and they'd just laughed about it.

"He's too shy to look at anybody, Mom," Miranda had said. Aside from anything concerning them, she had decided not to worry about it.

"I'm sorry, ma'am." John looked like he was about to get up.

"I best get to work feeding the livestock. Let me know any way I can help. I'll take over any of your usual chores until you're feeling right. You mind if I take Bo with me? He's a working dog. They need to work."

"Sure, you and Bo have fun. Listen, in case it wasn't clear, you can stay here and work as long as you want. We can make it legal if you want."

"Okay, ma'am. No need for more paper nor lawyers," John said with a finality that reminded her of her dad.

Mona stood up as John did and dropped her mug on the floor. It splashed tea and bounced, but didn't break.

"Sorry. I'm a little rattled," she said.

"You're entitled." He said. "Could I ask when's the funeral?"

"We don't know yet. I'll be sure to let you know. You can go with us."

"I'll be going with some friends," he replied. Why so abrupt? Mona thought he had the social skills of a wolf.

Bo was already waiting, turning circles in the mud room to leave with John, as if he knew what had been decided.

"I smell bacon." Mona heard Miranda's voice, low and raspy as she came into the kitchen.

"You want some potatoes and eggs to go with the bacon," asked Mona.

"No. I need the salt. Just toast and bacon, please. But, Mom, I could have made it myself. I get fat with your cooking. You use way too much grease. I can cook for myself."

"I know you can, but it helps me to keep busy. And, the fat part is all in your imagination." Was it? Mona was known for her love of butter.

Miranda hopped up on the island. Normally, Mona would tell her to get down, she'd crack the granite, but it didn't seem to matter.

"Mom, I can't believe he's *dead*. It's so horrible. I keep expecting him to walk in here." Miranda burst into tears and Mona reached over to hug her. This caused her tears to flow again, and as they let down into her stinging eyes it reminded her of breast milk letting down into already sore breasts.

"We'll get through this."

Skye came in. "Coffee," she said.

Miranda said, "Mom, sis and I were talking last night. We don't want you to be alone. We're so worried about you. We decided maybe we should put off college. We could come home to help you for a while."

"No way," Mona said. "You two going to college and graduating is the most important thing to me. We've had this discussion before. You're going back to school. This is going to be a little hard on you, losing your Dad, but I want you to both do your best. You don't have to get A's."

"Mom, are you sure?" Miranda asked. "Maybe one of us could stay. Or, we could take turns going to school."

"I'm one hundred percent sure. No, we're not even discussing it. I haven't decided yet if we can keep the ranch. It might be too expensive with Brian gone. I don't know if I can keep up with it, even with John here to help. We may have to sell." She couldn't believe what she had just said, and hadn't had much time to think about it. How could she manage the ranch herself?"

"Sell?" asked Skye. "But you can't. It's the family ranch."

"We love it," said Miranda. "It's so cool, the way you and Daddy fixed it up. I'd die if you sold."

"Don't say that," Skye said. "How could you say 'die' like that?"

"It's okay Skye. Not saying the word won't bring your dad back. Let's not get so touchy around each other. We'll discuss the ranch later. We're all emotional right now."

The girls took their food to the living room. End of discussion.

Mona fixed breakfast and by the time she cleaned up the phone calls started. Friends of Brian. Some she didn't even know, all expressing sorrow and wanting to bring something. Friends that once worked with Brian in Denver called saying they wouldn't be able to come, but would donate to his favorite charity. How could she not know if her husband had a favorite charity? She suggested they donate to the local farm-family fund for families who needed a little help, or to the Red Cross.

Wanda came over again to help with funeral arrangements. Funeral arrangements in Hawk were cut-and-dried. The coroner called from Glenwood Springs and said he was having someone from Denver come to help with the autopsy. It's been a couple of years since he'd had to do an autopsy, and never on someone who had died accidentally like Brian had. One of her best friends in Denver was a medical examiner, but the Glenwood Coroner said they'd recommend someone else.

The earliest they could have the funeral was the following week, and Mona needed more time, so she made the funeral day the 23rd. That was a Friday and maybe she'd be ready to face it by then. The thought of planning Brian's funeral brought another torrent of tears from Mona and the girls. Dread overtook her mood much of the day. With Wanda's help, they did the best they could to decide on the funeral details, the songs, even the suit that Brian would wear. The girls vetoed cremation. So, Brian would be buried in the nearby Hawk cemetery, as small as it was. His parents were buried further west, in Grand Junction, Colorado. The girls insisted that he be close.

By noon, exhausted again from the effort of existing without Brian, she fell into bed to sleep. She refused Wanda's offer to make her another cup of "hard tea." She didn't need to add alcoholism to her list of problems. Instead, she took a sedative, left-over from a prior dental surgery. Not exactly falling asleep on her own, but she figured at least she'd sleep a few hours.

Chapter 5

Friday, Hawk County Cemetery

They buried Brian on a cold and windy Friday in Hawk Cemetery.

Seeing Brian's casket among the tombstones and crosses of the cemetery filled her with panic and fear.

Mona and the girls had decided on a closed casket, and now she felt relieved about that decision. The three women, temporarily frail with grief and strong at the same time, clung to one another like survivors in a life raft.

They had never been religious in an organized kind of way, and that fact became a problem when planning Brian's funeral.

Brian had called them "recovering Catholics."

"That means we never go to church, didn't send our girls to church, and only pray in times of crisis," Mona had told the mortuary director.

"Don't worry—we will take care of the details," he had told her. And just like that, Mona turned over Brian's physical body and spiritual fate to the mortuary director.

The funeral was held at the small hill-side cemetery where her parents and Brian's were also buried. The air that day had the crisp mountain-air feel of fall in the Colorado High Country. It wasn't unbearably cold, the typical blanket of almost-warm signaling snow. You could almost smell the coming unpredictable snow that delighted skiers and terrorized ranchers who had to worry about the mortality of their cattle and sheep. The cold and wind sucked the last vestiges of moisture from the already dry air, and Mona's nose pinched as she breathed. The wind had a sharpness to it that promised to turn brutal in an instant. The aroma of wood-burning fireplaces comforted her. The Aspen trees had nearly finished dropping their orange and red leaves.

Mourners materialized bearing flowers and memorized condolences. There must have been two hundred people at the graveside for her and her girls. For Brian. My God, Mona hadn't realized that so many people lived in Hawk County. Everett McPherson, the local pharmacist, turned up in a full Scottish Kilt complete with bagpipe. Mona and the girls cried through *Amazing Grace* and *In the Garden*.

The minister, a Unitarian from Rifle, Colorado, gave a wonderful eulogy, which had been written by the girls.

"I'm sorry, Mom. I thought I could read it but I don't think I can without crying," said Skye. Mona knew that Miranda, slightly shyer than her sister, would never be able to do it.

"It's okay, honey," Mona said. "I told you it was fine if the minister reads it. You wrote the words. Daddy will listen anyway."

One of the local ranchers stepped up and gave a touching eulogy to Brian.

The most touching and haunting moment happened at the end of the service. Just when Mona was wondering what had happened to John Davis, he arrived on horseback along with four other local ranch-hands on their horses. They had dressed up the best they could with freshly ironed cowboy shirts and their best silver and turquoise bolo ties. One of the men's shirts had elaborate braiding along the seams, sleeves and yoke. John had on shiny black cowboy boots. His dress boots, Mona assumed. Each man carried a cowboy boot with mountain flowers, mostly Daisies, Bluebells, Lupine and Columbine. They stopped their horses, dismounted, and set the boots by the graveside. Most of the attendees dabbed their eyes with tissue.

Mona noticed in particular a young redheaded woman holding a young boy's hand. The pretty woman cried furiously into her handkerchief. As they left, a neighbor, a friend of Wanda's, asked Mona if she'd like the flowers brought back to the house. She said yes, that would be nice. Just the social effort it must have taken for those lone-wolf men to come together for her touched Mona to the soul.

Chapter 6

Friday, back at the Heartbreak Ranch

The funeral, which had taken forever to arrive, had come and gone in the blink of an eye. It wasn't yet over. There were guests to feed. They had invited everyone to come over and visit and eat. She struggled to hold herself together. It seemed to hit her the hardest when she looked at one of the girls, then they'd all start crying again. So, she avoided their glances, avoided them, at least until the day was over. The girls were so young to have lost a parent.

The losses brought on by Brian's death revealed themselves one at a time; a sudden thought, a glance at a photo, or a memory caused a deep feeling of desperation. Brian would never see their grandchildren. He would never see the girls graduate from college. They would never have another wedding anniversary. They'd never go on that cruise he had promised her.

Wanda and some other neighbor ladies had performed a true miracle in her kitchen. There was a standing rib roast, a ham, sliced turkey, scalloped potatoes, every salad and desert imaginable. It was too bad she had no appetite, but she was relieved that there was an abundance of food and drink for the guests. How could she have forgotten food? Many more people showed up to Heartbreak Ranch than had been at the cemetery.

"Wanda, I don't know how to thank you," she said.

The older woman patted Mona's hand with her own bony and weathered one. "You never mind," she said. "You'll have a chance to return the favor when I die."

"Wanda, don't talk like that."

"Like what? I'm an old lady. You don't live forever. Most of my friends are dead. It's up to you to throw me a party." The old woman winked at her, her lined face folding itself into its wrinkles. "I know I told you before, but I'm so sorry about your husband. You being so young, and all. It's a tragedy. You might always be alone from now on."

Mona pondered this possibility. Frightening. Depressing.

The women gathered in the kitchen, the men in the living room where someone had started a fire. Most were drinking beer, although the girls had gone around and offered brandy or whiskey too. Relief washed over Mona. The funeral was over. Tomorrow, she could start to think again. Tomorrow, she could grieve. Tomorrow she could figure things out; make lists, make plans. She'd have to reinvent her life after Brian and Mona knew it would take forever. She had always known Brian, it seemed. He had been the only one for her. The tears started to flow again.

"You all right, Mom?" asked Miranda.

"I'm fine sweetie. I'm fine, but I space out. Lack of sleep, I think. Every once in a while it hits me."

"I know the feeling. I'm so worried about you, though."

"Don't worry about her," said Ruth Anderson. "We're going to take care of your mom. We're neighbors."

Mona struggled to remember where Ruth lived. She and Brian had always kept to themselves. First the kids kept them busy, and then it seemed they had only needed each other. Mona would probably not see her again until the next funeral or wedding.

Brian had been Mona's best friend. Now she didn't have him. She'd have to become more social. He saved her from being alone. Maybe she'd make more of an effort to be friendly to the neighbors, to make friends in town, to look up old high-school friends. Just the thought made her exhausted. She doubted many of them had stayed around. It was hard to find work around here. The choices were service jobs in Vail, ranching, or some kind of independent business.

"I'm a strong woman. I can handle things. It'll be lonely for a while, that's for sure," Mona said.

"I wasn't a bit lonely when I lost my husband," Wanda said.

A hush fell over the kitchen and without looking Mona could feel the other women glancing at each other. It was the kind of quiet that carried rumors and accusation and allegations on its wings without a word uttered by anyone. Wanda had lost her husband to thyroid cancer a couple of years back, and that it had been a long hard struggle. Cancer was a tough subject for anyone, and country women seemed to run scared from the word. They could give birth at home with no anesthesia, or bandage a horrible farm equipment accident, but mention the word *cancer* and they scatter like cockroaches when the lights come on.

The women went on slicing meat and putting gravy and sauces in bowls.

"Guess I'm the only one can ruin a funeral," muttered Wanda. She carried her dish into the living room and the women continued their talking, starting up the chatter again like a flock of crows; a *murder* of crows.

"Does anyone know who that redheaded woman was at the funeral?"

The hush fell over the room again. This hush was more severe than the hush Wanda had caused.

"Did I say something wrong?" Mona asked.

"No, honey," Wanda said, who'd come back into the kitchen carrying an empty platter. "I overheard you gals talking. It's Marla Rodgers. Crazy women, that one." The women were all head-down working on their casseroles. The strange hush fell over the group again.

"Crazy, how?"

"She just is. Shows up at the strangest times. I was surprised she showed her face at the funeral." There was a murmur of agreement and again the scattering of women across the kitchen.

The kitchen cleared and everyone went into the living room to eat. The weather was nice, so they opened the French doors leading out to the back yard and people took their plates out there. A gentle wind scattered leaves over the back yard. Small comforts seemed bigger now, more significant.

***

Before Mona knew it, it was dusk. One of the men had kept a fire going in the fireplace and there were still about thirty people, Mona guessed, in the house in various rooms. Whether they stayed or left, it didn't matter.

The scotch bottle and snifters came out. Mona only had five snifters, so some of the men had their drinks in blue-rimmed Mexican glasses. They didn't seem to mind. Mona brought out the best bottle.

"Brian was saving this scotch," Mona said. "We picked it up in Scotland five years ago when we were there. He was saving it for a special occasion, but now I want to share it in his honor." Mona tipped her head back and tossed the shot down her throat.

Soon, Mona felt like she could fall asleep. She heard a throat clearing and Mark Eckland, the owner of another Hawk County ranch stepped in front of the fireplace. He faced Mona, who sat on one of the sofas. The Ecklands' property was a few miles from Wanda's ranch, which bordered Heartbreak on the Southwest side. Mark Eckland was an old guy, probably mid to late sixties. Mona knew that he had been in Viet Nam along with her late uncle, Adam. Her uncle had died over there, a fact that had devastated her father and the rest of the family. The story was Mark had tried to save her uncle, but Mona had never paid much attention to the story.

Like most of the ranchers, Mark's skin had become leathered like an old saddle from years in the sun. His green eyes stood out from his brown skin. He had the middle-age spread and chicken-thin bowed legs that a lot of the guys had from years of truck driving and horse riding. He also had worn what looked to be his best bolo tie, this one made of black onyx in the shape of a bucking bronco. It stood out as bright as his eyes against his black shirt. He had on black cowboy boots; probably his dress boots.

"Mona," he started. "I'm Mark Eckland, your neighbor. I know you met me personally maybe once or twice, but don't know if you remember me. I work for the BLM. Bureau of Land Management, in case you don't know. I had occasion to work a bit with Brian. That's my wife, Isabel, over there." He pointed to a petite stylish woman who appeared to be a decade or so younger than he. She raised her glass to Mona. Mona nodded to her. She seemed a little uncomfortable, maybe even a little bit bored or out-of-place.

"Do you remember us at all?" he asked.

"Of course I do, Mark," Mona said. She was embarrassed that he'd had to introduce himself. They were neighbors, for God's sake. The truth was her parents never socialized much with the neighbors either. They always waved at people from a distance, or nodded their heads to acknowledge their existence.

Mona saw Mark Eckland all the time driving his BLM pickup around Hawk. Mona knew that he'd worked for the Bureau of Land Management. Mona didn't know what he did exactly, but he was always waving at people. She knew there house was spectacular and expensive. Years ago, Mark and Isabel had razed the old ranch house on their land and built a house grand enough for people who lived in Vail, but a little ostentatious for down-valley people. Not bad for a government guy.

Brian hadn't talked especially fondly of Mark; saying how Mark was always joking how he liked to come by at least twice a week to check on things. Brian had thought it was as though Mark thought he was slumming or something. But, Mark certainly seemed nice enough now. Brian had been envious of Mark's job. How many people could get paid by the government to drive around a government truck all day and wave at people? And, he'd come to Brian's funeral. Mona always wondered how they afforded the big house, unless Isabel had inherited money.

He raised his glass. "He was a good fella, Brian was," Mark said. "I never saw anyone so intent on being a farmer. On purpose, that is."

There was a soft laughter in the room and a couple of "hear-hears" after which everyone took a healthy swig of scotch.

"Thank you Mark. It means so much to me. Only, I have to correct you. Brian said he was a rancher, not a farmer. He intended to raise sheep and cattle," Mona said.

Mona guessed that Mark Eckland knew the difference between a farmer and a rancher. He certainly would know that ranchers considered themselves slightly superior to farmers. Her dad used to say that ranchers put their land to use by grazing and raising cattle to sell and not trying to eke a living out of the soil.

"I want to second that," said John. "And for the record, Brian was set on raising sheep *and* cattle on the same ranch."

There was laughter among the men, who seemed to understand John's explanation. Ranchers usually chose between cattle or sheep. When her parents were alive, their land was mostly a farm and not a ranch. In reality, most of the land was nothing more than grazing. Her parents never had the money to farm it or put more than a couple hundred head of livestock on it. They made a little off the BLM lease, but it wasn't that much. Mona knew that local ranchers sometimes put their cattle in the high pastures on their land and got a little BLM money.

There was an awkward silence. Miranda must have noticed, because she got up and turned the music up a little more. It was a soft country station. She nodded toward Skye, who sat on the sofa. Both girls had cups of something and

Mona pretended not to notice or care if it was alcohol. She just could not deal with it right now.

Someone else stepped up. Mona felt touched that these eulogies had happened spontaneously.

"I'm Travis McClain."

Mona had expected him to come, especially since he had been with her after she called the ambulance.

"Travis. Thanks for coming."

"You know I always had the highest regard for you and Brian," he said. "And, it was a sad day last week when . . ."

"I know," Mona said, wanting to save herself and the girls from hearing the story again.

"I know you were here that day, and I want to thank you for helping."

"I want you to know I'm here for you. Whatever you need, you just call. I mean that." He tipped her glass toward her.

Again, another round of sipping. Mona hoped there wouldn't be more; she was growing very tired and wanted to go to bed. It was only nine, but it had been the longest day of her life.

Wanda seemed to sense this, and suggested that everyone leave so the family could get some rest.

Skye stood up and said she wanted to say something.

"Are you sure you're up to it?" Mona asked.

"I want to tell the story of Heartbreak Ranch," she said. "How it got its name, that's all."

Mona smiled her agreement.

"When we first moved back here, Miranda and I were all sad and everything about moving away from Denver. Denver was where all our friends were. It was our home and we were sad. We're city girls at heart. I know that Mom and Dad grew up here and everything. My sister and I talked about it lots. But, we didn't think it was fair that we had to leave our home. So, we cried all the time. Daddy had started playing an Elvis tape that had the song Heartbreak Hotel on it. He said he always played it when he was a kid and felt sad." Skye had started crying softly, but everyone listened intently.

"I remember that," said Miranda. "It did help a little."

"Anyway," Skye continued, "One day we were at an auction. You know, one of those farm auctions." There was a soft laughter. Farm and ranch auctions were common; they all knew what they were and they were never good if it was your farm being auctioned.

"It was Henry Brown's farm," said Miranda.

"Good old Henry, bless his soul," Wanda said.

"I found a white chest for my room. Kind of a wood thing with the paint chipping off. And, we found this cast-iron sign for the gate; the one that's out there right now."

"The HB brand," someone said. "HBR."

"Yes. And right away, daddy said that maybe we could buy it and call the place the Heartbreak Ranch. He said we should name it that for all the ranchers who had to auction off their stuff. HBR for short. We had to have an "R" made for the iron sign. And that's how it got its name. And, I love it. And, I'm going to miss my dad."

"And, so am I," said Miranda from her place on the sofa. "So much." She started crying again and Skye went over to comfort her.

Soon after, everyone started to leave. Before Mona knew it, the place was cleared, the dishes cleaned and the house straightened. She thanked the women for all they'd done and promised to have them over for lunch or something before long. Would she keep the farm now that Brian wasn't here? Could she pull off owning and running this ranch on her own—with only John to help out? Again, the tears stung her swollen eyes.

Chapter 7

Sunday, Heartbreak Ranch

Morning now brought relief as often as it brought dread; sometimes the emotions occurred adjacent to one another. The ablutions of the morning, once such an automatic thing, took effort now. Her warm and comfortable bed beckoned to her most mornings. She looked at the clock now and it shocked her to see that it read almost noon. The thought of seeing her two girls lifted her spirits.

Downstairs, Mona put on coffee for herself. The girls were up and puttering around in the kitchen. The aroma of bacon cooking wafted to greet Mona.

"Have you seen John this morning?" she asked Miranda.

"Don't worry, Mom," said Skye. "He did the chores already."

"I don't intend to make him do everything. I feel so guilty about that."

"Mom, we *pay* him to do the chores." Mona looked at her youngest daughter. Her thick brown hair and soft brown eyes made her the spitting image of Brian.

"You haven't seen how little he's paid. Besides I need him for the heavy work—the things I can't do."

"He gets part of the estate, doesn't he?" asked Skye.

"Where did you hear that?" Had she talked to the girls about the land that would be given to John? Had her parents talked to them?

"Miranda," said her big sister, "You told *me* not to say anything, then you go and spill it."

"Girls, it's okay. We should talk about this. Tell me please where you heard that John is getting part of the estate."

"We heard some of the women talking, that's all."

"At the funeral?"

"Here at the house, after," said Miranda. "We were eves-dropping." So—her parents had probably told Wanda. Or, maybe Brian had told someone?

"It reminds me why I hate small towns," Mona said. "Everybody is into your business. Plus, it's hardly ever true. Think of the tabloids. It's mostly fake news." "Mom, this is a nice town. It's the country. Do you know how lucky we are that people care about us?"

"You didn't think so when we were talking about moving here," Mona said. "Remember the crying and angst we went through?"

"Well, now we love this place. Anyway, we've got our college lives and friends."

"Let's get back to the subject of John Davis," Mona said. She took her coffee and a couple slices of bacon the girls had cooked to the breakfast nook.

"Come and sit with me."

"You want toast?" Skye asked.

"That would be great," Mona said. "I'm famished for the first time in days."

"I know how you feel," Miranda said. "I still feel a little sick to my stomach sometimes, though." A big sigh escaped from her youngest daughter.

Mona looked at the girls from across the table. She saw one pair of golden brown eyes and one pair in sparkling blue with gold flecks.

"Let's talk about this. John is getting a parcel of acres at the edge of the property. Grandma and Grandpa promised it to him," she explained. "He's got a dream to build a place of his own. I can't blame him and I don't know why he hasn't asked for it sooner. You remember I told you that my brother, your Uncle Bob, died in an accident and a few years later John came and helped Grandma and Grandpa with the ranch? Grandpa had lost a brother in the Vietnam War and he was still hurting from that. God knows I wasn't much help to my parents. Of course, I was young then, but I regret not being a bigger help to them. Anyway, John deserves part of the ranch. He's not asking for much. We've got over three thousand acres. That's a lot. Granted, most of it is up the mountain and useless, but its acreage."

"I thought *estate* meant money," said Miranda.

"Estate can mean money, but it can also mean any kind of property. A person's estate is what they leave behind. In our case, what were Brian's and mine will go to you two. After I die."

"Don't talk about it, Mom," said Skye. She wiped a tear from her eye.

"I just want to explain about John. He came to me with a contract that your grandparents signed for him. We're going to give it to him early. He shouldn't wait until I go or sell the place."

"Why didn't he get it when Grandpa died?" asked Skye.

"That's a good question," answered Mona. She didn't want to let the girls know that their dad had any ill feelings toward John. They'd had a big blow to their young psyches in the past week. She hadn't suffered anything like that at such a young age. Or, had she?

She thought of her big brother, Bob. She strained to remember how he looked and the sound of his voice. How could she forget about Bob and how he was killed so suddenly in the car accident? Her parents had never been the same. People avoided them like the plague after that, as if it were their fault they had lost a son, as if death were contagious. Mona felt a stab of guilt that she hadn't been more sympathetic to her parents. They had gone into themselves after their only son died.

"I don't know why John wanted to bring it up so near the funeral. Who knows why people don't talk about things at more appropriate times? But, he deserves his own piece of land. He wants to build a house. His dream is to have his own place. We can understand that."

"Oh," said Miranda. "That's probably okay. We were thinking that he wanted everything."

"I don't think John's got it in him to make a demand like that," Mona said. "I think he's a pretty good guy."

"The neighbors seemed to think we'd be evicted off the land and that's what John wants. We were worried. We're just trying to watch out for you," said Skye.

Why hadn't Brian discussed this with her if he knew about John's share of the property? Why hadn't her parents told her?

"I wish you would have told me this sooner. Just remember that you can't believe things you hear second-hand. We'll have to all watch out for each other now," Mona said. "It's just the three of us."

"Too bad Dad doesn't have any relatives left," said Miranda. "That whole side of the family is just gone."

After breakfast, Mona sat down to the task of opening all the sympathy cards and sending thank-you notes to people who helped and provided food.

She heard Bo scratch at the kitchen door. She let him in. The dog had begun going with John to do the chores each day. He came back to the house to eat. John had a key to the back door and let himself in to get coffee. Some days they left the door unlocked; that's the way her parents had always done it. Bo drank some water and went into the foyer to lie down on his blankets. The girls had moved them from the kitchen, because he seemed determined to sleep in front of the stairs. They'd moved the blankets to the side so nobody would break their neck tripping over him.

Almost everyone who attended the funeral also sent a card, and there were many more. There was nothing from the redhead that Mona noticed at the funeral. She had hoped for one. She hoped for anything to give her a clue about who she was and why she had cried so hard at the funeral. Mona had become obsessed with and she wasn't sure why. Was she jealous of the woman? Of her red hair? Or, was it some kind of intuition—the kind that Oprah always said to listen to?

Chapter 8

Two weeks later, Heartbreak Ranch

New normal became a comfort. Mona put a beef round roast in the crock-pot and added some peeled potatoes. The girls asked her why she had to cook with all the leftovers in the house, why she'd bothered to freeze much of the leftover food, and she hadn't wanted to tell them that she felt it was disrespectful to Brian to throw the food away. John was doing a good job of eating the leftovers, so she wouldn't worry about them for now. She'd just wait for the food, now labeled "funeral food," to be gone.

That day, the girls told her of their decision to go back to school.

"We worry about leaving you here alone, but we don't want to waste your money on school," said Skye. "We've already paid for the semester, and we wouldn't get it all back if we dropped out. I know that you worry about money sometimes."

"Never say that education is a waste of money, please. Girls, I wouldn't have it any other way. You'll go back and come home for the holidays. I've got a lot to keep me busy. You've both got cell phones. Just call me. You know how badly I want degrees for both of you. I was the first in my family to get a degree, and I want the two of you to keep the flame going."

"Are you sure you'll be okay?" asked Miranda. "We're so worried. It's only been a couple of weeks since Dad died." Her brown eyes filled with tears. Mona paced around the kitchen as the girls sat in the breakfast nook. She seemed a little calmer when she moved around.

"I don't want you to worry. I'll be fine. You know your dad wanted you to be educated. This is the best thing you could do to honor him. Besides, I've got a lot to do. I might have to sell this place."

"Mom," said Skye. "Promise me you won't sell Heartbreak Ranch. You can't sell," she said, her voice rising. Skye smoothed her long golden hair with two hands.

"Girls, I don't think I can manage this big place. The place isn't any good for growing crops. The property taxes on this place are unreal."

"John's here to help. It's not like he can't do the work," said Miranda. "This is your heritage. You can't just throw it away."

Mona's youngest daughter sounded just like Brian. She was the more socially conscious of the two daughters, but it sounded like they both wanted her to stay. Mona took the easy way out. "I'll give it some thought," she told them.

***

After dinner, as her two daughters packed, Mona logged into the Internet in her office, which was a small alcove off her bedroom. Where was the anxiety coming from? The procrastinating? She walked around the alcove, pacing to calm her racing mind. She gazed out the bay window that framed the alcove. She started looking at real estate sites. She needed someone to appraise the place. At least, it was paid for and with the proceeds she could buy a place in Denver, maybe in Cherry Creek. She'd be a little closer to the girls and their colleges and she wouldn't have to worry about running a ranch on her own. She could try to get her old job back.

She'd never loved being a project manager for computer firms, but it was good money and she had experience. She had been good at it. At least she thought so.

She guiltily hid her screen as the girls popped in and out of her office, asking where one of their possessions was located. She gathered all the papers she could find to take to the lawyer so they could get probate started.

Mona convinced the girls to wait until morning to leave. The Sunday traffic had become unbearable as hordes of weekenders to Vail and Breckenridge threaded their SUVs and trucks through Eisenhower tunnel on the way home to Denver.

Chapter 9

Monday, Heartbreak Ranch

Before she knew it, it was morning and she was up a little faster. Monday. Maybe each day would get easier. Hadn't someone at the funeral promised that? Or, was it just something "they say." Wanda had told her that it wasn't like that; there would be good days and bad, maybe for the rest of her life. On Monday morning, Mona helped the girls pack up and head off for Denver, making the girls promise to follow one another during most of the drive. They both would miss morning classes, but the professors would understand. John waved at them from the corral as they left, and Bo barked at his side.

Travis drove up in his pickup truck shortly after they left and Mona had him come in for coffee. He bent quietly over his steaming cup.

Travis bowed his full head of blond-streaked hair over his coffee. His Stetson rested on his knee. He raised his head over the steaming cup. Mona had noticed the folder he carried the minute she saw him. She understood by seeing Travis' shaking fingers that he had brought with him Brian's autopsy results and the death certificate. He'd offered to pick up for her.

Delaying the inevitable, Mona served coffee and gave Travis a plate of scrambled eggs and bacon. She had taken a plate to John earlier.

She sighed to get rid of a feeling of dread. It only helped for a few seconds before it overtook her.

"Are you feeling stronger, Mona?"

"My strength never left," she lied. "I still feel the grief."

"It's a process. I hear it takes one thousand days."

"That's what they say," Mona said. A platitude.

"You're going to be surprised at the autopsy report, I'm afraid," Travis said. He looked a little nervous.

"Why?"

"Because Brian died of an accident, not a heart attack."

"What kind of accident?"

"He drowned. There were signs of electrical burns on his neck and hands, but the cause of death was drowning. He never had a heart attack at all. No stroke, no heart attack He had water in his lungs indicating that he took it in after he was knocked unconscious.

"I'm disturbed by the electrical burns," Mona said.

"There's an electric fence out there, isn't there?"

"Sure, but I've grabbed it myself. I probably touched it the day he died. It gives you a jolt, but I don't see how a person could get burned. Besides, we always kept it at low voltage."

"Do you want to see this, or read it later?"

"Give it to me." Mona took the document and tried to skim over the graphic details that nauseated her. Soon, she began to feel faint. She sat down hard in the chair and put her head down.

"Sorry, Mona."

"I thought I could."

"It's different when it's someone you know and love," he said.

"Please, tell me what it says."

"Basically, something knocked him unconscious and he drowned. His heart was perfectly healthy. There were a couple small burns on his neck and on his hand where he grabbed with his bare hand. Remember, he only had on one glove?"

"My God. How could this have happened?"

"I don't know, but I'd have John check all the fences to make sure something isn't haywire. It says here he could have had an unexplained seizure, but there was no sign in his brain of a stroke or what they call a 'vascular event.'"

"I'll have John ride the fences and turn off the chargers to the electric fences. I'll have him recheck the voltage. I don't know if it had anything to do with why Brian died, but I don't want anybody else hurt."

"You use the solar chargers?"

"Yes. There's no landline electricity out there in the fields. Besides, we don't have a huge herd of cattle to keep in. We've only got a couple hundred at the most. We've never had a problem with the solar chargers."

"Well, I've got to get going. There's some problem down at the diner. I think old man Hanks is harassing somebody again."

"Thanks for dropping this by, Travis."

That afternoon, Mona got the courage to read the entire autopsy report. The pictures were the worst, so she turned them over quickly. Her stomach churned.

She had a certain satisfaction from reading that Brian's internal organs had been in good shape. The report showed no arterial damage or heart disease. If he hadn't been killed, he would have lived a very long life. Brian would think that is funny. It was good genetic news for her daughters. Still, she couldn't help wondering why Brian would have passed out in the field. Knocked out. Did that mean someone hit him? She studied the report. No signed of head bumps or injuries. Strange. Some kind of allergic reaction to something maybe? Brian had never been allergic in his life. It had to be the electric fence. The one that he had crawled through a thousand times.

Mona went to the bunkhouse to catch John before he went out to the field. Too late. He had already fed the barn animals and had taken Bo out to the field. She left a note on his bunkhouse door to come to the house so they could talk about the fences.

***

Back in the house, Mona logged into her computer to do some research on electric fences. Every rancher uses barbed wire or "devil's rope" as some of the older ranchers called it to keep livestock from roaming off the ranch.

Mona found a website that showed how electric fences work. She learned that most are designed to carry between five hundred volts and ten thousands volts. Wire fence is strung along posts and insulators are placed at the top at intervals. The length of the fence determines to a certain extent the voltage. She read that a fence could kill an animal or person if the voltage is high enough. The current is the "bullet" and the voltage is the "trigger" and if the voltage peaks enough along the fence it could kill someone. She knew that their fence was only about three thousand volts, much lower than the ten thousand limit, but she was disturbed to discover that a person could be electrocuted with only two hundred and fifty volts. There were lots of variables, such as tallness of weeds and grass under the fence and wetness of the soil. She might have to have someone come out and examine the fence.

John knocked on the back door and Mona called him in. When she explained what had happened, he seemed shocked.

"We check the fence every week. We've never lost an animal not even a rabbit to that fence," he said.

"Something went wrong if Brian was burned by it. And, I'm wondering if he could've been knocked unconscious by it."

"Could it be he just stepped into the ditch and grabbed the fence?"

"Sure, but would that knock him out? Besides, his boots have rubber soles. Wouldn't that have insulated him?"

"I just don't know. Brian did have me buy a battery charger to charge a couple of the solar cells. They weren't getting enough sun because of that Hayman fire haze."

"Could that be what happened?"

"I don't know. I'll find the charger. I think it's in the barn."

Shortly John was back saying he couldn't find the charger.

"I'll look tomorrow." John left without another word.

Chapter 10

Tuesday, Heartbreak Ranch

Brian had been dead a little over a month before Mona fully fell into her new morning routine. She walked the ditched with John and Bo every morning, just as Brian had. October now, the fields no longer needed irrigating, but Brian and John had made it a habit to keep the them clear of dead animals and debris. She wondered if her new habit annoyed John, who occasionally told her he'd do it himself, she didn't need to bother tagging along.

The three of them covered a few miles each day, fanning out in a different direction each day, sometimes finding a stray cow from another ranch or a raccoon caught in the barbed wire fence. Mona had bought herself a pair of pink Wellington knee-high boots as an alternative to her green pair.

"Your color's finally coming back," John said, studying her face. Levi's are still baggy though.

Mona clutched her chest at the still ever-present tightening.

Winter had not yet frozen the ditches completely, but had left crusts of ice, which they broke up with shovels. Soon the water would be frozen solid, but until then they could water the livestock without taking water from their well. They could drink from the thawed stream that ran through the ranch. The cold fall wind seemed to cut right through their heavy mustard-yellow Carhartt jackets, and she'd added an extra pair of wools socks under her Hunter boots.

"I don't know what I'll do when it's too cold for me to go on these walks with you," Mona said.

Her comment was met with John's silence. He'd probably rather be alone with the dog. She thought she detected a sigh coming from him.

Mona hit at the hardened ground with the shovel she carried.

"It's clay," John said. He'd actually spoken two words in a row after a half hour silence.

"What?"

"Colorado soil is all clay and silica, like kitty litter. Rain makes the dirt soak up the water and makes these massive clay mounds, which crack and shift when it dries out. Damned dry year," he said. "I'd like to haul in some top soil to plow in next spring."

"Been a bad year," repeated Mona.

They hadn't split into their customary separate ways, although John was probably looking forward to the moment.

Bo liked him, Mona could sense it. The dog's shifting loyalty became more apparent every day. Maybe the dog could sense the grief coming out of her pores. She'd read about dogs that could smell diabetes on a person. Bo looked up at her at times as if he felt some kind of guilt for abandoning her.

John strode along the ditch with his shovel, expertly dipping out debris and gently moving the clay soil so that the when and if it rained, the water could go in its groove and not flood any particular piece of pasture. Mona cringed each time his shovel hit a rock and made an annoying scraping sound. Mona watched his boot each time he did it. He needed a new pair. He hated rubber boots and so wore his cowboy boots to the fields each day. The Tony Lama boot had seen many years of wear and as he lifted it to place it on the shovel, Mona saw the worn sole. Maybe for Christmas. Of course, she'd need to get his size somehow. .

She'd have to redefine her life now. She felt waves of loneliness and fear. She missed the simple things like their morning talks over coffee and breakfast and sitting by the fireplace at night with a glass of wine. And of course, she missed him at night, in bed. She missed touching him. Feeling him. Him touching her. Was she losing her sanity?

Mona looked out at the expanse of green pasture as they walked southeast. The colors took her breath away for a moment, the purple of the higher country of Vail Pass, the beauty of the ghostly white Aspen devoid now of their quaking leaves, the green and brown of the pasture with its almost perfect lines of brown water separating it into large squares. The rest of the acreage loomed to the south as part of the mountains, rocky like their name and almost useless. Her father used to lament that the ski industry hadn't decided to buy their acreage for millions, but it seemed the land was exactly in the wrong spot, too far down-valley from Vail, too rocky to make for good skiing. Her dad always said they were on the high plains, neither mountain nor flatland.

"It's almost like a patchwork quilt," she said.

"Your mamma used to say that," John said. "You're like her some. She was a good woman."

His comment took her back. She never thought she was anything like her mother. How could she be like the woman Mona always thought was cold and closed off to the world?

"I mean that to be a compliment," John added. "You're much prettier than she was, ma'am."

"Oh, I didn't take it otherwise." Mona realized there was no use explaining to John. He seemed to draw his own conclusions, and he was maddeningly correct most of the time. She didn't know how he read people's faces so accurately. John's walk told Mona that he couldn't be talked out of anything, not matter how much she tried to explain herself. She'd known him for decades and yet she knew little about him.

Mona had to walk briskly to keep up with John and Bo. Bo seemed proud to show off his daily work to Mona.

He looked back at her, twirled and barked every once in a while as they walked along.

"We're going to have to go by the spot where we found him," John said in his matter-of-fact tone. Mona almost didn't catch was he was trying to say for a moment, but realized he wanted to spare her feelings and was asking if she wanted to stop and wait for him.

"No, I want to go there," she said. "What if a piece of his spirit is still there?"

"I don't believe in ghosts, Mona," said John. "Besides, if he was there, I suppose he'd be glad to see you."

Mona smiled at that.

They walked along and soon they were at the spot where she and Bo had found Brian dead that day. John quietly sculpted the ditch in case of flooding and checked the fence. It happened to be the spot that needed the most work, which is why Brian had been there that day. Mona watched John work the shovel. He straddled the ditch. His left hand reached out to grab the post of the nearby fence. He grabbed carefully. Mona watched for a while and then looked down to pick up something golden brown she saw about four feet away.

It was a glove. Brian's glove. She remembered taking one off him to check his pulse and the glove was in the way. She had clutched that glove and had ended up carrying it all the way to the hospital and then back home. She remembered putting a lot of thought into the glove at the time. Should she throw it away, since Brian obviously had lost its mate? Or, would he be angry that she had thrown away a perfectly good glove. She remembered giving it a big sniff of its earthy leather. She still had the glove clutched in her hand when she arrived home hours later, hours after Brian was gone. Now, it was on top of their bedroom dresser, waiting for Brian. She never knew or cared about the other glove, but here it was. She was amazed that neither Travis nor the coroner had noticed it.

There was something that bothered her about the gloves, but she didn't know what. This one had holes in it and a brown scar across the palm. Of course, she had never paid much attention to Brian's gloves. Maybe the mark was from years of wear and tear and grabbing the barbed wire fence. She saved the glove to be united with the other on top of the dresser.

"John, did you turn the fence off?" she asked. She pointed to his gloved hand that now held two of the four fence wires. She could hear a slight hum as the wires came closer together.

"Yes, ma'am. But, I turned them back on. We need to keep the animals in and keep coyotes and wild dogs out. You know that Wanda's had problems with dog and coyote packs killing her sheep. It's pretty much on all the time. Through my glove it just feels like a little bite. I'm used to it."

"To tell you the truth, I don't buy that the fence had anything to do with Brian dying. Me and Brian, and your daddy before him has been mending fences and clearing irrigation ditches for years. You can touch these things and not get as much as a bite. Unless you step in a ditch while you're doin' it. Even then the bite's a little bigger but not enough to kill a person. It might be hard to let go of the fence a little because your hand starts contracting. But, you don't die. I still think maybe he had some heart problem that knocked him out."

"Just please be careful around the fences," Mona said. She examined the glove with its brown line. A burn mark? She felt a frustration that John had gone against her wishes and left the fences on. "I wish there was a better way to deal with animals."

"Will do," he said. "Come-on, Bo, let's get this job done."

Mona followed him around for the rest of the morning. No wonder Brian had given up going to the gym. There was enough aerobics and weight lifting in walking ditches than a normal two hours at the gym. And, she and John and Bo were at it most of the morning.

"You work hard, John, and I appreciate that. We'll go to the court-house and get your acres turned over officially." Mona hadn't found a comfortable time to bring up the subject of John's inheritance, and he hadn't mentioned it again. What better time than walking the fields with him.

"I appreciate it ma'am. I've saved a little money to get the house started. I'll do a lot of it myself."

"Don't you have friends who can help?" Mona regretted the question immediately. She didn't know of a more condescending question. She had been asked that a time or two herself, since she and Brian hated to ask for help. Brian had always said that depending on strangers was for desperate people.

"Nah," he said. "I have only a couple of buddies I'd be willing to ask for help. They were at the funeral. Those guys are busy."

"Yes," I remember them," she said. "Well, the girls and I are here for you, for what it's worth."

"Getting the land's all I ever wanted," he said. "You ain't nothin' without forty acres. I 'spect a hundred makes me a rich man."

"I don't know if I agree with that," she said. She huffed and puffed to keep up with his six-foot strides. It was almost like he was trying to walk fast enough to lose her. Bo kept looking back, checking on her. The dog seemed to be showing off a bit for her.

"I think you're stealing my dog from me," Mona observed.

"No ma'am," he said. "He'll always be your dog at heart. I suspect he misses Brian and that's why he wants to hang out with me. Wish Brian hadn't had him neutered though. Shouldn't ever neuter a good cow dog. Takes away their spunk."

Mona heard herself launch into her speech about pet responsibility, at the risk of sounding like her youngest daughter. It was the same speech she had given Brian when he hadn't wanted to neuter Bo. What a lot of the ranchers took for spunk was just plain old testosterone-induced aggression. She wasn't sure having a dog chasing after chickens and sheep was a good idea. She hadn't wanted to have the dog run off and impregnate all the female dogs in the county. But, it was becoming apparent that that's how a lot of the neighbors had gotten their cow dogs in the past. Brian had told her that they get a good mutt-mix at the dog pound, usually a non-spayed female puppy, and let her get pregnant with a certified Border collie or sheep dog.

Bo's a good dog, though, aren't you boy," he said to the dog. "Even if you ain't got balls no more."

Mona felt her face flush, but it didn't matter, because John never gave her a look. Talk of genitals and reproduction came second nature to cowboys and she wasn't sure why she felt shy about it.

John stopped and hesitated on their way back. Mona assumed it was his signal to talk.

"What is it?"

"About that battery charger that was in the barn. It ain't there anymore and I don't know where it went."

"Oh God! Where could it have gone?"

"I don't have a clue. You need to believe me. But I'll keep looking."

Chapter 11

Tuesday, Heartbreak Ranch

Mona had seldom gone up to Brian's loft office before his death. Clutter everywhere. Man Cave. She could smell the still-new oak from the floors and wall and ceiling beams. Masculine but clean, the room still smelled somehow like Brian. The old leather arm chair he'd refused to give away worked perfectly as the only furniture, but for the desk and chair that served as pedestal for a large computer and printer. She loved the room, but thought it was wasted as an office. The space, with its sloping ceiling, would make a perfect guest room, but it felt like sacrilege to change it now.

The first thing in sight in the room was the dormer window-seat. The window looked out into the open-space in the back to the rolling hills and the orchard that her father had carefully planted. It was beautiful now, the peach and apple trees having bared their branches completely now stood in a foot of multi-colored leaves. The few apples that had survived the birds and squirrels, now rotted on the ground below the trees, fermenting and giving the blue jays and crows one last pleasure before they were completely gone. Mona had completely forgotten to pick them.

She turned from the window. The only flaw in the room was the trap door in the wall that the contractor hadn't wanted to cover up. "In case you need to get to the plumbing or something," he had said. Other than that, a person could live up there. There was even a small closet-style bathroom up there.

It was the first time she had entered the renovated loft since Brian had died, but now she was desperate for facts. Easier stuff first. More risky stuff later. Better not to jar the psyche with too much information. So, with fear like one facing an unnamed illness, she pushed on.

She put out a request on the Internet with a couple of realtors for appraisals on the house. She'd had one come out on Monday to appraise it and the agent had promised to email it. In a flurry of determination, Mona called her lawyer, the one she and Brian had used in Denver, to get probate started and petition to have herself declared executor of his estate, since he had died intestate. Until that was settled and she had the death certificate, she could not get into the accounts that were in Brian's name only.

She sat at Brian's desk. Mona logged in to get her email. Maybe she would use this as her office now. It was nicer than her cubby-hole office off the bedroom. She could use that space as another closet, maybe.

Nothing about probate in email. Disappointing. The appraisals from a number of realtors about Heartbreak Ranch stunned. They came in around two million dollars, not including the range acreage, which could be sold separately. The total could approach four or five million. It sounded high considering how little her parents had probably paid for it. They'd once said they got the whole piece of land, house and everything for under thirty thousand. Of course, that was decades earlier. Mona knew though that since they had inherited the property, she'd most like have to pay a high capital gains tax when she sold. Still, she hadn't had to pay inheritance tax on it when her parents passed it down to her. They'd be happy about that. Or would they? She pictured her pragmatic and steadily joyless parents.

Brian must have known the value of the place, although he didn't talk about it. She had left the property taxes and money issues up to him, even though she had been more educated in accounting and mathematics. He had wanted that responsibility and Mona acquiesced to him, even though she sometimes had misgivings about it.

So, she had the tax issue to consider. If she sold, the tax consequence could be huge. Still, there would be a lot left and she wouldn't have to worry about upkeep of the ranch.

She could sell and buy something really nice in the Cherry Creek area in Denver. She allowed herself a five-minute daydream of an estate in Cherry Creek, walking distance to Cherry Creek Mall. Still, finding a buyer at that price could be difficult. There were not many corporate millionaires anymore who wanted to buy a ranch to tool around on over the weekends. Who knew, maybe someday a ski company would come around and want some mountain property. Now, she sounded like her dad, who had talked and dreamed all his life of selling and never did.

She toyed with the numbers. What if she sold and spent half on a residence and used the rest for college and other expenses for the girls? She saw now the dilemma faced by ranchers and farmers. The problem was not wealth, which was tied up in the land and its structures, but cash to keep the place running, and paying property taxes. When and if they left the farm to their children, many times those children walked away, scared off by the taxes due. She didn't want to mortgage the place and end up more and more in debt. She was the opposite of "dirt poor." She was "dirt rich" and "money poor."

Guilt gnawed at Mona. Brian would not want her to sell. Why had he been more attached to it than she? After all, her parents had owned the place. It was *her* childhood home, not his. Maybe he was right and she was rejecting her roots. She had become, simply put, a snob. A city-slicker snob who didn't want to admit she came from a country hick background. She decided to leave the realm of the future and just deal with the financials as they were. She remembered some advice someone gave her at the funeral; don't get in too big a hurry to change your life. Maybe that was good advice.

Mona dug around in Brian's papers, and there were lots of them. She tossed things that were outdated or no longer relevant, finding some pleasure in tossing things out. To her surprise, Mona found a life insurance policy that Brian had taken out on himself for four hundred thousand and bought just last year. It came as a shock. For Brian to buy anything without talking to Mona was very strange. He'd always been so negative when discussing life insurance. She put it aside. She'd have to call the insurance company, but didn't think she could do it without crying. She realized it meant that she could keep Heartbreak Ranch. She'd wait for morning and try it then. She went down the back stairs from the loft into the kitchen and put the kettle on for tea.

She didn't allow herself to think about the insurance. Could Brian have committed suicide and made it look like an accident? The thought was unbearable. He hadn't been depressed. She couldn't remember one time he seemed depressed. It wasn't like Brian to think of life insurance. And how would he have done it, died while making it look like an accident?

She sat and drank her tea. Her appetite had evaporated again, but she realized it was past two and she hadn't eaten since breakfast. She took some turkey and sourdough bread and Swiss cheese out of the fridge and made herself a sandwich. She didn't even put mayo on it. It probably wouldn't help her feel any hungrier. She sat and sipped the comforting tea, took small bites from the sandwich and thought of Brian. In the back of her mind was the life insurance. Money can't make you happy, but lack of it can sure make you less miserable.

Miranda called from her dorm room at Fort Collins. Colorado State University was a more casual, down-home type university and Mona normally felt confident about her youngest daughter's safety and Miranda was staying in the dorm, which was cheaper and meals were included. Mona heard a lot of complaining about the food, but she had eaten there herself during Parent's Week, and it wasn't that bad.

Miranda patched-on Skye in Boulder so they could all talk. C.U. was more known for its party atmosphere and rich students, but Skye was handling it well.

"How are you Mom," Skye asked. "We're so worried."

"I can't believe Dad's gone," said Miranda. Mona knew she was crying.

"I'm going to be okay. I'm keeping busy. I'm doing paperwork, finding out what Dad used to do so I can help John. Remember that grief is a process. Your sadness will come and go."

"We're coming home this weekend," said Miranda. "We decided you shouldn't be alone."

"No," Mona said. "Your homework will suffer if you do that. Besides, it's not always safe for you to drive over Vail pass. It's getting to be winter; the blizzards will be coming. I'd just worry about you each way."

"Mona was met with silence on the other end, so she knew that's what they were hoping for too.

"You can come visit at Thanksgiving. We can catch up then."

"Mom, we've got something else," said Miranda.

"Miranda!" said Skye. "We decided."

"No, we should tell her."

"What, already?" asked Mona. It must be about money, she thought, judging by the tones of worry in their voices. "Is it one of the cars?" They both had fifteen-year old cars that Brian had bought cheap and fixed up.

"No," said Skye. "It's about Dad. I suppose we should tell you. I know how small towns work."

"Already? You've barely lived in a small town."

"We got a taste of it at the house after the funeral."

"A taste of what?" asked Mona. Now she was worried.

"We heard a couple of women talking in the kitchen. We were coming down the back stairs into the kitchen and I guess they didn't know we were there."

"And?"

"Well, one of them was talking about how dirty the fridge is," Miranda said.

"Miranda," chastised her sister. "Get to it."

Mona was still smarting from the fridge remark. She tried to keep the place clean, but it was almost impossible to get everything. And, it wasn't like she had advance notice.

"That old woman, what's her name?" asked Skye.

"Wanda?"

"Yeah, Wanda," said Miranda. "I can't believe we've lived here two years and you still don't know her name. Anyway, she said that Dad and that redhead at the funeral were having an affair."

Silence again.

"What? Tell me," Mona said. Mona's heart seemed to leap out of her chest and while she had managed to keep her voice calm, she was screaming inside.

"She said they were having an affair and that her little boy might be his."

"Girls, there is NO way that is true." Mona's stomach lurched at the thought. It could be true.

"Thank god," said Skye. "We don't really need a brother on top of all this."

"Skye, what a great way to put it," said Miranda sarcastically. "Way to go. Like we're thinking of ourselves here."

"Girls, it's okay. There is absolutely no truth to this. You know people were jealous when we moved in because we seemed like city slickers. I'm glad you told me though. I can put Wanda straight."

"Mom, no. Don't say anything. We'd be so embarrassed," said Miranda.

"It's not you who should be embarrassed. I'll give it some thought. But, I don't want you two to think about this again. It's just a couple of old women making up stories. That's all. Your Dad and I were very close."

"Ooh, we don't want to hear about your sex life or anything," said Miranda.

Mona laughed at that, talked to the girls about their classes, and hung up. A sick feeling gnawed at her stomach. She felt like she'd been punched in the gut. Why did this redheaded woman keep popping up into her life? Maybe it would have been better if they hadn't said anything. Or, maybe Mona hadn't paid enough attention while Brian was alive. Could it be true? Had Brian been having an affair? Did he have a child—a son?

Chapter 12

Wednesday, Heartbreak Ranch

Grooming and feeding the horses each morning, a job she'd hijacked from John, soothed Mona. The earthy horse smell connected her to the ranch in a way she hadn't experienced since she was a small girl. It floated in the air around her, saturated her hair, followed her in a cloud of musky scent all the way back to the farmhouse each day, forcing her into a daily shower that might have gone by the wayside, pushed aside by the heaviness of grief.

Two of the horses greeted her almost like a dog would, with excitement and a swish of their tails and a steep bow of their shiny heads. They snorted their greetings to her as if they were attempting to speak to her. Bo usually came with her and tried to nip at the horses' heels, as cattle dogs are inclined to do.

John's horse stood back a little, looked beyond Mona, as if she would be a traitor to John by greeting Mona. She fed them a mix of oats and molasses, made sure they had fresh hay, mucked out their stalls and changed the straw. The straw supply had fallen low, and she realized that Brian had done the supply ordering, so she made a mental note to go over the supply records. She had to find out if he had ordered lately. Another thing to add to the to-do list. Mona stroked the equine coats smooth with the wire brush, letting the distinct musk smell from the horses comfort her, even as she knew the odor infiltrated her clothing as certainly as cigarette smoke. She craved a Starbucks latte. She knew driving to

Vail for one was crazy. Hawk County had not now, nor would probably ever fall under the spell of Starbucks.

It was then, that Wednesday morning near the end of October that Mona decided for certain to keep the ranch. This was home. This was where she belonged. It was as if the life she had before had been a detour. The life insurance would allow her enough working capital to keep it going without sacrificing the girl's college funds.

The knowledge that she would stay boosted her mood. It meant she could commit herself totally to this ranch, to the house, the community. Her musings turned to fantasy. She could run for mayor, for city council. Everyone would respect her for her vast experience. Experience told her that these random daydreams might be fantasy and not practical. You couldn't outrun your roots so easily in this part of the country, and her family had been outsiders of sorts, primarily because they kept to themselves in a self-inflicted ostracism. The Stewarts. A strange and stand-offish bunch. No hard-won degree and work history would free her of blue-collar politics.

Occasionally, Brian would creep into her musings. Then, she was forced once again to face the fact of his death. He would not be with her to share the ranch and to grow old with her. He would not see the girls graduate or be there at their weddings.

After Mona finished her chores and exchanged a quick conversation with John to make sure he hadn't been told by Brian to order supplies, she retreated to the house. It was nine o'clock, and she hadn't eaten.

John had started coming into the house early to eat. Sometimes he went to the Hawk Diner in town. He had always seemed to be a loner, something that Mona appreciated about him. She didn't need another family member to worry about and yet she needed someone to talk to, if just to make sure her voice still worked each morning. He was perfect that way, always around when you needed him, but disappeared when you didn't want company. Mona suspected that he had a keen sense for people and their moods the same as he had for the livestock he sometimes bought and brought home from the Denver Stock Show.

Mona found a packet of ramen noodles in the cupboard and put it in a bowl with water and popped it into the microwave. It didn't seem appropriate to cook an entire meal for herself and so she had begun eating like a college student again.

She added butter and salt to the noodles when they were done, feeling slightly guilty for making them even more unhealthy. She threw away the spice packet, which sometimes gave her a migraine. She carried the bowl of steaming noodles up the back-stairs to Brian's hideaway office.

She booted up Brian's computer and unlocked the desk drawers with another key she found on his key-chain. The desk was stuffed with papers, but they were neatly put into folders in alphabetical order.

She looked for something labelled "farm supplies" since she was most urgently worried about ordering for the winter. She found them under "ranch upkeep." Mona was relieved to find that Brian had ordered supplies. They were to be delivered, and he had paid by credit card. She'd have to let John know to look out for them. She'd have to get John to keep track of inventory levels for her.

Then she found something surprising. Tucked in the supplies file was the receipt for an electric fence charger. He had paid nearly a hundred dollars for it. She kept it out for later investigation.

She emailed the two girls and told them that she decided to keep the ranch. She knew they would be happy about that, and Mona didn't want to wait for their Sunday call to tell them, even though she had only hours to wait. A text seemed a little abrupt, so she opted for email. She made a mental note to send them each a treat package. She liked to put goodies and cosmetics they used into boxes and send them each a surprise.

Mona decided to read and empty Brian's email boxes, both the sent and received. She would have to close his email account and order one under her own name. She felt her blood pressure rise a little as she added that to her list of accounts she'd have to rename or take Brian's name off. She realized then that the emails she sent out would have Brian's name on them as well as her own, since they had shared a box.

Most of the emails were from friends or to order ranch supplies, or to inquire about beef prices and that sort of thing.

However, there were some from Marla Rodgers that disturbed her. That red-head again. She only found three, and two of them were in the "sent" box. Brian made a habit of emptying the email deleted box.

The emails shocked her with their raw emotion.

"It hurts me so bad not to be able to see you," Brian had written. "In many ways you are the love of my life, but I have to do what's best for the kids."

There it was, the ugly truth. She gasped. Short and hurtful, thought Mona. She immediately started dissecting the note with her emotions. Had he left room for Mona in that note, between the lines? Love of his life? What Mona wouldn't have given for a note or sentence like that from Brian.

She felt sliced in two and the hurt felt more than the hurt of his death. A different kind of hurt. Betrayal. Such a personal love letter to someone else. So, Brian had loved Marla and had broken up with her. No wonder he'd seemed so moody the last few months. Angry. Mona had chalked it up to the fact that they both had second-thoughts about their move from Denver.

From the three emails she found, Brian acknowledged a past affair with Marla, but told her he had to stick by his word and not see her any more.

After reading the notes, Mona had to take a break. She got up and walked to the dormer window and looked out on the land. This new grief came cloaked in anger and jealousy. Mona knew he had loved her. She thought they were close and had a great marriage. They had never lost any of their intimacy, even during stressful times. Maybe it wasn't the way Brian had wanted it. But, if only he had told her. But, how would she have reacted? Maybe they wouldn't have moved here. Maybe he'd still be alive. Maybe there's been no "Marla" in their lives.

Why had he needed Marla? She knew she would never really know the answer. She could fabricate her own reasons why Brian needed someone else. Only Brian knew and he was gone. She cried for a while, and then went back to the computer. She was tired of the burning in her eyes when she cried. Tired of the ever-present dread, the loss of appetite. The sick feeling in her stomach remained long after the tears dried. She put the "Marla notes" aside. She couldn't bring herself to remove them from the computer yet, but she would remove them later so there would be no chance of the girls finding out. They didn't need to know about this affair. To them, it was a rumor, started by nosy small-town women, and Mona would try to keep it that way. She remembered her daughters commenting about Marla and what they'd heard at the funeral.

Mona continued sifting through the email, deleting those that she wouldn't need later. She replied to some of them, informing the sender to contact her via email, explaining that Brian had passed away. She didn't give any details. She knew it might be considered rude to inform people of a death by using email, but she didn't need to add another task to her list. She told them to change the email Id to hers for any further messages. She would let the email account go for another month or two, then delete it.

Mona turned to Brian's paper files. They were many in number and neatly hung in three of the desk drawers. She found more information on Brian's life insurance policy.

She found a copy of Brian's life insurance application. He had to take a physical to get the life insurance. She had been unsuccessful in getting him to go to a doctor in ten years, so it surprised her that he had done it on his own. Had he known something about his health that she hadn't? A copy of the physical was in the life insurance file. He had been in perfect health. He would find that ironic now, she thought. She kept the folder out so that she could call tomorrow to check on it.

Many of the folders were information on the livestock; the sheep, the cattle, breeding the cows, births, that sort of thing. She knew she'd have to educate herself more on this now. Ranching was more complicated than she thought. There was a science to it if you did it right. Mona found a folder on deciding how much feed to buy for the year. There was one on animal health: vaccinations, vitamin shots, yearly exams for the animals. Brian had done the record keeping, and she didn't think John wanted to do anything that smacked of paperwork. It would fall to her. This would be her job now, and she'd have to step up to it.

The farm income folders painted a grim picture of ranching. Ranching and farming were just not that profitable unless you were a big outfit. Most of the successful ones incorporated and diversified into other businesses. They sold. Sold out. Those same companies were the ones that now sometimes produced outbreaks of disease and inferior products.

Heartbreak Ranch had enough acreage, but it was rocky and ill-suited for growing more than pasture. It was good for grazing, but her father had never built up the livestock to a point that it was truly profitable. He had probably had a fear of being too big because that would mean hiring more people. He had been too much of a loner for that. Revenues were only around forty thousand a year, some of it from the "grease wool"—uncleaned wool from the sheep shearing each year. There were ten thousand in farm subsidies which explained the few hundred acres of soybeans in the south fields. Mona had never quite understood why they grew them. They had to bring someone in with a machine to harvest them. Ten thousand for the beef they sold.

When you took out John's embarrassing twelve thousand salary and tax money there just wasn't that much left to keep the place going. Forty grand seemed a paltry sum compared to her former salary of almost a hundred grand. She'd need the life insurance to stay above water. She sighed and vowed to remember her decision to keep the ranch. Maybe when she felt better she could do some free-lance computer consulting. She could work remotely and she still had a network of friends in Denver.

The thought of Brian with Marla lingered in Mona's mind. She looked Marla up on the Internet and social media. Almost nothing. A familiar hurt made her stomach clench. She had loved him so much, still did. She couldn't imagine ever having an affair, although she understood why affairs happen. She had seen enough office affairs in her past life. She never thought she'd be one of those women who didn't know what her husband was up to. Mona forced herself to think of the task at hand, even though the thoughts of Brian's affair intruded constantly.

There were several folders marked BLM. Mona knew that to be the Bureau of Land Management. Brian seldom mentioned it, except to mention visiting Mark Eckland. Mark had worked for BLM his entire career and had been friends with her parents. She leafed through the binders. There were pages and pages of plotted charts, maps. She set them aside, unable to determine immediately what they were.

Tucked behind the BLM folder Mona found a leather-bound logbook. She took it from the desk and opened it. The entries were all the same, but went back to 1982. There were over thirty years of entries, but there was only one for each year. There was a date and an amount. The amounts started off at fifty thousand and the most recent were one hundred fifty thousand. Good God. Were her parents paying the Bureau of Land Management? For what? They had never mentioned it to her. But, in fact, they never talked about the ranching business to her. Her father probably figured she wasn't interested or didn't understand it. And, he was right about that for most of her life. Brian hadn't mentioned anything either. She took out the book to keep on top of the desk. She'd go visit with Mark and ask him.

Maybe the money was going *to* her parents instead of being paid by them. They had a shared BLM grazing lease, but she always thought it didn't amount to much. Maybe they had more land than Mona thought. That didn't make sense to her either. Why would they have kept a thing like that quiet? She knew the BLM sometimes paid for certain things like care and upkeep of rescuing wild horses. Her parents had talked about that but had never pursued it.

John in particular said he was interested in the wild horse herds, which had grown over the last decades in the western states. He always said you could have your own huge horse ranch in no time by rounding them up and breaking them. To Mona it seemed like a gold-rush fantasy. The whole thing puzzled her. There was way too much money being logged here to come from a grazing lease.

Mona took another break, and then turned her attention again to Brian's computer. She checked the cookies log to figure out what Internet sites Brian had visited. This was a job she had done for the last company she worked for. For market research, they had told her. They needed to know which sites people visited most often, so she had to scan the cookies file which was copied from each individual computer to the network cookies file. She had felt like a snoop then, but now curiosity drove her on.

There were no porn cookies in the file. Mona was relieved. That would be the straw that broke her if she found out her sweet husband was into porn. There were some cookies that pointed to the BLM website. She went to one of them, but it required a user-id and password. She'd have to look for it later. She knew Brian always used his first initial and last name for a user-id. It was usually perfect for the requirements for most user-ids. She tried BMORGAN. She put her own password in the password square. She wouldn't know what he used as a password. The computer came back with a message that the password was incorrect. So, he did have a user-id with the BLM. Maybe they hadn't talked about everything after all, she thought. She felt irked that he had so many secrets from her. Well, just two, she rationalized. She felt anger well up. She sent an email to the BLM site saying that she'd lost her husband and his user Id and password. She'd check on this website later.

Mona took a break and went down the stairs to the kitchen. She made a cup of tea. The clock said it was noon. Her stomach growled at that news. The ramen noodles had worn off two hours ago. She searched the cupboard for anything she wanted to eat. Turning to the fridge, she found some ham and slapped it between two pieces of sourdough bread. She sliced off a chunk of cheddar cheese and put it on top of the ham before she closed up the sandwich. She carried her meal upstairs to finish the computer work. On the way upstairs, Mona realized how quickly the day was going. Since Brian had died, the days crawled. On the other hand, it seemed like yesterday that she had lost him. Time distortion.

She sat at the dormer window-seat and ate her sandwich and gazed out over the rows of neglected fruit trees. The sandwich tasted wonderful. Maybe she was coming out of the shock of losing Brian. She knew she'd lost weight because her pants were a little loose on her. She figured it would come back with a vengeance because she hadn't intended any weight loss. If only she could go ten minutes without thinking of him or of the sight of his body lying in the field.

Sandwich finished, she sat at the computer and searched. She cleaned up some old files she wouldn't need. She kept anything to do with ranch business. There were some links to Shepler's, the country wear store and to other outfitters. Maybe the girls would want cowboy boots for Christmas. She already planned to buy John a new pair.

Mona called it a day and closed up the computer and Brian's office. Too late to nap and too early to go to bed. The house was too quiet. Bo had pretty much deserted her. She went downstairs and turned on the television for noise. She turned it to a cooking channel, something without a plot to follow. Maybe she'd go ask John to come up for dinner. She remembered the dinner bell her mother kept on the back porch. She would ring it to beckon John. She decided to make her mother's meatloaf and mashed potatoes. Then, she'd see if he wanted to eat with her. Otherwise, she'd eat meatloaf the rest of the week for lunch.

The girls called while Mona was preparing dinner. They were excited and happy that she was keeping Heartbreak Ranch. They all cried a little talking about their Dad. It had been that way since he died. Mona knew that eventually they would be able to talk about other things, about happy memories.

Once dinner was done, including fresh-baked biscuits, Mona rang the dinner bell. Why had she cooked so much food? She saw John's truck in front of the bunkhouse and smoke coming from the chimney. If he weren't interested, he just wouldn't show up. That is what her mother used to say. Mona used to think it strange and a little rude. She remembered a girlish crush she once had for John. Now, she thought maybe she had been mad at him for not showing an interest. It was a good thing he hadn't. His lifestyle and hers were completely different. At least, she used to think so. The truth was that he was closed off; they would never connect emotionally or even socially enough to have a polite conversation. It was the way John was and that's the best it would ever be. He was a brother to her.

John showed up at the door and stomped his feet. The fall air was crisp, almost cold.

"Yes, ma'am?" he said.

"You want dinner? I made more than I can eat by myself."

"That sounds good. I was just about to open a can of chili."

They ate the good food in silence. Mona was grateful not to have to make idle conversation. John ate hungrily and that made Mona feel good. She gave Bo some meatloaf and gravy.

***

The next day, Mona called on Brian's insurance. She needed to report his death and start the process going. The money would relieve some of her worries.

"Yes," the woman on the other end of the line said. "Someone already reported his death."

"Who would that be?" she asked.

"A woman named Marla Rodgers."

Shocked, Mona took a breath.

"Marla?"

"Yes. I understand you're the ex-wife."

"No. I'm the wife," she said angrily.

"I'm sorry," said the woman. "Then I misunderstood. You are the beneficiary on the account. We wondered about that since the other woman's name was not on the policy."

"Well, thank God for that," Mona said.

"But, we're looking into this case," the woman said. "I can't tell you more than that, but because of the circumstances we'll be looking into this. It's been flagged"

"He died from an accident. That should be clear."

"I can't tell you what they're looking at, but the agency has opened a case."

"And, how long does that take?" Mona asked.

"It could take up to a year. Sometimes even longer to get it settled."

Chapter 13

First Day of November, Heartbreak Ranch

November brought powdery snow, freezing temperatures and little relief for Mona. Unable to do much outside besides trekking to the horses to feed and brush them, she baked cookies. She baked nearly all day: chocolate chip, macadamia nut, oatmeal raisin. She arranged them on plates and covered them with plastic wrap. Then, she set out to deliver them to neighbors who had been so kind to her after Brian died. It would give her a chance to kindle some kind of relationship with the people that Brian had obviously become so close to.

That list included Marla Rodgers. Since Mona had decided to stay in the community, it would do her good to know her neighbors better. Besides, she needed to find out more about Marla.

Mona felt happy and full of purpose baking the cookies and packaging them. She boxed them and loaded them into the back of Brian's pickup truck, the cold biting at her through her wool gloves. It had been a mild fall, if you didn't count Brian's death. Now though, winter had arrived with a vengeance.

She visited Marla first. She wanted to get the visit over with. Who was she kidding? She had put on the whole charade of baking cookies and delivering them just to meet this Marla character.

Mona's knees almost knocked together with fear as she pressed the doorbell on Marla's rented foursquare house.

The nerves weren't only from the cold. The house was one of those late forties clapboard houses with a cute little porch. Her house was as close to downtown Hawk as you could get. Mona wasn't sure there was a downtown. If you blinked your eyes driving down I-70 towards Glenwood Springs, you would miss it.

Marla looked surprised as she opened the door. She opened it just a crack. Mona realized how unfair the surprise visit was, and decided to just drop the cookies off and go. She wanted to see this woman in her natural habitat. Marla wore plaid pajama bottoms and a tight white T-shirt. Jealousy stabbed at Mona. Even in horrible clothing and no makeup, Marla was unquestionably beautiful. Her body was great even after having had a child. She had creamy white skin, bright blue eyes, and that curly mass of red hair.

Mona could hear cartoons playing on the television or computer in the background. Her son must be home, she thought. She was dying to see the boy, dying to see that he looked nothing like Brian.

"Come in," said Marla. "Please."

"No. I'm just dropping off cookies for you. And, your son. I want to thank everybody for being so kind after Brian died."

"Come in," she said. She opened the door wide and let Mona in.

"Maybe for a few minutes," she said. Mona noticed the quivering of the cellophane wrap on the plate of cookies she held. For God's sake, Mona, get it together. Feeling like a teenager jealous of the new cheerleader, Mona stepped inside the small house.

"I've got coffee on. I'll make you some."

Mona hesitated too long and now was committed to a cup of coffee with the woman Brian had been having sex with. What was the matter with her? She was now a stalker.

The house smelled musty, the way other people's homes smell sometimes. It wasn't the musty smell of dry books or dust. It was more like borderline poverty. Maybe the smell was her imagination wanting to make up imperfection in this young woman. She could see most of the rooms from the entryway. The young boy's toys dotted the hardwood floor of the living room in front of an unlit fireplace. A bowl of cereal, looking like candy floating in a sea of white milk, sat on the floor beside the fireplace. Lots of cheap knick-knacks, the kind you could pick up quick at a dollar store, were placed willy-nilly around the room. The old furniture gave the room a drab feel. The boy was sitting very close to the television, mouth open, and the cereal forgotten. Still, to Mona's dismay, Marla lit up the room.

The boy's brown hair and eyes disturbed Mona. She had hoped he had Marla's flaming red hair. She struggled to remember her high-school genetics. What if he had red hair? There'd still be a chance he'd be Brian's, but you could never be sure. Yes, you can, she thought, with a DNA test. She wondered if Marla's hair was dyed the rich red color, but her complexion belied that conclusion. Marla had the creamy skin and scattered freckles of a natural redhead. Damn it, thought Mona. There might not be a way to rationalize out of the fact that Brian may have fathered a son. Mona struggled to hold back tears that threatened to unmask her fear.

"He looks like him, don't you think? His name is Nathan. I gave him my last name so people wouldn't talk. Nathan Rodgers." Marla asked as she came in carrying a tray with china coffee cups and a carton of cream. The delicate china seemed out of place. Maybe it had been her mother's china.

It seemed that Marla had seen straight through Mona and her "cookie" pretense.

Mona's stomach sank and she prayed her face wouldn't flush. She thought of how she and Brian talked about having another baby. It looked to Mona like he had done it without her.

"Who?" Mona asked. Her heartbeat sped up and her hands began shaking again. She didn't want to take the cup of coffee from the tray and betray her nervousness.

"His dad, of course," said Marla.

"His dad?" Mona took a deep breath, steadied her elbow against her side and took the delicate china cup. She shook her head at the cream and steadied the cup with both hands as if warming them with the hot china.

"I don't understand," she said. Mona knew herself to be a terrible liar.

"You have to know that Brian was his dad," she said. "I was about to go to court to get child support when he died so suddenly."

"So, you and my husband had been seeing each other?" *Smart Mona.* No, they'd gone to a clinic for IVF.

"We were in love, Mona," she said. Marla's use of her given name startled Mona. Maybe Brian had talked about her to Marla. What could he have told this young woman about her?

"Really," Mona said. "I just don't know what to say. Was there a paternity test?"

"No, Brian refused to take it."

"So, he didn't think your son was his? I'm sorry, should we be talking in front of him like this?"

"Oh, he's too young to really know what's going on. He's a little over three, if you were wondering." Marla said.

"You'd be surprised how much they pick up and understand," Mona said. She did the math in her head. Brian would have been with Marla for a long time if Marla was being truthful.

"Well, he might as well learn young, that's what I think," said Marla. Marla looked very young, probably under thirty and most likely under twenty-five.

"Can I ask what you do for a living?" asked Mona. She wanted to find some flaw in Marla. She hoped she was on public assistance.

"Well, I can't possibly work full-time with Nathan at home. I really want to be a stay-at-home-mom. I get a little money from the state for him. I do a little dancing at night for tips."

"Welfare?" Mona asked. She had really wanted to utter the word, *dancing*, but went with the safer one.

"It's called the WIC program for women and children who need help. I don't want to be one of those working mothers who leave her kid with someone. I want to raise my son myself. Of course, I was trying to get child support for him. I'm still going to try for it. I just want you to know."

Normally, Marla's words would have given Mona reason to debate. She'd met many stay-at-home mothers during her working career that maintained a moral superiority for not working. But, in Mona's opinion, people had different reasons to work. She and Brian couldn't have provided the girls with much on his income. The corporate world had never really suited him and he'd had to scrap his way up to the bottom of middle management. They'd chosen for her to work too and give as much time as they could to the girls.

She had no beef with stay-at-home moms; it was Marla she had problems with. So many problems.

"I think I'd better leave," Mona said.

"Thanks for the cookies," said Marla. "You'll be hearing from me again."

"Do you have a lawyer?"

"I'll have to get legal aid or something," Marla said. "You know, if Brian hadn't died, he would have just given the money to me. I'm sorry you lost your husband, but I lost him too."

"Brian was an upstanding man," Mona said. "If Nathan is his, something will be done."

Mona went to the SUV and drove down the road. Then, she stopped the car by the roadside and cried. The pain seemed worse to her than the pain of Brian's death. There was something else there. Anger. She knew she would probably not get another chance to talk in depth with Marla. She regretted those things she didn't ask. Had Brian loved Marla? What did Marla have that she didn't? Mona knew it was better she didn't know the answer to these questions.

She decided to drive to Wanda's place next. It was a long enough drive to let Mona cool off and gather her wits. She needed some kind of "mother" to talk to and Wanda seemed to be the only option.

Wanda's place was way off the beaten path, only because you have to drive a couple miles into her property to get to the house. Sometimes she got socked in during the winter, as Wanda put it. She had to buy her groceries for the entire winter just in case. Wanda had a great log-style home that she and her husband had built on their original house site and they'd continually updated and renovated it.

"Come in," Wanda said eagerly. "I've been waitin' for you to come see me."

"I know," Mona said. "I've been meaning to visit since you invited us to drop by."

The small old bird-like woman had more energy than was appropriate for her age. Her house had all western-theme furniture and furnishings. The furniture looked new and looked straight out of an Arhaus or Restoration Hardware. She led Mona to the large living room with its wall-to-wall stone fireplace. A wood fire raged in it, wafting the delicious smell of apple wood burning. The wiry woman old woman lugged a bundle of wood to the fireplace and added each small block one at a time.

"Had to chop all this wood myself with my little banty hen arms." She had a way of wheezing at the end of a laugh. Maybe COPD?

"Coffee?" she asked Mona.

"No, no. I got my coffee at my last stop. "I'm dropping off these cookies to thank you for all your help."

"No need," Wanda said. "But thank you. I don't bake for myself since my husband died. Course, I eat like a horse. Never know it by lookin' at me. All skin and bones, and all. A little fat makes a girl sexier, don't you thing? Strange thing about age, all that weight you try to keep off when you're young melts away when you get old. You're left with an old wrinkled sack of skin with a little fat around the middle." The old woman picked up some skin on her arm and let it drop back down. It took a few seconds for the crepe-paper skin to settle back down into its loose wrinkles.

Mona laughed and felt immediately more comfortable. The woman had a way about her. You just knew she was saying what she thought.

"Does anyone help you with the ranch since your husband died?" asked Mona.

"Oh, it's all pasture now. No livestock or anything like that. Some of the ranchers pay me to let their cattle graze the pasture. Keeps it down that way so I don't have to have someone mow. That way they don't have to drive them up the mountain to graze on the BLM land. They wouldn't have to do that. It's not like I'd go round up their herd and chase them off. Place is all paid for, so there's only taxes to worry about. Damned taxes. If I have any fencing or anything needs to be done, I just hire one of the local cowboys to do it. With social security, I don't have no worries. My husband always called it 'social insecurity'." Wanda let loose the wheezy laugh again.

They sat in front of the fire on a new-looking leather sofa. A matching club chair and ottoman stood on one side of the sofa. A Navajo rug, an authentic-looking one, hung above the fireplace.

"I got this new furniture after he died," Wanda said. "I noticed you looking at it."

"Very nice," Mona said.

"Expensive, too, if you don't mind me saying. Harold never much liked me buying things. I always wanted new furniture. Then, after he went, I just went hog-wild. It's an adjustment when they die, though. First you grieve a little. Then, you realize you're free to do whatever the hell you want to do. Then, you don't realize how much you miss them. Even Harold, the mean old coot."

"I didn't mean to be a snoop. You certainly deserve to buy whatever you like. I was admiring, that's all."

"Oh, I know," Wanda said. "But, at my age, I prefer to just say things right out loud. There just isn't enough time.

For instance, I think you came over here to have a 'come to Jesus' discussion with me."

"A come to Jesus?" asked Mona.

"Yup, I just want you to come out and say whatever you need to. I don't spect you have many people to talk to about things."

Mona was not sure whether Wanda was talking about herself, or about Brian's death. So, she decided to open the conversation. If she had learned anything in business it was how to open up dialogue. Certainly, she hadn't learned it from her parents.

"I just left Marla Rodger's place. I dropped some cookies off to her to thank her for coming to the funeral."

"Ah," Wanda said. "And, you saw the boy?"

"Yes."

Silence from Wanda.

"Do you think he is Brian's?"

"That's the gossip, honey. I hate to say, but I'll never dodge the truth with you. Course, nobody knows but God and Marla. Not even sure Marla would know for sure, you know what I mean. That's the gossip anyhow."

"My God, maybe I made a mistake trying to stay in this town," Mona said. "Maybe that's why Brian was so eager to come back here and to stay here. He had to talk me into keeping my parents' house. It must have started before we even moved. Or, while my mom was sick and we were coming to help. I can't stay here now." She couldn't hold back her tears.

"No, dear. You belong here. Your girls belong here. Don't let a little trouble drive you away. It's much worse that way, you know. You only take your troubles with you. And besides it gives people more to talk about when you move on. You don't want something like that forcing you out of town. Hold your head up high. You didn't do no wrong. Not even with all the unwed pregnancy scandal."

She'd never thought of it as a scandal, but she supposed it was a scandal in a small conservative town where young pregnant girls were usually sent away to have their babies and give them up.

"You know that it was Skye that I was pregnant with? I don't apologize for her. Ever."

"Oh—didn't mean harm. But, just speaking what it was back then. You two was so young when you went off and got married."

"We didn't run away—we went to college."

"Maybe we should change the subject." Wanda handed her a tissue.

Mona blew her nose. "It's just so much with him dying and not being able to talk to him about this. That's all."

"It will be alright, dear."

"Please tell me what you heard about Brian and Marla."

"Just that they were having a little fling, that's all. Then, Marla turns up pregnant and everybody assumes it's Brian's. But, between you and me, there isn't one man hasn't dipped his stick in Marla Rodgers."

A surprised "oh" escaped Mona's lips.

"Don't be so shocked," Wanda said. "My husband got around a little in his day. Truth be told, it happens all the time. Men can be dogs."

"I'm sorry. That must have hurt terribly," Mona said.

"It's something that makes women seem bitter over time," Wanda said. "It hardens you inside. Truth is, the older you get the less it matters who they went to when they was young. Just as long as they brung you home from the dance. But, word is, that Marla Rodgers has been to the doctor more than once for complications."

Mona chose not to ask the woman about those complications. She knew that gossip was usually only half true and you could never tell which half.

"There's more to worry about," Wanda said. The old woman looked worried.

"Tell me."

"This one's bad," Wanda said. Her expression changed from amusement to concern.

"There's talk around Hawk that you killed Brian. That you were so upset over his affair and the boy that you killed your husband."

"My God," Mona said. "How could they think that?"

"Mona, I don't think that, but I don't think Brian died in an accident. Farmers have accidents, but not with electric fences. Somebody did this, mark my words. You were the one to find him in that field. So they say."

It was more than Mona could bear, but the cold chill that ran through her bore witness to the truth. Wanda had said out loud what Mona hadn't wanted to think.

Mona didn't try to defend her or explain herself; because she knew it wouldn't do any good and could make her look guilty.

The two women sat and ate cookies and drank hot tea and milk. Mona dozed off.

When she woke, the room seemed darker, the fire burned down to embers and she had a wool blanket covering her.

"God, I fell asleep," she said.

Wanda came in from the kitchen. "Shhh," she said. "It's alright. I don't spect you've got much sleep lately."

"I better go."

"Nonsense. I've put on chicken and dumplings and you're staying for dinner. I must have known you were coming. I don't often cook chicken and dumplings anymore." The old woman seemed pleased to have the company, so Mona stayed.

"Just let me go freshen up," Mona said. "You don't know how much I appreciate this. It's almost like I'm all alone these days, so this helps."

"Bathroom's that way, around the corner," Wanda said pointing to the back of the house. "Help yourself to anything. I don't have them fancy soaps most people buy these days."

The bathroom had one of those great old claw-foot tubs that had become fashionable again. It was even in great shape. The tile had been changed lately, and there was still evidence of her husband's illness, like a makeshift handicapped shower that was carved out of one corner of the large bathroom. Mona looked in the medicine cabinet for toothpaste. She'd use her fingers to freshen her mouth, which felt like she had been asleep for days. When she opened the medicine cabinet, something fell with a thud on the sink. Mona picked it up and examined it. It took her a few moments to figure out what it was. A stun gun. Mona turned it over in her hands. It was a hand-held kind, not the kind that shot wires at someone.

"You okay in there?" asked Wanda. She knocked on the door.

"I'm fine," yelled Mona.

She put the stun gun back on top of the cabinet, took out the toothpaste.

Mona rubbed the minty paste onto her teeth and rinsed her mouth. That would have to do. She went to the kitchen. It smelled wonderful. Wanda had served to heaping bowls of chicken and dumplings and had baked biscuits.

"This looks so wonderful," Mona said.

"How long since your last good meal?" asked Wanda.

"I suppose right after the funeral when you brought over all that good food."

"Nonsense. You barely ate a bite that day. I was really worried about you. When Harold died I ate like a horse. Course, I was expecting his death. It was a relief after caring for him for two years."

They sat down to eat. The food tasted wonderful, as if it was the first meal Mona had eaten.

"I didn't break anything in the bathroom," Mona said.

"Something fell from the top of the medicine cabinet. I wasn't snooping—just needed a little toothpaste."

She wanted to ask Wanda about the stun gun but didn't know how to open the conversation.

"Oh, it was probably that damn contraption that Travis gave me. I won't use a rifle like a lot of folks around here. Don't want to kill nobody. I'll have to find a better place for it. I don't want any kids to get ahold of it. Not that any kids come around here anymore. Kids are scared of old people and don't go around them much if they don't need to. Don't worry about that thing. Same thing happened when the Ecklands came to visit."

"You mean the BLM guy?" asked Mona.

"Him and his wife. Isabel, I think. She's a hoity-toity one, that one. Her thousand dollar purses and all. Who in hell would pay five hundred dollars and more for a pair of shoes? I heard she paid a thousand for one pair. Not that I've been shopping with her, but that's the grape vine. She's a good fifteen years or more younger than Mark Eckland." Wanda made a little tsk sound.

Wanda would surely cringe at a three-dollar cup of coffee too.

"Well, it was nice they dropped by."

"It was when Harold was so sick. Almost everybody dropped by, but there was nothing anybody could do. He suffered so," she said. "One visit was all folks could muster. They'd take a look at my sick old man and see their future starin' them right in the eye. Chases folks off faster than a sink full of dirty dishes. And, there's nothing worse than an old widow. Unless it's a young one. A young widow or a young divorcee is a crime in a small town according to most people. Nothing worse unless it's an unwed mother. They reek of trouble and responsibility."

"I'm sorry to remind you." Mona could see Wanda getting worked up thinking about it. Turns out there was something worse than and old widow or a young widow: a middle-aged widow. She was now a middle-aged widow. Not an identity she wanted.

"Don't worry about that, honey. I remember I'm a widow every minute of every day. You'll see that yourself. It probably gets better over time. People are so afraid of reminding you, but there is no way to forget."

They ate in silence for a while and Mona felt grateful for the hot food and company.

"Don't you worry about gossip," Wanda said. "Nobody ever died of being gossiped about. I suppose a few have died gossiping about others, though." Again, the wheezy laugh coming from the old woman.

"I don't worry so much about me, but I do worry about the girls."

"They're stronger than you think. I saw them at the funeral. They're great gals. And, so smart to go to college and all."

"I know that," Mona said.

"Speaking of gossip, I know you've probably heard the gossip about me and my husband." Wanda had put down her fork and her eyes had a kind of fear.

"Gossip?" Mona asked. She had heard the gossip about Wanda assisting her husband's death, but wanted to make sure that was the subject Wanda had in mind. The thought of her seventies husband having an affair seemed comical.

"Harold suffered more than you can imagine. Cancer is a horrible thing," she said. "I put him out of his misery, that's true. If they want to cart me away to prison for it, so be it."

Mona realized this was Wanda's version of a bold confession wrapped up in stoic fear. Mona reached out and touched Wanda's hand. She didn't really want to hear any detail, but Wanda persisted.

"They were giving me Valium prescriptions. To bear *my* pain, if you can imagine. If I took that stuff, I couldn't stay awake to take care of him. I saved them up until I had two bottles worth and gave them to him all at once along with his morphine. He went right to sleep, happy as you please. He was so weak he just surrendered to it. I'd do it again. They never left quite enough morphine to do the job and I had to make sure it worked the first time."

"I understand, Wanda. Still, I don't think you should repeat that story to anyone else."

"I just wanted to say it out loud. I hope the Lord forgives me."

"Wanda, just for the record, I don't think what you did was wrong. I think you should forgive yourself. I think you husband would be glad you helped him."

"Let's talk about something else that has been bothering me," Wanda said. "Harold used to tell me to mind my own beeswax, if you know what I mean," she said.

"What is it?"

"That damn BLM truck going up and down the road all the time. For twenty damn years. What business did that man have botherin' your parents for all those years?"

"You mean Mark Eckland? Maybe they were friends or something."

"Friends, my ass," Wanda said. "The Ecklands were too high-and-mighty to socialize with your people."

"Really," Mona said. She was surprised at the anger in Wanda's voice.

"There's something about those people that I never liked," she said. I always thought they was after your folks land. You know how the government is. They'll take your last dime. Thank God it didn't come to that."

By the time Mona left Wanda's house it was almost ten at night. She'd have to deliver the rest of the cookies the next day.

Chapter 14

Monday, Heartbreak Ranch

It seemed to Mona that Bob Higgins, Insurance Adjuster, had driven two hundred miles from Denver just to deliver Brian's life insurance settlement.

Why wouldn't he simply call her? Mona stiffened her resolve and asked the adjuster some tough questions. Her parents seldom talked about money unless it was to complain about the lack of it. After Mona was ten or so, she never heard them speak of money again. After her brother was killed, her mother quit "fixing up" the house and bringing in flowers in the spring.

Mona had already done the math in her head as well as on paper. She needed the four hundred thousand from the life insurance policy for the ranch and for her girl's education. The policy had been a welcome surprise and now she wasn't sure she could make it without it. Her mood spiked from depression to hope. She didn't want to take a loan out on the land. She didn't want to sell any of it off either if she didn't have to. She knew that it would be difficult to sell parcels that didn't have good access to electricity and water rights.

Bob Higgins informed Mona that they'd have to investigate before releasing any money, and it was probable that none would go her.

"It's not that you ever really had the money, now is it? That's how we have to think of these things," asked the skinny little man as he sat on Mona's living-room sofa sipping a cup of coffee. It was as if he were clairvoyant. He seemed sadistically happy about delivering bad news to Mona. He reminded Mona of a professor she had once, with his short-sleeved checked shirt and bow tie, always ready to dole out a mediocre grade or two or lower it if you complained. Bob Higgins had on shiny cowboy boots under his Docker pants. Probably thought he'd be going to cow-country, as anyone outside of Denver sometimes thought.

"No, it's not like that," Mona said. Money carries an emotional impact, Brian had always said. It's not always about the money, he'd say, sometimes it's about the emotion that goes with it. Money cannot make you happy; lack of it could make life hard.

"You know, Mr. Higgins, this isn't only about money. It's not about me wanting a windfall. It's about what Brian wanted for me and the girls. It's about his having paid for this life insurance. I think it's about giving my husband what he wanted and what he had coming to him. It's not fair that he paid the premiums and went to all that trouble for nothing."

She had believed he was coming to deliver the check personally, which she had thought nice if not odd. She thought Mr. Higgins would also sell life insurance to her. She thought she'd buy a half million dollars worth of life insurance so that the girls would be taken care of should she die before they finished college.

"I'm afraid there will be a delay with this case," said Mr. Higgins. "We have opened an investigation into your husband's death. There's a note on here that another young woman called about the claim. Of course, her name isn't on the policy, but for some reason she thought it was."

She felt her windfall fantasy dissipate like the morning fog as she poured tea for the two of them.

Mr. Higgins drank his coffee from a hearty pottery mug and ate a biscuit that she had pulled from the oven.

"This is a really good biscuit," he said. "Home baked?"

"Well, I baked it, but now you can get those great frozen ones," she replied. Inside, she was in turmoil. Maybe she needed a representative with her, a lawyer or something.

"I thought you country girls made everything from scratch." He munched on his biscuit, upon which he had slathered butter and honey.

Country girls? She looked at him, not wanting to continue the small talk. She didn't want to spoil any notions he had about her or who she was. She was probably more educated than he, but she didn't want to tip her cards. She smiled as she thought about getting her Bachelor's Degree from the same school that Skye was attending. She looked at Higgins again and tried to decide how much to open up to him.

He had a small piece of melting butter on his lip, which made Mona shudder.

"I'm an investigator," he explained. "This could take a very long time."

"How long would that be?" Mona asked. She thought Mr. Higgins was observing her for signs of guilt. Maybe she was letting her imagination get away from her. No need to be paranoid.

"Maybe up to a year. Sometimes takes longer. If we find anything unusual, that could invalidate the claim. What I notice right off-the-bat is that your husband hadn't had the policy for long. He bought it a little over a year ago. Very unusual for a person with two children nearing college age."

Mona's heart sank. She didn't need this kind of ongoing issue about money. "Clearly, that's what you're hoping," Mona said. "Is this common to do this these days?"

"Do what?"

"Intimidate beneficiaries?"

"I'm not trying to intimidate," he said. He had softened his tone a little, almost defensively. "But, the autopsy indicates that your husband, died in a field. Most of these deaths are heart attacks, and yet your husband was a young man with no signs of heart disease. Why would he pass out and drown in a ditch? The report also said that perhaps he had been knocked out by the electric fence first. How could that happen when electric fences are not known to kill? In cases where the decedent is young and healthy, or apparently healthy, we look into it."

"Here's what I think happened," Mona said. "I believe you'll see that he was electrocuted. He had grabbed the fence and was standing in water. That probably knocked him out and then he drowned before he could recover. The charger we were using could have been faulty." She felt very much like someone making up a story, but she had thought about it over and over again. How could he have died out there in a ditch that barely had a foot of water in it?

"You might be surprised that we thought of that already. We did an experiment, and it's just not possible. There are not enough volts in an electric fence to kill a person. Even small animals can get away with contact with an electric fence. Even fences with the maximum allowed voltage of ten thousand volts don't usually kill. It's because those are used on lots of acreage and sometimes miles of fence. So, the voltage is diffused over a longer area and is diluted."

"Could the fence have malfunctioned?" Mona asked.

"Not likely, although we'll check out that possibility. Where's this charger you talked about?"

"That's the thing. Our handy man can't find it."

"What's his name?"

Mona hated dragging John into this, but gave his name.

"I'll talk with him after. Where is he?"

"The bunk house. You can see it in the distance to the right of the house."

Bob Higgins wrote down something in his notebook. Mona hoped it was her query and not what he wanted for lunch.

"Have you seen the autopsy photographs," asked Bob.

Mona's stomach clenched. She knew she wouldn't be able to handle the reality of that. "No. I don't think I can. I've read the text."

"Okay then, that's understandable," he said. "But, we see some marks that could be from a stun gun. One possibility is that he was stunned and then drowned."

"A stun gun?" Mona asked. "But, it's not possible. They already put 'accidental death' on Brian's death certificate."

"That's true, but until our investigation is finished we just don't know. These small-town coroners don't always catch these things. They just aren't used to looking for anything out of the ordinary. They are not trained in the techniques the way a medical examiner would be."

"What are you thinking?" Mona asked. "That somebody killed him?" Saying the words out loud to Bob Higgins put a voice on her thoughts over the last few weeks. How could Brian have died? He was so strong, and despite Miranda's and Skye's beliefs that their parents were old, Brian was a young man. If he had not died accidentally in that field, he would have lived to be a very old man. He had always been so health-conscious. Mona didn't try to wipe the tears off her cheeks.

"I'm sorry to upset you," he said. He did look distressed that she would cry. You'd think he'd be used to it. He wrote something in his book. The look quickly passed and Mona wondered if he had faked the concern.

"Do I need to get a lawyer?" she said. Something about his demeanor made her ask. Shouldn't have asked a question that made her look weak.

"Oh, no. I don't mean to scare you," he said. "I'm just explaining why we cannot pay on this claim for the time being. If we end up paying this claim, I'd say it's a year down the road. If not, we feel it's best you know as early as possible. It's a lot of money."

"Right," Mona said. "Can I ask what you'll be doing next?"

"My team will be going to the field where he died, looking that over. We'll interview everyone who had contact with him before and after his death. We do quite complete investigations. Many of our people were once in the police department or were lawyers or private investigators."

"That's fascinating. I want you to know that I more than anyone want to know what happened to Brian. I loved him so much. And, the girls miss him so much."

"I'm sorry for your loss," he said.

***

As soon as Bob Higgins drove down the road, Mona called Travis McClain. Maybe he'd be willing to help her. She had previously struggled with calling Travis. Maybe he'd think she was coming on to him, since she had lost her husband. She already imagined the women in Hawk and beyond discussing her flirting habits. She couldn't confide in the girls, and could not think of anyone else who could give her some objective advice.

It seemed to Mona that Travis arrived at her kitchen door almost as soon as she hung up the phone. She opened the door to let him in and then waited while Travis shouted out to John Davis. John had been keeping the place going, almost silently, like a large quiet elf working wonders in the night.

"I don't know what I'd do without him," Mona said. "He works so hard. Never complains."

"Your parents used to say the same about him, Mona," Travis said. "Especially later on when your Dad got sick and couldn't do any more."

Travis looked at Mona in a way she remembered Brian looking at her. She smoothed her blond hair. She had put on mascara and lipstick and not much else. She felt self-conscious around Travis. He had a way of looking at her like he was inspecting her face for every detail. Sometimes she caught his eyes wandering down her body. Brian had stopped looking at her that way except on occasions where she'd be dressed for a party or stepping out of the shower.

"You look beautiful, Mona, if you don't mind me saying."

Travis had an "aw shucks" quality about him that was both annoying and endearing. She could almost forgive him for the ogling.

"I shouldn't have called," Mona said to Travis as he came in through the mudroom. Mona remembered when he used to follow her around like a lovesick puppy dog. He was younger than she. Still is, she reminded herself. She shook off the guilt-inducing thoughts of attraction and former crushes.

"Nonsense. You want me to take my boots off here?" Travis asked. "They're muddy."

"Sure, go ahead and leave them there," she said.

Travis took off his boots near the door and walked into the kitchen.

"Tea or coffee?" Mona asked.

"Normally I'd drink coffee, but I'll have some tea with you."

Mona smiled at the reference to coffee, as if he had to explain his taste for tea.

Mona made the tea in a china teapot and brought it and the cups to the breakfast nook.

"I'm sorry to bother you, Travis. I need some advice."

"I'm good at that; at least I think I am. I want to say something first," he said. His hands shook a little, making the china cup ring a little against its plate. She should have given him a "man-sized" mug.

Travis cleared his throat. "I know there's been some awkwardness between us. But, I want us to be friends. If anything else develops between us, then so be it."

"Travis. I don't want us to be awkward around each other either. I need a friend right now. I won't be ready for dating for a while. If ever."

"I'm a patient man, Mona."

"But, Travis, you should be finding someone younger."

"Please don't say 'your own age.' We're just not that far apart in age. When you're sixteen, a few years are a lot, but when you're our age, what difference does it make."

"Travis, I'm thirty-six. I've got grown children. I just want to remind you. You should be thinking of having kids."

"Got one," he said.

"You do? I don't remember you having a child."

"We lived together for two years. She didn't want to get married, but moved to Nebraska. I found out about Chad two years ago. He's six now. I was only twenty-seven when he was born. I didn't even know I'd had a son."

"Travis, I'm sorry. I didn't know."

"Don't be sorry. He's a great kid. I go see him a few times a year. Take the drive out to Nebraska. This year, we'll go see the Nebraska-Colorado game."

"So, you pay child support?"

"Every month. I know what you're thinking. Am I sure he's mine? I had a paternity test done. He's my son, alright."

"Travis, you surprise me."

"Sometimes, Mona, you don't make the choices, but someone else makes them for you. I wouldn't choose to father a child and not marry his mother. Not in a million years."

"I know that about you."

Travis looked a little sheepish as he drank his tea. He gulped down the rest of his cup and Mona refilled it.

"I didn't come here to talk about me," Travis said.

"I need some advice. Can I trust you to keep it between us?"

Travis looked down at his bootless feet as if inspecting his socks.

Unless it involves a crime, then you know that I've got a duty to follow the law."

"No, it's not like that; at least, I don't think so."

103

"Tell me, Mona. I've got a memory like an elephant. If you tell me anything I shouldn't hear, I'll pretend I'm a priest. I *am* catholic. Lapsed."

"I got a visit from the insurance company today," Mona said.

"Health insurance?" Travis asked.

"No. It seems Brian had a life insurance policy."

"Thank God," Travis said. "I was worried about you and the girls and how you'd make it. I know how hard ranching is."

"It's not so easy collecting. They're opening an investigation of Brian's death. They don't think it was an accident."

"What are you saying? Do they think you had anything to do with Brian's death?"

"All they're saying is that Brian didn't have a heart attack or anything, so it is strange that he died out there in the field. Of course, we knew it wasn't a heart attack. It's just a mystery what really killed him. I was thinking maybe the fence malfunctioned or something. Maybe he was electrocuted, although not enough to kill him. Maybe it knocked him out or something. There must be something else going on."

"I have to say, that bothered me too. But, I don't know about your fence theory. I've seen cattle caught up in those things for hours and they live through it. Makes them a little jumpy, but doesn't kill them, even when they're standing in knee-high water."

"They found what looks like stun gun marks on his neck," she continued. "I don't know what it means."

"Man," Travis said. "A stun gun? I don't think the coroner made any special note of it. I'm trying to think who has one of those." Travis looked at Mona, and for one second she saw a question in his eyes.

"Not me," she said. She felt like a child telling her father she didn't do it.

"Oh, I didn't think it was you."

"Yes you did," Mona said. "I saw it in your eyes."

"My dad always said I had a 'tell' in my face," Travis said. "It's my job to look at all sides," he said.

"I know, and I don't blame you. Let me just tell you everything that's bothering me about this," Mona said. "Can I do that without getting into trouble?"

"Like I said, I'll keep it in this room," Travis said. "I want to help you and the girls."

"I was at Wanda's house yesterday. I accidentally found a stun gun in her bathroom."

"Mona, did you touch it?"

"Yes, I did. It sort of fell down off the top of her vanity in her bathroom."

Travis looked worried. "It's not good you touched it, to be honest." Travis didn't mention that he had given the device to Wanda.

"God, I didn't even think about it. It hadn't occurred to me that it would be a problem."

"Let's don't get stuck on that. I can't imagine Wanda having anything to do with this. Please go on," he said.

"That's all I know about the insurance company case. I'll deal with them. On another subject, do you know Marla Rodgers?"

Travis blushed red, heightening the blue in his eyes.

"There's that 'tell' again," she said.

Travis blushed even more. "Everybody knows Marla," he said.

Normally, Mona didn't like that kind of gossip about other women.

"I'm more concerned about her and Brian. Did you hear anything about them?"

"I'm sorry, Mona. It's true. Everybody in town knew it."

"And her son?"

"I'm just not sure. He could be Brian's but I'm just not sure."

"He looks a little like Brian," Mona said. She had started crying.

"Damn, Mona. Sorry you're hurting like this. It's all you need."

"I'm not as worried about me as I am the girls. Although, I don't mind saying that it hurts almost worse than his dying. I know that's bad to say. I'd be mortified if anybody found out, and yet I want to do the right thing for the boy."

"Nobody needs to know," Travis said. "You can trust me."

"But, everybody in town knows. They're bound to hear."

"Then, maybe you should tell them before anyone else does. Nothing sets you free like the truth, that's what I believe."

"That's good advice. But, I want to make sure the boy is Brian's before I do that. I don't want them to worry. If he turns out to be Brian's, they'll have a new brother."

"God, Mona, but you've got a big heart."

"Don't say that yet. I'd still like to brain that redhead who slept with my husband."

"Well, Brian must have had a screw loose, sorry for saying."

"Thanks for the vote of confidence," Mona said. "It will get straight. There's something else bothering me. What do you know about my parents and their relationship with the BLM?"

"You mean Mark Eckland? He *is* the BLM in Hawk County."

"Yes. There was a log book I found in Brian's records. They were my parents, actually."

"Eckland gets around. Seems he has a lot of power in this county, but never did figure out why. He's got money. God knows why. BLM's a government job."

"Well, it just doesn't seem right that Brian never said if there was some business deal between our ranch and the BLM."

"Why would you think there was a business deal?"

"Because, I found logs. I don't think I should get into it right now, but it involves years and years of money."

"Going to the BLM, or from?"

"From," Mona said.

"Some of it must have gone to the Eckland's," Travis said. "Just look at how they live."

"What do you mean?" asked Mona.

"Big new house. Must have cost five hundred thousand at the time he built it. In Denver, it would be over a million. That's a lot for a house in Hawk County. How'd he do that on a government salary?"

"Does his wife work?" asked Mona.

"Isabel? You kidding? She fancy's herself a socialite. Nobody likes her, though. The woman's got shoes more expensive than my truck. I wouldn't really know—but that's what the ladies around town say. I'm exaggerating, of course."

"Of course," Mona said.

"So, do you think something could be going on for him to be making extra money?"

"I'm sure of it," Travis said. "I just haven't put my finger on it yet."

"It isn't like this is New York City and he could be shaking people down for money, is it?"

"No, I don't suppose it is," Travis said.

"Do you want some pie or something?" asked Mona.

"I've got to get going. They're going to wonder what's happened to me if I don't call in or show up back at the office. But, I'll give some thought to your problem and we'll talk again," he said.

"Thanks, Travis. I feel better just getting some of this off my chest."

"You call me, you need anything," he said.

"Travis, if you want, come by for Thanksgiving dinner. The girls will be home. John will be eating with us. I'm sure he'd appreciate the male company."

"I was wondering what I'd be doing for Thanksgiving. Sometimes I end up eating at the Hawk Diner. Sounds wonderful to me."

"Good. We eat about four."

Chapter 15

Tuesday, Heartbreak Ranch

Mona shivered against the cold November air as she stood in front of the Ecklands' home. A few flakes of snow floated down on her and the grey air signaled more before the day ended. She drew the basket of homemade cookies close to her so that the wind couldn't them into hard little hockey pucks. It was hard enough to cook at high altitude and get the recipe right; then a person had to keep the product protected from the oxygen-deprived atmosphere.

Isabel Eckland opened the massive wood front door of her and Mark's home. The impressive house sported a stucco and stone facade, with lots of natural brick and fountains surrounding the huge yard, almost as if Isabel had envisioned a moat. A red tile roof, as out-of-place in Colorado as a palm tree, topped the house. This house was like no other in Hawk County. Mona had a memory of driving by it as the couple built the home.

It seemed the original ranch-style brick home had been razed and this grand new mansion replaced the more modest one. What had once been pasture for sheep or cattle was now a massive manicured lawn. Aspen and blue spruce stood sentry on the expansive the green yard, which was dotted with little mushrooms sprinkler heads. Lawn lights led the way down the slate path. Mona felt a pang of envy and pushed it away, reminded herself that she also had a beautiful home.

Maybe the Ecklands had inherited some money. She knew that Isabel hailed from Colorado. Wanda didn't think Isabel's family had much money. They were ranchers like everybody else. Maybe she had some rich relatives back East or something. Besides, once you had the land, and the Ecklands had plenty of that, you could build whatever you desired on it. Maybe Mark had done much of the work himself.

"Come on in," Isabel said. Isabel was a petite and pretty woman. She reminded Mona of Audrey Hepburn with her slight bony frame and short dark hair that matched big brown eyes. Mona wondered if she smoked. Did this scrawny woman ever eat? There was an ever-so-slight smell of cigarette smoke, as if Isabel walked through a smoky room and the particles had clung to her. Tiny lines crawled upward from Isabel's pretty mouth as if she had puckered and unpuckered it many times during her lifetime. Even so, she looked twenty years younger than her husband. She most likely was.

Isabel perfumed the air as she walked, and the waft seemed to be Chanel No.5. Mona remembered the expensive aroma because her boss used to wear it. She had warned Mona not to wear the same perfume because the aroma might be slightly different on each of them and they might clash. It made Mona laugh at the time, but what did she know about perfume and its dynamics? Who knew that when one woman wore a fragrance, another wasn't allowed to wear it? Her mother had not taught Mona such things.

Mona followed Isabel into the foyer of the house. The house was beautiful, but seemed too large for such a small woman. Mark was big, big and soft around the middle, so maybe he liked things on a large scale. If he was in his sixties, then his wife was probably early forties.

Mona noticed the tall ceilings with its crown molding in the foyer.

"You have a beautiful home," Mona said. As if she doesn't know.

"I just love it here," Isabel said, her voice slightly more perky. "We've worked very hard for what we have." The statement was not so much an apology as an explanation for a question Mona hadn't asked. Maybe Mona's face showed her ever-so-slight envy. Isabel had probably encountered plenty of envy in Hawk. God knew, she probably learned it or inherited it through her DNA. Hawk County was pervaded with a poverty mentality, an invasive fear that you didn't deserve such riches and if you dared acquire them, someone else would take them away.

Mona doubted that Isabel ever had worked outside her home, which wasn't uncommon for wives in Hawk County. There wasn't much to do besides ranching and there was usually enough work for a ranch wife. Lots of ranch wives did heavy chores as well, from driving tractors and wheat combines to driving fence posts. Mona doubted Isabel had ever wielded a shovel or driven a tractor.

"It's a beautiful home." Mona, you're repeating yourself. She'd done it often lately. The constant anxiety Mona felt seemed to have affected her memory. "I recall driving by here as you were building. It's positively gorgeous. Is this a working ranch?" asked Mona.

"Oh, God no. My daddy was a rancher and I was determined I wouldn't be married to one. Mark makes a good living working for the government. Of course, it's not your ordinary government job. He's pretty far up there on the food chain. Great benefits too. We're keeping the property for investment purposes. And, because we love it so much here."

This woman was not afraid to give personal information. After all, what business was it of Mona's?

"That's great," Mona said. She wondered about the "good living" part of Isabel's statement. What was top government pay? A hundred thousand? That qualified as a good living, but it was another huge jump to "luxury living." Everything in the place reeked of money, much more money than a government salary. Mona was no expert, but could tell quality when she saw it.

Isabel led Mona into a living room where a large marble fireplace enclosed a wood fire where a fire burned softly. A silver tea set including a sugar bowl with sugar cubes and little sugar tweezers sat on the mahogany coffee table. More Isabel's style, thought Mona.

"I appreciate you calling before you came," Isabel said. "And, it was nice of you to bring cookies."

"Well, I wanted to thank Mark for coming to the funeral. I'm a little late getting around to everyone." Mona had thought it might be her only chance to meet Isabel, to get to know her. She wanted to talk with Mark, but there was something daunting about that goal. She'd decided to work her way up to it by going through his wife first. Maybe Isabel could offer some insight into her husband's relationship with Brian. Isabel asked about Mona's girls and told her how sorry she was for them, losing their daddy and all like they did. Isabel shook her head expressing pity for them.

Mona fought the tears but knew the sorrow came out in her voice. She hated that this tiny woman had made her feel sorry for herself. "Thanks so much. At least they're older. Not that the loss is easier on them, but I suppose it's easier on me not to have small children." Mona heard herself rambling, but her nervousness drove her on. Sudden silence would scare her even more. She could hardly back out now. Would it be harder if the girls were younger? She hadn't thought about it.

"You and Mark don't have children?" Mona hated the question even as she asked. She knew her question came across as rude and possibly hurtful, but she came here to get personal information and she wasn't about to back off.

Isabel didn't hesitate. "No. Never wanted them. I suppose Mark did at one point, but it never worked out. By the time I thought I might want them there was a hysterectomy."

"I didn't mean to pry," Mona said. "Please, have a cookie." Isabel seemed slightly embarrassed and mad at the same time. Mona couldn't blame her.

"Mark will like these," Isabel said. She took the cellophane wrapped plate and carried it into the kitchen. "From the lips to the hips," Isabel said as she left the room. It was clear that none of the cookies would touch Isabel's lips. Or hips. Mona wondered if they'd go right into the trash can after she left Isabel's house. It hardly mattered; after all, it wasn't about the cookies.

Mona poured herself a cup of tea and started to put sugar into it.

"Oh, you poured your own," Isabel said. Mona heard disapproval in her voice.

"I'm sorry; I thought I'd save you the trouble."

Mona had broken some tea-pouring protocol.

"Oh, it's okay I'm just a stickler on manners, that's all."

"I'll remember next time." Mona knew there would not be a next time, but the sentence had slipped out. Too late to take it back.

"I know that Mark was close to Brian," started Mona. "I never got to know your husband. He seemed quiet but nice." Isabel's voice and manner had a touch of a sneer, as if she thought Brian was a country bumpkin.

"Oh, he's always a lot friendlier with the men than with women. I prefer it that way," Isabel said. They both laughed a little, but Mona wondered if she knew about Brian and Marla. Of course, she does. She probably started the rumors.

"Brian read a lot," Mona said. "He read everything about politics and the environment. He was really quite educated. We never got to travel as much as he wanted to." Mona fought back the tears that had become inevitable when she talked of Brian. She felt the urge to defend him, to bring up all his good qualities.

Isabel spent about fifteen minutes talking about her world travels and objects d'art she had purchased along the way: a Faberge egg which had a special place on the mantle, china from Harrod's in London, a gold statue from Egypt. Isabel explained they never wanted to go anyplace like Africa or Australia. Only "civilized" places. Places with good plumbing. She expressed disappointment at the plumbing in Ireland. And Egypt.

"You'd think with Ireland being so close to London they'd have better facilities," she said.

"I suppose it has something to do with the oppression of the Irish by the English," replied Mona. "But, I hear they're catching up now with technology." It was hard coming up with something to say about the plumbing of other countries.

"I wanted to ask about Mark and your husband. They seem to have known each other better than I thought."

Isabel bristled. "I try to stay out of Mark's business dealings."

"They had business? It's just that I found some papers."

"Yes, I think Mark might have worked with your parents on some matter." For someone who stayed out of her husband's business, Isabel seemed to know something she wasn't revealing.

"Yes, classified, but then why would my husband have information about the BLM? There seemed to be some kind of business arrangement."

"I'm actually glad you came over today," Isabel said. "Because, Mark had been talking about retrieving anything BLM related from Brian. Now that he's gone, I think he's going to ask you for them. Or, you can destroy them, if you like. Mark would prefer that he takes all of Brian's papers related to the BLM. They're really top-secret government documents. It would be a crime, actually, if they fell into the wrong hands."

"That sounds very ominous. I'm wondering why Brian would know anything about it if it were top-secret. He didn't work for the government or anything. It's all very troubling to me, not knowing what was going on with his life. But, about the papers; I think I'll destroy them," Mona said.

"I think it's best that we stay out of their business," Isabel said. Don't destroy them; give them to my husband so that he can deal with it properly and legally. It came out as a warning and her tone made the hairs on the back of Mona's neck stand up.

"I think you're right about that," Mona said. They finished their tea and Mona said her goodbye and left the house.

***

The visit had only served to make Mona feel worse and even more worried about what Brian had been up to. Still, Mona had found out something about Mark and Isabel. It just didn't add up. Where had they gotten their money? Of course, they could be deep in debt, but how much of that stuff could have actually been put on credit cards?

Shaken by the visit, Mona played it again and again in her mind. As soon as she got home, went to Brian's attic office, found all the BLM records, and stashed them in the cubbyhole in the wall of the office. She made a note in a log on her computer that she had visited the Ecklands' home. She needed some kind of record.

If she saw Isabel again, she would tell her that the records had been destroyed. Mona also copied the records from Brian's computer onto a CD and put the CD with the rest of the BLM records. She'd hang onto them as long as she felt necessary and then destroy them. Maybe it was nothing and Isabel just didn't want her close to her husband. Mona had noticed something she'd never thought about, that some of the rancher's wives considered her a threat now that she had become a widow. She had lost not only her husband, but also her social status in this small community.

***

The next day, Mona called Travis and told him about her disturbing visit to the Ecklands.

"Mona, I've known Mark for years. He mentored me in some ways. Taught me some things about ranching business and about the ranchers around here. Isabel isn't the friendliest woman. She's got problems, but you have to take anything she says with a grain of salt."

"I guess that's good advice, Travis. Still, it was disturbing. I was shaking by the time I left there. I had a nightmare about her last night."

"I think you should let it alone, to be honest. Don't do any more poking around. If you need some information, why don't you ask me and I'll get it for you," Travis said.

Mona didn't press him further about Mark Eckland. It was clear that Travis liked him. It seemed that everyone liked him. Was it because of his money? He didn't seem to have anything else much going for him, but maybe he had more knowledge than Mona gave him credit for.

"I'll see you on Thanksgiving for dinner?"

"Oh, yeah. Thanksgiving. About four you said?"

"I'll see you then."

***

The Wednesday before Thanksgiving, Mona hadn't shopped, hadn't even ordered her usual fresh turkey. She drove further down-valley to Glenwood Springs to the grocery there. Driving to Vail would be closer, but the Glenwood supermarket would be less expensive. Besides, it was ski season and Vail would be crawling with celebrities and photographers. She hoped for a fresh turkey, but knew she might have to settle for a frozen one and hope it thawed before morning. She took her time ambling through the store, picking up potatoes, bread and breadcrumbs for stuffing, vegetables, fruit, and nuts. She was out of everything. She still felt shrouded in fog.

Mona was happy the butcher found a fresh turkey in the back, a Butterball that someone had cancelled. It was a huge one, and that suited Mona fine. She'd have leftovers to make soup.

Halfway through her grocery jaunt, Mona noticed people staring at her. The first one she noticed was a woman who stared from a distance, over the top of a mound of grapefruit. Then, another woman came up, said hello, and they whispered and sent telling glances in Mona's direction. Sympathy for a new widow? Mona was new at this new state of being. Tears came to her eyes and she tried to shake off the feeling. Another man and woman, a couple, it seemed, stared and whispered to each other. The grapevine seemed to have made it down the valley to Glenwood Springs. Maybe more people knew Brian than she thought. If that were true, though, why hadn't they shown up at his funeral? Then it occurred to her that maybe they weren't feeling sorry for her, but thinking she had murdered her husband. A chill came over her. She hurried through the rest of her shopping. She hoped she hadn't forgotten anything. On the way home Travis called to say he wouldn't make it for Thanksgiving dinner – he was going to visit his son for the weekend. So, it would be Mona, her two girls and John for dinner.

***

A feathery powder snow started falling on Thanksgiving morning. The girls had arrived the night before, had stayed up nearly all night talking in front of the fireplace. Mona had risen when she woke at two, had crept downstairs and covered the sleeping girls with quilts, put more wood on the fire and went to the kitchen to start preparing the turkey. She knew she had plenty of time, but she couldn't sleep and had to do something.

Mona had learned to ride the waves of sleeplessness that came with her grief over Brian. Sometimes, she'd wake and couldn't believe that he was gone. It was as if he had gone away on some trip somewhere and would be back soon.

Sometimes she imagined she heard his voice calling her name from another room. It was chilling when she heard it, even though she knew it was her exhausted mind playing tricks on her. Most of the time she had a sick feeling in her stomach each time she woke. Instead of lying in bed staring at the ceiling, she'd started getting up. Doing something productive usually made her feel better. She was lucky that she didn't have a day job and could nap occasionally during the day if she felt the need.

Mona felt some of her old joy return as she chopped, diced, sliced and boiled. She got the turkey going about five in the morning, which was plenty early. She'd need the oven room for rolls, stuffing, and sweet potatoes later. The girls got up around seven. Mona asked them about breakfast. Usually on holidays they wanted only cereal, choosing to save room for the large meal later in the day. John stopped by the back door to check on dinnertime and then left to do daily chores.

The girls showered, dressed, and then took over the kitchen. They had both started cooking lately. Maybe it was the absence of a kitchen to cook in that made it seem like a luxury. Skye made homemade salad dressing and cut up vegetables for salad. Miranda made homemade dinner rolls, starting with yeast and using Mona's heavy-duty mixer with the bread hook. Mona had never really used it. Brian had made bread occasionally and all three of them used to love the smell of fresh-baked bread.

Mona straightened the house and left the kitchen to the girls. She took the girls' things upstairs to their respective rooms. She couldn't resist searching through their bags, a habit she had picked up while they were in high school. She felt guilty while doing it and took care to put the belongings back the way they were found.

Skye's bag spilled when Mona accidently turned it upside down. Something fell out. Mona turned the object over in her hands, inspecting it. A stun gun! Why would Skye have a stun gun? Protection, maybe? It was mildly disturbing, perhaps more because it made Mona worry that Skye wasn't safe at school.

Mona went to the kitchen where the girls were happily preparing whipped cream. She asked Skye about the stun gun.

"I'm sorry. It fell out of your bag accidently."

"Sure, Mom. You were snooping, weren't you?"

"I was just looking for dirty clothes to wash," Mona said. "I didn't mean to pry."

"Dale gave it to me. He had two that his parents bought him."

"For what?"

"Just in case someone follows me or something. I've never had to use it."

"Do you even know how to use it safely?"

"Of course, I do," she answered.

"Please, just be careful with that thing."

"Don't worry about us, Mom. It's you we're worried about."

"Let's call John to dinner."

With the turkey dinner a success, Mona quickly cleaned the kitchen. They had brandy in front of the fire and talked. John opened up and talked constantly. The girls looked at each other and at him and let him speak. Who knew that it took liquor to make the quiet man talk?

At one point, John revealed that he and Brian never got along very well. He said he had a respect for him, but they never were buddies or anything.

"Your dad wanted me to tear up the contract between your grandparents and me. It just wouldn't be right, you know. It'd be like giving up my retirement. It's the only thing I've got."

"You know, John, you don't have to worry about that any more. The land is yours and we're glad we have you here," Mona said. He certainly picked strange times to become talkative, she thought. She wouldn't have wanted him to discuss this in front of the girls, but she decided to let it pass.

At six o'clock, Mona put together sandwiches of turkey and cranberry sauce with stuffing on the side. John remained and Mona opened yet another bottle of wine. She hoped she'd sleep that night.

The girls started prompting John. They had probably never heard him talk so much and Mona feared they might be using him for entertainment.

"Aren't you tired girls?" Mona hinted that they might like to go to bed, although they hardly ever went to bed before midnight.

"Mom, John's talking. Don't be rude. Besides, it's only seven. What are you thinking?" said Skye.

Mona rolled her eyes at her but her oldest daughter ignored the look.

"I've seen things that have the other hands talking about aliens and such, but I know that it's people that cause such things."

"What are we talking about, John?" asked Mona.

"About the two-head calves, the miscarriages in the animals. Happens occasionally, everybody knows that. But, the old-timers say we never saw so many as the last twenty years. Something causes nature to get so out of balance. It ain't no aliens, I'll tell you that much."

Mona had heard her father talk to the other ranchers about abnormalities in the animals. They didn't talk about it in front of the women. Mona remembered her mother laughing about it with Wanda. Men that think women are too delicate to hear such things. Her mother had thought that was a hoot. Finally at nine o'clock Mona had enough and insisted that they end the evening. The girls helped Mona escort John to his bunkhouse. Bo followed him inside.

Chapter 16

Monday, Heartbreak Ranch

When Brian came to her in her dreams, as alive as ever, he talked to her about routine things, as if he were away on a business trip and she happily greeted him and life was again normal. Waking brought the plunge into reality, the deep sickly disappointment.

She had heard Miranda and Skye talking about how they were worried about her.

"She never moved his things. His moccasins are exactly where he left them before he died. Did you notice his medicine is still on the dresser, his cologne still on the bathroom shelf? It's just weird. She's going off the deep end."

Hearing their words didn't hurt her because she knew they were right. It brought musing to her. What exactly was the "deep end" and what is the way there? How does a person have a nervous breakdown?

It hadn't been a conscious act or decision on her part to leave his things as they were. It had, after all, only been a few months since his death. Instead Mona had an inability to take the action to move them; in fact, she hardly noticed any of it. His things integrated themselves into her reality and Mona felt that to move them might disrupt things. His clothes belonged beside hers in the closet. His shoes had their place under his side of the bed. His pillow belonged on the right side of the bed. Normal order reigned in her house. Except for Brian's absence, everything seemed the same. Random thoughts entered her mind. She'd be without a partner for the rest of her life. She'd be a bag lady. Maybe the last time she Brian made love was the last time ever for her.

And so, she cried as she took his clothes from the closet, his cologne from the shelf, his medicine from the dresser. Reason reigned in her mind at times. She'd never be bag lady. When have you seen a rancher who is homeless? The last and final thing a rancher has is his land. That fact is what makes ranch auctions so tragic.

John had not spoken much to Mona since Thanksgiving. She wasn't sure if he was angry or embarrassed about his drunken discussion after dinner that day. She had been prepared to talk to him about it. She thought sure he'd stop in the next day for coffee and an apology for getting drunk during Thanksgiving dinner, but she hadn't seen him all day. She checked on the livestock to make certain he had done the chores, which he had. He must have had a horrific hangover that day after Thanksgiving, but still got up early to do the chores. She heard Bo bark a few times, so Mona knew when he went out to the pasture or into the barn. Bo's bark and excited whining had turned into an audible cue to tell her time of day. Was she avoiding John, or was John avoiding *her*?

She puttered around her house and tried to find places for Brian's things. She fretted about John. She missed having someone, even someone as repressed as John, to talk with over dinner. She'd let him stew a few days and then take some cookies or something to him as an icebreaker.

As she pulled all Brian's things down from the closet and out of the drawers and separated them into piles. One pile for the Salvation Army donation, one for John. John and Brian were about the same size. Mona created one pile to keep. There were favorite things of Brian's that she was not ready to give away nor ready to see John wear, like his best Stetson hat, his favorite pair of cowboy boots, the embroidered western shirt her mother had made for him. She couldn't part with the thirty year-old buckskin-fringed vest that he had bought for the Aspen bluegrass festival. She folded those things carefully and put them into her cedar chest.

Mona also thought about what John revealed on Thanksgiving. She wanted to talk to him more about it. She wanted to know everything that he thought was suspicious about the property.

Mona remembered her parents talking about the underground testing for oil during the sixties, and how it had felt like earthquakes while they did them.

Mona had been curious about it for years. At first she thought it was testing of the earth the same way you would take a biopsy from a person. She thought at the time they should take smaller chunks of earth so as not to disturb it. Later, she read that it was nuclear testing designed to loosen shale enough to cause oil to pool. Once it pooled, it could be sucked out of the soil the same way you'd suck the soda from the bottom of a glass with a straw. She had asked her mother if it was dangerous. Now that she thought of it, Mona realized that it wasn't much different from the "Fracking" that environmentalists railed against today, except it was much worse because it involved nuclear energy and radiation. Why, when men do things unlike women, they do it with big explosions and not with finesse? And, why do they not clean up the mess after?

"Just don't drink ditch water or eat snow," her mother had told her children. "It could be radioactive even after all these years." Mona still thought of it when she saw soft clean snow falling down from above. She had never again raised her face to the snow and let it fall into her open mouth. She had passed it along to her own girls, telling them not to let the snow fall into their eyes or mouths.

Mona's father had told her all the underground testing would provide jobs in the area. Mona learned later that he'd hoped to get one of those jobs to bring in some extra money and benefits.

A chill went through Mona. Could her land be radioactive? The thought terrified her. Cancer. Genetic damage to her children and grandchildren. She knew she'd have to look into it. Another random thought; at least Brian won't die of cancer. Brian had been terrified of cancer. There seemed to be so much of it in Hawk County. But then, it seemed like there was more cancer in the whole country. She and Brian had discussed it many times. Maybe people in the past never lived long enough to get cancer. But why? Maybe they had died of cancer and nobody knew what it was. And why were so many young people getting it? What if cancer was not the worst thing that could happen? There were all kinds of devastating birth defects and nerve diseases. Mona shook off the dark thoughts.

She heard Bo barking wildly. Someone had come into the yard. It was the only time Bo barked that way.

Mona met Mark Eckland at the door.

"Mark!"

"I didn't even ring the bell," he said.

"We don't get many visitors. Bo usually warns me but . . ." Mona nodded toward the bunkhouse and the distant sound of the barking dog.

"Please come in," she said.

Mona noticed Mark was carrying a briefcase. Did he have business with her?

"I've come for Brian's records," Mark said.

"Oh," Mona said. Mark had caught her off-guard. What records? Of course, Isabel had probably told him right after she left their house that Mona had files and information that Mark might be interested in. She played dumb.

"I'm not sure I understand," she said. "Brian never discussed anything with me about business with you. But, maybe we should talk about it."

"Can I sit down?" Mark asked. He pointed his chin toward the great room.

"Sure, I'm sorry to be rude. You want coffee?"

"No thanks. I've had my fill this morning."

They settled on the sofas, facing each other. It felt good to have someone to talk to, even if Mark wasn't there to socialize. She felt vaguely conscious that her house wasn't nearly as grand as his. She probably wasn't nearly the homemaker that Isabel was. He looked around at her things and she felt as though he was critiquing her house.

"I'm glad you came. I want to ask you about your business with Brian. With my parents, for that matter. I don't think I understand it," Mona said.

"Mona, you don't need to understand. If you let me on Brian's computer and into his records, I'll just take what's mine and leave you alone. It's government business." Mark's words had the "don't worry your pretty little head about it" tone.

"I can't do that without really going through his records and understanding what they are. Maybe it would help if you would explain it to me. Obviously, Brian was not telling me everything. Maybe I need to have a lawyer look at it."

"I don't tell my wife everything either," Mark said. "There are things she's just not interested in. Other things she just plain shouldn't know."

"Like 'men's business'?" Mona asked.

"I know that in Denver, you were . . ."

"One of those women's' libbers?"

"Well, frankly, yes. You weren't raised that way, Mona. I knew your mamma and papa." Mark made it sound like she had been serving time in prison or something. She knew she was somewhere in the center, neither Democrat nor Republican, neither liberal nor conservative.

"No one knew them better than me," Mona said. "I loved them, and that's why I'm keeping this place going. They didn't have a son to take over and so I think a daughter will do just as well."

Mark let out a "hmmmph."

"I'm not sure we need to agree on my political beliefs," Mona said. She felt increasingly uncomfortable by Mark's presence. She regretted not getting John a cell phone. Her mind wandered. Maybe she'd get him one for Christmas.

She could call him if she needed to. It would take some convincing on John's part.

"You're right. So, if you'll take me to Brian's office. In the attic, isn't it?"

"Sorry, I'm not going to do that," Mona said. "I won't just let someone go and take Brian's things."

"Mona, let me warn you. I will get a warrant. I've got lawyers."

"I didn't know you were with law enforcement."

"I *am* the government, Mona. I've got power."

Something about how he said sent a chill down her back.

"I'm sure you do have power. But, not in this house. I'd like you to leave."

"I don't want bad blood between us, Mona. I'm sorry to bother you. I'm sure you won't do anything irresponsible with his records."

"Can't you tell me what this is about?" Mona asked. "What is it that you're concerned about?"

"Like I told you, it's government business. It's top-secret and I need to make sure it doesn't get out."

"Well, you don't need to worry about me. Besides, what do I know?"

She showed Mark to the door. He left so quickly in his truck that he kicked up gravel and dust that didn't clear for five minutes.

Mark's visit left Mona shaking and upset. She cried for a while, then decided to do something concrete. She went to Brian's loft office to search his computer again. She needed more information, and it seemed Mark Eckland was the only one who had it.

Logged into Brian's computer, she did an Internet search on Mark Eckland. She came up with about ten relevant hits and some completely irrelevant ones. The top ten were Mark's name on BLM meeting minutes, none of which revealed anything of interest. She did find a record of his service in Iraq. She printed the record. She knew that he had served with Mona's uncle in Iraq and that the story was that Mark was with him when he died, and had in fact Mark had been a war hero. Despite searching on this, Mona found nothing further on the Internet about Mark's service.

She went through her parent's logs again, but they were so cryptic, that Mona couldn't make sense of them. It troubled Mona that Brian had never talked about it. Why would he withhold something from her? The only answer Mona could come up with was that the logs and the business with the BLM were insignificant. It didn't matter, and Brian didn't want to bother her with it. It had to be. They talked about everything. Not about Marla, she thought. Her stomach sank with despair when she thought about Marla.

She turned again to the computer, thinking there had to be something she had missed. She found herself surfing the Internet again, randomly choosing words of interest to search: radiation, BLM, Colorado.

With a spark of hope that comes with Internet surfing, Mona thought of the BLM web site that she had been unsuccessful in getting into before. She tried again. This time, Mona put "Marla" in the password, hoping that it wouldn't work. It did. Again, her stomach sank. It was as if this last clue had flung her into reality. Her husband really had been "seeing" Marla. Beautiful red-headed Marla.

"You'll have to buck up", she told herself out-loud. Something else bothered Mona about the password, other than her jealous reaction. Who had Brian been trying to keep out of the web-site? His wife? She was probably the one person who wouldn't have known the name. The wife is always last to know. Some things Mona would never know for sure. The one thing she knew was that her girls would not know the depth of Brian's deception. Not if she could help it.

Mona turned her focus to the BLM web-site, which was massive.

She did searches on the web-site for Brian Morgan. To Mona's great relief, there was nothing about Brian. Mark Eckland's name came up in several copies of meeting minutes, which were so boring Mona couldn't imagine anyone actually reading them. But, she decided to skim a couple of the pages for information. Nothing pertinent.

She searched the web-site for "Colorado." She got three hits. One of them was for Rocky Flats in Denver, a nuclear plant that had been the focus of environmentalists for a couple of decades. There were two for Rulison, Colorado. Rulison was a small town, if it could be called that, down-valley from Hawk, near Rifle, Colorado. In fact, it was more of an area than a town. There were a couple of beaten down trailers there. That was about all Mona knew of Rulison, although she remembered the name from her mother's stories about the testing.

The articles were huge, and so Mona printed them off. She'd read them later. She skimmed them while they printed. The articles outlined Project Plowshare, a government project to use nuclear weapons for peacetime purposes. Mona felt a chill at one sentence. A nuclear device more than twice as powerful as the bomb that exploded over Hiroshima in 1945. It seemed the purpose was release natural gases and oil from shale deep within the ground. It seemed that later the project was partially funded by a private oil company. Mona remembered the talk. It was 1969 when her parents felt the man-made earthquakes. They were told it was nothing to worry about. The government had it all under control. There was some broken glass and shattered car windows, and then nothing more was said. Her family had been used to the talk of nuclear energy. It sound so much more benign when called "energy" and not "radiation."

She continued reading. The experiment had been largely a failure. Her father talked about the oil boom and then bust over twenty years ago. The gas produced by the test was too radioactive for safe use. This fact sent chills through Mona. Also, the document said, oil shale proved too expensive to process and many Western Colorado people, mostly men, lost their jobs with the large oil companies that had invested in the area. There was nothing else but ranching and not much money in that. The entire history of Colorado's

Western Slope, the land that lay to the west of the Continental Divide, was one of failed promise. Still, the rancher prevailed.

A handful of demonstrators, largely dismissed as tree-huggers and hippies had organized and demonstrated against the use of nuclear energy or nuclear testing.

The articles piqued Mona's curiosity, but she felt she had gotten off-track. It was all so "déjà vu." Once every decade or so oil and gas companies tried to wring gas and oil from the saturated shale in the Western states. Every time—so far—they'd been unsuccessful.

She piled the printed reports for reading later. She had a feeling she'd be doing a lot of reading with Brian gone. She had lots of lonely evenings to fill and luckily she liked to read. Television was an occasional diversion. Reading really took her away from her problems.

Mona shut down Brian's computer and went downstairs to make tea. She didn't bother locking the office door. It just made it harder to get into the next time. Late afternoon had become a lonely time for Mona. Her mood would go down with the sun. She decided to call John over for tea. If he weren't in the field, he'd hear the cast-iron dinner bell on the back porch. Mona rang it vigorously and waited. Sure enough, John showed up five minutes later.

"Yes, ma'am?" he said. He held his had sheepishly in his hands like a small boy. Bo came into the house with John.

"Hi Bo, I've missed you," Mona said. She tossed him some leftover cheese from the fridge.

"I wrangled your dog away from you, didn't I?" asked John. "You want him back?"

"John, I think Bo is better with you. He needs the work. Don't you boy?" The dog wagged his tail wildly at Mona. He had been Brian's dog, not so much hers, but she loved him just the same.

"I didn't cook dinner, but I've got leftovers. I've got turkey and ham that I froze from Thanksgiving. You want to join me for dinner?"

"I wasn't sure you'd still be talkin' to me," John said. "After the fool I made of myself."

"Don't think twice. It happens to the best of us," Mona said. "Besides, it got me thinking about things."

Mona heated up dinner and baked some fresh biscuits and they ate quietly. After pie and ice cream, Mona brought out the box with some of Brian's things that would go to John. "I'd like you to have these. And, this silver jewelry. These are some silver bolo ties and a couple of turquoise and silver bracelets that Brian bought in New Mexico. The girls don't think they want it," Mona said.

"Thanks ma'am," John said. "I'm honored. And, whenever you want to borrow Bo, you just whistle."

***

Although it was only eight o'clock, Mona went to bed. She had lately been in the habit of taking a shot of brandy before going to bed. It helped her sleep.

Mona woke from a vivid dream. It hadn't been a nightmare really, but what her mother used to call a "worry dream" where things were not quite right, not quite what they were meant to be. She was cold and pulled the quilt up over her shoulder. Then, the barking.

Mona looked out her bedroom window, from which she could see the back of the bunkhouse. There was no light on. A glance at the clock told her it was one o'clock. She'd never get back to sleep and sighed at that knowledge. She'd go down and get tea, make a fire and read.

She pulled on her robe for warmth.

More barking, louder this time.

She hurried down the stairs and looked out the kitchen window. Nothing, still no light on at the bunkhouse. Bo continued to bark; a different bark than normal, more urgent. Had something happened to John? She opened the back door off the kitchen and yelled at Bo. It had no effect. Maybe he had seen an animal; a coyote or raccoon. It wouldn't be unusual. She thought of the sheep and hoped the coyotes stayed away. She couldn't afford to lose livestock to coyotes or cougars.

She heard a thump upstairs in Brian's office. She froze, a chill of fear running down her spine. The old house sometimes made noises, the creakings of a century old house moving with the earth. But, this was different. She thought of a raccoon again. Maybe she'd run to the bunkhouse to get John, since he probably had his cell turned off. She backed into the corner toward the phone. She debated calling 911. It would take them an hour to get out to the house and if she was wrong, if there were nobody in the house.

More thumping. She looked toward the back stairs to Brian's office. The light was on. Had she left the light on to his office?

She started up the stairs to the office grabbing a broom she'd left at the bottom of the stairs. Her knees knocked together from fear. Her heart pounded in her chest and her hands shook. Why was her cell phone never in her hand when she needed it? Maybe she left the window open up there. She tried to remember. Almost to the top of the stairs, something hit her. She heard it before she felt it, a dull thud that signaled metal against her skull. It was a hard hit and knocked her painfully down the stairs. She felt something brush past her, then darkness.

Chapter 17

Monday night, Heartbreak Ranch

Dazed and dizzy, Mona opened her eyes and felt hot breath on her face. She heard a rhythmic sound, kind of a whooshing. Panting. Her eyes stung and the tears that rolled from her eyes seemed to be caused by physical pain. Then her memory kicked in. She felt terror, as if in a waking nightmare.

My God, somebody's in the house.

She mustered her energy to get up, fearing another blackout. Her head, in the back, throbbed with bolts of pain. She felt back there. A goose-egg. She wondered for a moment if her pain and dizziness were caused by a stroke. *But, there wouldn't be a lump unless I hit it when I fell.* The fear of fading to darkness overwhelmed her. My God, what if had she died right here on the stairs? What would the girls do then?

The panting continued, punctuated by worried whines. "Bo," she said. "How'd you . . ." Mona's leg throbbed. Not as much as the leg. Another current of terror rushed through her. She wondered why Bo wasn't barking. What kind of guard-dog was he? Then, she realized that if Bo was in the house then John must have let him in because the dog had been with him in the bunkhouse.

What if John was hurt too? Her mind went to her closet up in her bedroom where Brian had kept a loaded hunting rifle. He had called it his twenty-two and had said it was not big enough to be dangerous unless he shot someone directly in the head with it, but big enough to scare someone away. Just the sound of a shotgun being cocked, metal on metal, was enough to scare someone away. But, the rifle would be too far away. The only time in her life she thought she needed it and it was never handy. Her heart thudded with fear. Her hands shook.

"Mona, are you alright, ma'am?"

Mona heard John's voice. She looked up and he had bent over her. He looked frightened. He picked a hell of a time to be quiet.

"John?"

"Yeah, it's me. What happened?"

"You tell me, John. Somebody was in the house. Did you see anybody?"

A passing thought made Mona wonder if John would hurt her. He did have a key. Only he and the girls had keys to her house.

"Bo woke me up barking. Like to break my eardrums, he was barking so loud. I heard a car, maybe a truck drive away real fast. I came runnin' to the house and found you like this. Did you fall?"

"No, John, I decided to sleep on the stairs. I was thinking about calling an ambulance."

Mona caught the confused look pass in a second across John's face. Then just as quickly, it dissipated. He never did understand sarcasm.

"Sorry. I'm grouchy. Someone was in the house, John. I think I heard somebody rustling around in Brian's office in the attic. My God, somebody broke into my house." She understood now the feeling of violation a person has when robbed. Her feeling of safety had vanished out the same door the intruder had escaped.

John helped Mona up and sat her up on a chair in the kitchen. She felt dizzy. She had a nasty bump on her head, but didn't think she had a concussion. Of course, she wondered if a person with a concussion would know it or not.

"You want me to call 911?" John asked.

"No. Are you kidding? But, please sit for a minute while I get my bearings," she said. "I think I need ice for my ankle." She could move it, so didn't think it was broken.

"We could call Travis to come out," said John. "He could go after this guy, whoever it is."

"No, I don't want to create a big fuss. They probably think I'm a big drama queen or something."

"What's a *drama queen*?" asked John. He brought her ice and had put on the teakettle to make tea.

"Never mind," she said, irritated that John was failing to understand her.

Bo stuck by Mona's side too and she let them tend to her. The dog's expressive eyes showed concern. She felt safer. After all, if Bo trusted John, why shouldn't she?

For a second she doubted John again. But, she had heard the truck drive away. She'd remembered it in her haze of struggling for consciousness. So, it couldn't have been John.

"Who do you suppose it was, John?" she asked. She immediately thought of Mark Eckland. She wanted someone else to say it first. Obviously, he had wanted Brian's records and Mona would not let him have them. Who else could it have been?

"Don't know why anybody would want to do that. Maybe they wanted his computer?" suggested John. "And, there's something else."

"What?"

"The other ranch hands always said there was money hid in your parent's property. Maybe in the house. Maybe he was after that." John looked a little sheepish. Mona figured he had thought about it for a long time before saying anything to her.

"Why would they say that?" Mona asked.

"Just one of those legends that gets around by word of mouth. They also say there's gold buried somewhere above Wanda's place. You know how it is. Everybody wants to go on a treasure hunt. I doubt there's any gold buried in that old woman's property. But, the story about your parents has been around a long time. That they had a lot of money squirreled away in this house. The way they were able to send you off to college the way they did and nobody else could afford to send their kids to college at all."

"There's nothing stashed away. Not in my house. You can pass it around that there isn't anything hidden in my attic. We've had the place renovated, remember? There's nothing stashed on the land either. Besides, it's not as expensive to go to a state college as you'd think."

It explained why so many contractors were eager to do work for her and Brian. Maybe they wanted access to the house. It also explained all the torn down walls as they renovated—some of them Brian didn't think needed to be torn down.

"Yes ma'am. Didn't mean to make you upset. And for the record, I never said it was in the attic. And, I myself never poked around much. I always gave your parents their privacy. I always thought of myself as a guest here. Still do."

Mona realized that she wanted John to be more open with her. She knew what worked with the girls and it wasn't criticism. John, like many born-in-Colorado men, said more with body language than most people did with words. What he had just uttered to her was the most candid she thought he'd been for quite a while.

"I'm sorry, John. It's just that I feel violated right now. Somebody broke into my house, hit me, and stole God knows what out of my house."

"He didn't touch you did he?"

"You mean rape?" she asked. "No. I would have told you if that had happened."

John cringed. "I know, ma'am. And, if I find out who it is, I'll take care of it for you."

"What does that mean?"

"Oh, don't worry. I wouldn't kill nobody. I would just mess him up a little bit."

Mona wondered for a brief second if that applied to a woman. It seemed a little odd that he didn't seem to date or bring any women around. Of course, how many women would go for a semi-hermit ranch hand that lived in a bunkhouse? To his credit, maybe that's why his dream was to build a house.

"I appreciate it, but let's let the law take care of it. Just to be clear, I don't want you to hurt anyone. You could get in serious trouble."

"Sometimes the law can't help," said John. "But, you want me to do anything for you or the girls; I'll lay down my own life."

"And, you know you're part of this family and we'd do the same for you." Mona would have to think about laying down her life for her ranch hand, but it seemed like the right thing to say. She knew she would give a kidney to each of her girls. But, would she do that for John? She'd have to think about it pretty hard. She wasn't even sure she would have given one to Brian. But the girls, she wouldn't have to think about it for a minute. She'd give both her kidneys to save her daughters.

"You want to talk about what we should do now?" asked John. "You said you don't want me to call anybody."

"Let's not think about it until morning. Would you stay here? On the sofa?" Mona felt suddenly self-conscious about what she was wearing. She had on Brian's old flannel pajamas that were three sizes too large and over that her flannel robe. She must look slovenly, but it hardly mattered. It wasn't like she was trying to be attractive for John.

They locked up the house, Mona left John on the sofa and Bo beside him. They lit a fire in the fireplace and she gave them two blankets to keep them warm before she went up to bed. She slept fitfully, one ear open for noises. Her head and leg throbbed despite the extra strength aspirin she had taken. She longed for the stash of painkillers she had thrown away because they had gone past expiration.

***

When Mona woke again, she smelled brewing coffee downstairs. Her head still hurt and she wondered again if she had a concussion. It hardly mattered. If she hadn't died last night she probably was not going to. The last thing she needed right now was more town gossip. A trip to the emergency room would certainly stoke a couple of good rumors.

She showered, dressed, and limped downstairs. It looked like John had started the coffee, made himself some toast, bacon and eggs, and had gone out to do the chores. There was some bacon left on the counter under a paper towel. It was eight-thirty, according to the kitchen wall clock. John had cleaned up after himself. Come to think of it, the guy was fairly clean. She'd never seen the bunkhouse look messy. Of course, she didn't go in there often either.

"I need to work on my schedule," Mona said out loud. She felt scattered and unproductive, although she was unclear what she was supposed to accomplish. She sometimes missed the regimented and grueling routing of corporate life.

She ate something quick and then called Travis to report the break-in. He'd come out later to write up the report, he told her. Travis hadn't seemed overly shocked or concerned, although it could have been the "by the way" attitude that Mona had been careful to convey. She'd "buried the lead" as her journalism friend used to say. She'd started out asking him how his day was and talking about the ranch.

Mona went upstairs to assess the damage to Brian's office. Whoever it was didn't get Brian's hard-drive, which Mona had feared. Maybe this person didn't know much about computers. He took the monitor but not the hard-drive. Why take a monitor unless you thought the data was on it? No wonder the person had seemed so awkward and clumsy. It wouldn't have been easy to lug a monitor down the stairs. It would prove to be almost useless to the thief. Someone more computer-able might simply have downloaded her files or broken into her computer electronically.

Some of the paper files were gone too, but he hadn't found the cubbyhole in the wall where the important stuff was stored. Whoever it was got a pile of unpaid bills. Mona was glad she hadn't mentioned the cubbyhole to anyone, not even the girls. The question arose about what would happen if she died. Who would know about the information in the cubbyhole? She would have to worry about that later. For now, she didn't want her daughters in danger because of a few documents. She wasn't a hundred percent sure of John yet.

Someone had raised the ante here and Mona didn't know why. But, she had to be careful whom she told what. She hadn't told Wanda, which was good. Wanda, though a good soul, had a big mouth. Mona needed to be more careful with her own mouth, unless of course she wanted everyone in the valley to know.

She decided not to volunteer the information to Travis. He looked at the office superficially and didn't poke around too much.

"Anything missing, Mona?" he asked. He walked around the office, peering at things.

"The computer monitor."

"Oh, yeah," he said. "Any other damage?" He didn't seem to think it odd that they took only the monitor. Mona wondered how familiar Travis was with computers. She took her own knowledge for granted, having worked in business for a long time herself. Maybe they thought the data was stored in the monitor.

"Not that I could tell. Except to the back kitchen door. He broke the lock right off. John put on a new one. Sometimes I just leave it unlocked. I guess from now on, I'll lock it—not that it'll help much."

"Breaking and entering." Travis wrote something in his book.

"What should I do now?"

"Not much we can do without a description. Could be somebody driving through. Most break-ins around here aren't perpetrated by people who live here."

"Like I told you, I didn't really see him. He was dressed all in black. It's a blur."

"Well, maybe he'll try to fence the computer monitor."

"What would he get for it, under fifty bucks?" she asked. "That hardly justifies a break in. He was after something else."

"I don't know that much about computers, Mona. I'm just glad you weren't hurt."

"I *was* hurt." Mona started to cry much to her dismay. She never liked baiting sympathy, but she felt truly pathetic.

"I'm sorry, Mona. Please don't cry. We'll find out who did this," Travis said. He put his big burly arms around her and she felt a stir of actual feeling in her body.

"No, I'm sorry. I'm just emotional right now. Let's just file a report and see what happens."

"You want me to drive by occasionally to keep an eye on your place?" he asked.

"No, you don't need to do that. John's here."

"Well, you should know I drive by occasionally anyway, just to watch over you. Besides, how do you know it wasn't him?"

Mona gave Travis her best shocked look. "Why would I have reason to mistrust John?"

"No reason. It's just that how much does anybody know about this guy. Even if he's been around for twenty years or so, the guy's a little weird. You know what they say about quiet guys? He did prison time, you know."

"As a juvenile. And, it was for a car accident. That could happen to anyone. My parents trusted him, that's good enough for me," she said, trying to convince herself. Travis had installed doubt into her mind.

"Anybody come around looking for the girls or anything? You know how young guys are?"

"No. Besides, why would they go to the trouble to steal a computer monitor if they were looking for the girls? That just doesn't make sense."

"Just throwing out ideas," he said.

"I'll be fine, Travis. Thanks for thinking of me."

"I always think of you, Mona. Always have." With that, Travis left.

***

Christmas was a simple but comforting affair. Mona ordered a pre-cooked honey-baked ham and it proved a delicious and easy choice. The girls reminded her that their dad always had to have turkey at any holiday. In fact, Brian had driven Mona nuts over his need to cook the turkey in a different way every Christmas.

Mona felt relief when Christmas vacation was over and the girls were on their way back at school. Her solitude had become habit; she'd wrapped it around her like a blanket and now the extra activity had worn her out. She still grieved for Brian and vacillated between the need for solitude and the intense need to be around people. The girls cried a good deal over the two weeks they were home. That made Mona worry about them, but they assured her that at school they could get away from it and be happy at least part of the time.

Mona obsessed about Brian and Marla. She could not get the image, imagined or not, out of her head. Nor could she forget about the little boy. She felt guilt about him. What if he was Brian's child and she was completely shutting him off from his half-sisters? But, if she brought him into the girls' lives, would they resent her or think less of their father? Mona thought about it until it drove her nearly crazy.

Something worse bothered her though. She felt certain that Brian had been murdered. She could not feel safe in the farmhouse until she found out who had done it. She would worry about the girls until she knew who had done it. She turned then to researching Brian's death.

***

The Tuesday after Christmas Bob Higgins from the insurance company surprised Mona with a visit. For a fleeting moment after she opened the door, Mona hoped he had come to hand deliver a check. Heartbreak Ranch's finances could buckle with two college tuition payments due and no money coming in. How had Brian kept it afloat? Mona figured she'd be out of money by April. She had already started looking for employment. Her employment options were limited unless she moved back to Denver or could find some job she could do from home. A year or so ago, there were lots of internet-based jobs which she could do at home, but now with everyone wanting a work-at-home job, it would take a miracle to get a job like that. That wouldn't stop her from trying.

Bob Higgins stood defiantly holding his briefcase. He had an assistant with him, a young man in an overly large suit. Either the young man had borrowed the suit from a larger man or had recently lost weight. This didn't look like a friendly visit. Mona's nerves jangled just looking at Bob Higgins, and his assistant annoyed her before he even opened his mouth.

"I'm Ryan Whitaker," the young man said. His right hand shot out for a handshake, which Mona returned. She didn't say anything, but opened the door and ushered them in.

Having sat them in the living room, she said, "Have you come with the insurance check?" She already knew the answer.

"Afraid not, Mrs. Morgan. As you know, we're investigating your husband's death."

"Yes, you told me last time you were here. Why would you need to make a personal visit unless you had something to give me?"

"I do, as a matter of fact, have something for you," said Bob. He briskly pulled up his briefcase and opened it.

Could it actually be a check? But, no such luck. Mr. Higgins pulled out a folded piece of paper much too large to be a check. He handed it to her.

"It's a search-warrant that I've asked Denver detectives to get. Local law enforcement should be here with it soon," he explained.

So, Bob Higgins had talked to detectives about Brian's death.

Soon Travis was at the door with two policemen from Glenwood Springs.

"I wanted to come, Mona. I'm sorry I knew about this the other day, but couldn't say anything," he said.

"I understand, Travis, but what is this about?"

"Insurance fraud, supposedly," Travis said. "They're doubting Brian's death was an accident."

"What are you talking about? Brian took that policy out on himself. It's not like someone else did."

"Mona, it could be anything. They want to rule out foul-play." Travis did his best to comfort her. He looked guilty about having brought the search warrant.

Soon men with big muddy boots overran the house. They ransacked Mona's house and she couldn't do a thing about it. Their muddy footprints tattooed the floors all over the house. They turned over drawers in every room of the house. Of course, as Mona knew they would, they came up with nothing. She breathed a sigh of relief that they hadn't found the cubbyhole in the attic office. It felt like her guilty secret, like the bottle of Valium she once hid from Brian.

"Travis, what are they looking for?" Mona asked.

Travis had a helpless look on his face. "I can't tell you that. I heard them talking, but I don't think I can tell you. Not yet."

Mona glared at him.

"It's a stun gun. They're looking for a stun gun."

Mona let out a gasp. She thought of her daughter's stun gun. Her brain spun. Maybe she should have taken the stun gun and tossed it. But, then she'd have something to hide. There was no law against having a stun gun and a lot of young people were carrying them.

Travis took Mona by both shoulders. "Is there something you need to tell me? Anything?"

"No. Well, Wanda had a stun gun at her house. The day I went over there."

"Mona, it's probably the one I gave her. You don't suppose she did something to Brian?"

"Why would she do anything with Brian? She didn't have anything against Brian. She loved my parents." She thought of Wanda, skinny and wiry as a Bantam chicken, trying to attack a man three times her size. It simply didn't make any sense unless she'd had help.

"Who knows why people do anything. I'll see if I can her to turn it over. You did the right thing."

Then, why did she feel so bad? Now they would be harassing Wanda. Wanda was a sweet old lady who had been kind to Mona. This was how she repaid her? Mona felt sick about them interrogating Wanda. She felt sick about all of it.

Chapter 18

New Year's Eve, Heartbreak Ranch

New Year's Eve sent little relief Mona's way. How would she keep the ranch going with a paltry income? Was Marla's son Brian's son? How would her two girls react to the possibility of having a brother? She had no doubt that eventually they would act with generosity and love. Still, Mona didn't want it to be true. *Please God, don't let this baby be Brian's.* This worry weighed heavy on Mona, but not as heavy as the thought that Brian might have been murdered. Not only that, certain people seemed to think Mona was to blame. The "Hawk grapevine" was becoming heavy with grapes of rumor and allegation.

She called Miranda and Skye around six o'clock on New Year's Eve. She told them to please be safe. They both assured her they were going to private parties. Of course, Mona knew that teens didn't always tell their parents everything, but she felt better having talked with them. The words were on the tip of her tongue, the words that would tell the girls they might have a brother. But the words stayed there and would not come out. Instead, shallow words about mundane subjects came out.

***

Winter had sucked the life out of most of the vegetation; evergreens had taken on a dusty grayish green as if the dry winter had drained the water from them. Mona began to feel joy at every snowfall that cleaned the air and cover the ground and bare trees with a blanket of white. Each snowfall seemed to bring peace to her. She took long walks through the snowy fields, letting the white powder rain down on her like cold powdered sugar. She had her fireplace going almost all the time now.

What had happened to Brian out in that field on that horrible day? What went wrong with the fence? If only Bo could talk and tell her what happened. If only Brian would come to her in a dream and tell her or show her what happened.

While Brian visited Mona almost nightly in her dreams, they never talked about anything of importance. They talked about her day, about how he missed her coffee in the morning. In her dreams she never asked him where he was or what happened to him on that day. How odd, she thought, that if there really were a connection, he could tell her how he died.

Mona heard a rustle of activity outside, Bo's urgent bark, and the heavy thud of a truck door slamming. Travis had come back with another search warrant, this time for the bunkhouse. Obviously they hadn't thought about that the first time. He was humble, apologetic. He was just doing his job, he told her.

In the distance, Mona saw John wave Travis and another deputy into his small bunkhouse. Mona had gone too, against Travis' wishes.

They found a shotgun, which Mona knew he had, and not much else that could be construed as a weapon. They didn't take the gun with them, most likely because Brian hadn't died from a gunshot wound. John lived like a Spartan. Mona felt a pang of admiration and envy looking inside John's living space. Who knew you could live with so little and be so content? He had a few pair of rugged and worn jeans, a few western shirts hanging neatly in his closet (which was an open alcove with a single closet bar), a few sport shirts, some underwear and not much else. Mona thought that if asked, John's prize possession would be either

Bo or the scrap of paper on which he had drawn his dream house.

Travis and the investigator he had brought with him left John's bunkhouse carrying a small paper sack. He waved at Mona as he climbed into his truck. She suspected he didn't want to bring the investigator into her house and let him see how friendly he and Mona had become. She waved back from the front porch and stepped back inside. She'd ask John later what had happened. She saw John head for the pasture with Bo. There was little to do out there this time of year except to look for stray sheep, which was rare. Sheep were— well, sheep; they stay together. There weren't really any ditches to clean and maybe an occasional downed fence. Mostly, Mona suspected, John and Bo both needed the routine.

Alone in her kitchen, Mona worried about John. And herself. Then, Mona turned her worry to Wanda. It didn't seem right that an old woman should be so alone. Her daughter rarely contacted her, although Mona felt she would show up in a New York minute when Wanda died. Wanda's property was worth a few million on a bad day. Wanda didn't answer her phone, but Mona knew the old woman was probably at home. Wanda was as predictable as spring lambing. Mona drove to Wanda's house, certain that her elderly neighbor would also receive a visit from law enforcement. It was best to be there for support if it happened.

Wanda met her at the door. She opened the door and walked toward the kitchen, waving Mona in.

"I'm putting on the kettle for tea," she yelled. "Make yourself to home. Just so happens I baked yesterday too. Just in time." Wanda was so thin and frail looking she looked almost like a bird. Mona doubted she ate much of anything unless she cooked for company. Looks were deceiving though; Wanda was known to do her own farm chores, even helping to brand cattle back in the day when she had cattle on her ranch.

Without waiting for Wanda to instruct her, Mona went to the living room and sat on the sofa in front of the stone fireplace where Wanda had a fire going. It took the chill off Mona, which was partly caused by nerves and the nearly constant anxiety that had gripped her since she lost Brian. She had been startled by the ease at which Wanda let her into the house. Maybe she didn't know that Mona was the reason for the search of her house.

Wanda came back with a wooden tray with a teapot, two cups, and sugar and cream. She looked haggard, even for a woman of her age. Never one for makeup or sprucing herself up, she looked wrinkled and old. She had on an embroidered sweatshirt and jeans, the entire outfit accessorized with heavy turquoise jewelry. Mona was always tickled by Wanda's affinity for denim. When Wanda dressed up, she usually chose a denim skirt with cowboy boots and added a large squash-blossom turquoise necklace that would sit heavily on her sunken chest.

"I wanted to make sure you're alright," Mona said.

"I'm alright. Same as always," Wanda said. This was about as depressed as Wanda seemed to get. Usually stoic and sometimes dryly funny, Wanda's moods didn't seem to fluctuate much. She reminded Mona of her own parents in that way. They'd come from that strong silent generation that suffered alone. They celebrated in solitude. They worried and plotted in silence. Allowing too much outward joy invited trouble.

Silence.

"Wanda . . ."

"I think I know why you came." Wanda said.

"Why?" asked Mona. She wanted Wanda's view before she spoke.

"It was about them men coming in here and ransacking my house." Wanda became visibly more agitated and Mona could tell it had been traumatic for the old woman. Mona's stomach sank with regret.

"The search warrant," Mona said. She'd been right; they had a warrant for Wanda's place too.

"Well, whatever you call it. They made a terrible mess. All they found was that damned stun gun. Glad the thing's gone. I'd never use it anyway. Why anyone would want one of the contraptions is beyond me. Would have thrown the damn thing out in the cow pasture under some cow dung if I'd known they was coming. Would have told them where it was if they'd asked."

"Wanda, you know they searched my house too," Mona said. "They searched the bunkhouse. I know how intrusive that feels. I'm not trying to minimize how you feel." Mona regretted her words. She felt herself slipping back into the office speak that businesses use to placate employees.

"I'm not the kind of woman who worries much about feelings," Wanda said. "It made me damn mad."

They sipped their tea.

"It's true what I told, you know," Wanda said.

"What's true?" Mona's heart beat faster; sure Wanda was going to say something about Brian.

"That I killed my husband," she said.

Mona put down her teacup. She had wondered if Wanda remembered telling Mona about her husband right after Brian died.

"I killed him. Smothered him. He begged me to do it. He suffered so while he was sick. Almost two years. He moaned all the time. Wouldn't go to the doctor toward the end, and the only way to get the drugs to help him would be to go to the doctor. What the hell is an MRI for anyway? To drain your pocketbook for no good reason, that's what."

"Wanda, I'm so sorry."

Wanda waved her arm toward Mona as if to say it was ok. "Someone told me to go to the Internet to get a prescription, but what does an old woman know about a computer? I was about to go to Mexico to get some painkillers, but what would I ask for? The last time I used a painkiller was when I had my daughter. Damned if I could remember what they used on me. We were in a terrible predicament, him and me. He wanted out he was in so much pain. Kept asking why God didn't want him up in heaven."

"Wanda, I'm sorry. But, I thought you were not going to talk about this. Remember our agreement not to tell anyone?" Mona remembered Wanda told her she'd given him pills. Nothing about smothering.

"Smothered him. Didn't have pills, otherwise I would've used 'em. I have nightmares about it, but I think I was the only one to help him. He went real peaceful. No struggle. He was too damned weak for struggle. When he saw me coming at me with that pillow I saw the thank you in his eyes. He never said things like thank you and I love you. Things just weren't that way in my day. I know he loved me though. Who would put up with an ugly old woman like me except him? He never wandered in his life that I knew about. That's the important thing. Me and that crusty old guy built up this place with our own two hands. Never told me he loved me, but I knew it the same way I knew the sun was in the sky for a reason." Wanda had tears coming from her eyes, but her expression hadn't changed. She was one tough bird.

"Wanda, remember that you must not tell anyone else this. It is between the two of us. I'm glad you told me the details just so you could get it off your chest. Now we're closer friends. But, you must not tell another soul. And, I want you to know that you're the bravest person I know and that I think you did a good thing to help him out of his pain. I hope someone does the same for me when my time comes."

Mona thought that her husband's death had weighed on Wanda's chest a hundred times the weight of her turquoise necklace.

Mona took Wanda's hands, which were ice cold and bony as chicken feet. She wished Wanda could have gotten help. Mona knew that a hospice would have helped Wanda and her husband but that he had been too stubborn or scared to go. Or, maybe they couldn't afford it.

"I never told anyone," Wanda said. "I was sure they were coming for me that day they came with the warrant. I almost shouted it out, just to get it over with. Almost told them to take me away and put me in prison. I did it, I killed him."

"Did you hear me, that you should not say this to anyone again? But you shouldn't worry about it either. Nobody is coming for you." She wasn't about to let this old woman get dragged into a controversy over a man nobody else tried to help.

"I heard." Wanda sat back. "Then, I realized it was about your Brian. Good God, why would I hurt Brian? He wasn't the easiest guy to get along with. We had that fight about him treating John right. He didn't do right by John after all the time he spent with your parents helping them and all after they lost their son and all."

"I didn't know you didn't get along with Brian," Mona said.

"Could take him or leave him, tell the truth," she said. "Good-looking isn't everything. Your husband could charm the pants off a snake."

"I'm sorry you felt that way about Brian. Really, he was a good husband and father. He was hardworking and smart."

"Then, why did you kill him?" Wanda asked.

Wanda's words stabbed at Mona.

"Wanda, I did not kill my husband. I know how the local gossip works. I know that he was seeing another woman, but believe me; I didn't have anything to do with his death."

"I was just testing you to see what you'd say. I don't see you doing something like that," Wanda said. "I'm a little worried that John might have."

"John?"

"Couldn't stand Brian, you know. Brian was trying to cheat him out of the land that he worked a lifetime for. Sometimes people mistake quiet for stupid. John isn't educated, but he sure ain't stupid. He knows about things and has the patience to read and find out about things."

There it was again. The issue about the land that John was promised by her parents. Why in God's name hadn't they given it to John while they were still alive? It was like them, Mona remembered, to make somebody wait a lifetime for something. After all, they had to wait lifetimes for the things they got. Had they been more generous with John, maybe much of this heartbreak could have been avoided.

"Wanda, I know how you feel. We're going to get to the bottom of this. And, for the record, I didn't know about John and the land. I should have known. Brian should have told me, but he didn't. My parents should have told me."

"I know you would've given it to him. I figured Brian didn't tell you. God knows why your parents didn't tell you. They probably all figured you give it to John too soon. God forbid he didn't have to wait the rest of his life for it."

"Wanda, I know that sooner or later you and I would have talked and you would have asked me about the land. I hope we're lifelong friends. I'm always here for you. I hope you know that."

"I would have given it to them, you know. If they had asked kindly, I would have given them the stun gun. They didn't have to wreck my place. Took me days to get it back to normal. Those people are animals."

"Well, they have their own ways of doing things. They can't just ask you for a piece of evidence in case you try to alter it in some way. You might have cleaned it or something," Mona said. Mona thought about her handling the stun gun. Her prints would be on it. It seemed like the universe was conspiring against her lately.

"If I had done something evil with it, why would I keep it? It doesn't make sense."

"That's true, Wanda. Did you tell them that?"

"Of course I did. Thanks for coming over. I feel better getting things off my chest. I feel so free now that you know. Remember, you can tell me anything. Tit for tat." Could it be that Wanda still thought Mona killed her husband and expected her to confess to her? Mona shook off the thought.

"Just remember not to tell anyone else about your husband. Let's give him some peace. And, I think you deserve some peace yourself."

Wanda nodded and they finished their tea in silence. Mona felt so comfortable now in Wanda's living room that she could have stayed forever, drinking tea and watching the fireplace.

***

That night, Mona dreamed of having an undiscovered secret. It haunted her all night. In her dream, she knew where someone was buried and was afraid Travis would find out. The dream seemed to go on and on. She had taken on some of Wanda's secret and now it would be a part of her forever. She had to trust herself to keep that secret. Sometimes the law and common sense seemed to cross boundaries.

Travis came over the next day, Monday, with some information he had on Brian's death. He told her it was what the detectives had come up with so far.

"I don't want you to read it," he told her. "I don't think you can handle the pictures and even the diagrams. I'm barely getting used to seeing this stuff myself. But, I want you to know what it says."

"I already read the autopsy—this couldn't be any worse." Adrenaline rushed into her bloodstream. She felt a little faint and wanted to sit down.

"Can I come inside?" he asked.

"Sure. Come on in." I'll get some coffee. Mona rushed into the kitchen and leaned for a minute on the kitchen island to steady herself until she felt better.

Mona brought coffee and coffeecake and they settled in front of the fireplace.

Just give me the bottom line," Mona said. "Accidental death?"

"Mona, they've classified this as a suspicious death and not natural causes."

"What does that mean?"

"It means an ordinarily healthy man dies suddenly. There were no witnesses, at least that we know of. Let me explain that an autopsy is supposed to determine four things; cause of death, mechanism of death, manner of death, and time of death."

"If you remember, the autopsy listed the cause of death as drowning, not heart attack. And, not electrocution. The combined electricity from the fence and the stun gun was probably enough to knock him out, but probably wouldn't have killed him."

"Oh, God. He did drown then?"

"Likely he was unconscious. I wouldn't worry about him dying in pain or fear. Also, as we knew from the autopsy, he didn't have a heart attack or stroke. He had little sign of heart disease. Sometimes aneurysm explains sudden death in younger people, but that was ruled out as well. There were no birth defects of any kind internally or externally. That's in case you worry for your girls. Sometimes there's some internal defect that causes death at a relatively young age."

"But, we knew all this, didn't we?" she asked.

"No surprise on time of death. He had probably been dead a couple hours when you found him. Mechanism of death is different."

"Tell me," she said.

"From the pictures taken at the autopsy, they found two marks consistent with the stun gun. They may not have found it if someone hadn't brought up the possibility. That's how small it was." Travis looked intently at her. Was he looking for signs of worry or guilt? It made Mona self-conscious. How does an innocent woman act? This was all new to her. This explained why the investigators had seized Wanda's stun gun. John wouldn't have one. He was against most self-defense items accept for a rifle.

"Travis, I have to tell you that the insurance adjuster is going along these lines too. They noticed the stun gun marks. I didn't want to tell you in case it led the detectives down a wrong path."

"You can trust me, Mona," he said.

"Travis, was there anything else?"

"Based on where the stun gun marks are, they think he was turned over so that he would drown in the ditch. He probably fell face-up first. That ups the ante on his death."

"What do you mean?"

"We're looking at murder. Someone went out to kill him. It doesn't look at all like an accident. If someone were playing around with the stun gun or threatening him with it, that's one thing, but if they were out to kill him, that's another. Some detectives are coming out tomorrow to make plaster casts of the area. Unfortunately, most tracks and footprints are likely washed away. That's the trouble with us rural people. That's what they'll say anyway, that we don't know what we're doing out here in the boondocks."

"Travis, what about the stun gun that they sent in for prints?"

"This is where it gets weird. My fingerprints were on it. Makes sense, since I gave the damn thing to Wanda way back when her husband was still alive. They didn't believe in guns and two people living alone like that are vulnerable. Especially since her daughter was a drug addict at one time. I got enthusiastic about stun guns because they don't kill. Usually. You can disable someone and still have time for the sheriff to get there to help you."

"Your fingerprints were on the stun gun?"

"Yes, but so were yours, Mark Eckland's, Isabel Eckland's. And Wanda's. It doesn't really say much."

"Why would Mark and Isabel's fingerprints be on the stun gun?" Then Mona remembered that Wanda had told her about the Eckland's visit.

"Maybe for the same reason yours were, Mona. They visited Wanda occasionally too. Isabel stopped by occasionally and so did Mark. Word was Wanda kept it up top of the medicine cabinet in the bathroom. You know how people tend to open the medicine cabinet in people's bathroom just to see what's inside. I've heard of people stealing medication and that sort of thing that you have to get a prescription for. Another possibility is I showed the stun gun to Mark Eckland before I gave it to Wanda. He was interested in getting one himself. It's amazing how popular they are getting."

"I remember now that Wanda said it had fallen out when she'd had Isabel over."

"They were friends—Wanda and Isabel?"

"I don't think so. I think it was a casual thing. Wanda was trying to be more neighborly, I think. I think it's odd that Wanda wouldn't have put it away given that it kept falling off the cabinet. Maybe the old woman is more sinister than we think. Maybe she knew people would pick it up and leave prints on it." Now she was implicating Wanda in Brian's murder. It was too crazy to think about, and yet she'd said it out loud.

"It's a little 'out there' to think she could hurt Brian. Not unheard of that an old person would commit murder—but, what's her motive? I don't see it."

Travis left Mona more worried than ever. She had plenty to worry about and not sure whom to trust. Could she trust Travis? He was so likable and easy-going how could anyone not like him? She decided to be careful what she told him. He wouldn't leave a copy of the report because the Denver detectives had not cleared it.

And there was Wanda. Could the old woman be so wracked with guilt about putting her husband out of his pain that she had gone crazy? Mona shuddered at that thought.

Chapter 19

Monday, Heartbreak Ranch

Mona never expected to hear Marla Rodgers' voice at the other end of a phone call, especially one that Marla had initiated. Who could forget the attractive voice that went along with the attractive woman? Just the sound of it plunged Mona into primal female envy. Couldn't Marla at least have the annoying Colorado twang?

"Mona?"

Mona felt annoyed again at the familiarity of her name coming from Marla. "Yes?"

"I need to talk to you. Can you come by?"

"I don't think that would be appropriate. I just don't think it's a good idea, at least until everything gets straightened out."

"I need money to pay my rent."

"Have you thought of getting a job?"

Marla's statement stirred a burning rage inside Mona. Mona felt like a shrew, like a jealous wife. Tears came to her eyes, and she struggled to keep the grief out of her voice. Mona had always thought that jealousy was the most destructive of emotions.

"Nobody in this town will hire me. I don't have any skills to speak of. Brian was helping me out, now I've got nobody. I'm out of money. I haven't bought myself anything in months." Self-pity seeped from Marla's pretty voice.

The image of Brian giving Marla money further enraged Mona.

"Marla, I'm barely making it myself. If you would agree to have your son tested to see if he's Brian's, then maybe we can talk. Have you tried welfare or something like that? I don't feel it's right. Did Brian by any chance let you know that he was sending two daughters to college? I think you should try state benefits again."

"It's run out. I'm supposed to apply for school now, but I missed the semester deadline."

Mona felt rage rise even more. She also felt envy that Marla was at a time in her life to think about college and not retirement. She knew she shouldn't fall into the trap of helping Marla. She remembered Brian's words that you don't really help anyone by giving them money. Was it true that he was giving her money? Could she trust what this woman was telling her? And, if he were paying her, why would he steal from his own family to give to this woman? Did that prove that Brian fathered Marla's son?

"I'm going to get a lawyer and go to court. I'll sue you for everything you've got," said Marla.

"Why should I listen to this?" Mona asked. "What have I done to you?"

"You were so dependent that Brian couldn't leave you. He wanted to, you know. And, don't think everyone in town doesn't think you killed him."

"First of all, I have always worked and have my own money. Why would I kill Brian? I loved Brian. I still do. And, how do I know *you* didn't kill him?" Mona asked. She felt childish the minute she said it, but rage continued to rise. She wasn't sure why she was torturing herself by staying on the line with Marla. Was she that lonely that she had to talk with her former husband's lover?

"And, why would I kill him? I loved him."

"I loved him. He was married to me." Mona slammed down the phone. Her hands shook. She paced to disperse the fury she felt. Soon the anger turned to grief and she cried for nearly an hour. That was all she allowed herself.

Mona knew she had to find out for sure whether Marla's son was Brian's. She could never quit worrying about him otherwise. If Brian had fathered a child, Mona wanted that child to know his half-sisters. She wanted to have some part in his life. The thought pained her, but if it were true, she would do the right thing and help them out. And, she had to find out who killed Brian before she ended up in prison for something she didn't do.

"Brian, why did you do this to us?" Mona raised her arms upward. Then, she dried her eyes and called Wanda.

Mona could count on Wanda to be straight with her.

***

"I'm too old to mince words," the old woman said. "It's true the whole county's talking about you, saying you probably killed your husband because he was messing around with Marla. They all think her son looks exactly like Brian. They feel sorry for you. Those that don't feel sorry for you blame you for being one of those liberated women. Some people root for Marla because she's young and pretty. You're young and pretty too, mind you. But, the fact is, every man in the county lusts after Marla."

Wanda's words stung Mona. Was Wanda being cruel just to hurt her?

"I can tell by the way everyone looks at me in the grocery store that they're talking behind my back. It's the same way they looked at me at school after my brother died." Mona surprised herself by bringing up that dark time after her brother died in the dreaded car accident. She was crying uncontrollably now. It had been like a bad dream. Her parents closed off and changed after that. It was as if they had become ice from within. She seldom heard them laugh together after her brother died in that car accident.

"Yes, that was a sad time for your parents. Like to kill them, as I remember. People look at you the same way whether they think you did somethin' bad, or somethin' bad happened to you. They'd look at you that way if somethin' good happened to you. Doesn't make no difference. They'd look at you the same if you'd dare to win the lotto. It's our Scottish roots. That's what I believe. They didn't have nothin' when they came over here and don't want nothin' here. Don't want anybody else to have it either."

"That's a different way to look at it, Wanda."

Mona tried to shake off the negative attitude. There were plenty of good people in the area. She thought of the people who had turned out for Brian's funeral. She must be depressed, she decided.

"You keep your head up, dear. I don't know if Marla's son is Brian's. I don't suppose anybody knows but Marla, and I doubt she knows it for sure herself."

"So you don't know? Tell me everything you've heard."

"How would I know except for what gossip everyone else has heard? You must think I have more friends around this place than I do. Counting you, I think that makes two, maybe three. I know everybody, mind you, but they're not really my friends. All I know is what I overhear. Most people think Marla's pretty. They think she's been around and that she's been seen around with Brian. That's all I know."

"I guess I really don't want to know anyway."

"You're lucky. You've got two beautiful smart daughters and a fine ranch. I think you're going to do just fine. And if it means anything, I think Brian loved you more than you knew. You're a beautiful woman inside and out. Hell, Marla can't hold a candle to you, Mona. I'm here. You need me, you just holler."

Mona touched her own straight sandy hair, which seemed inadequate compared to Marla's thick red mane. Marla was voluptuous in many ways. Even her hair was voluptuous. No wonder Brian had fallen for her. Who wouldn't? Wanda's attempt to cheer her up hadn't worked. Her mood deepened, darkened.

***

To make Mona's day a little worse, she got a call from Travis who broke the news that the Colorado Bureau of Investigation was looking at her case to see if they had reason to make an arrest.

"Arrest me?" Mona asked, her heart speeding up. "How is that possible?"

"They seem to think they've got motive. The insurance policy. Money's a powerful motivator. When it comes to husbands and wives, it's almost always one of them. That or a girlfriend."

"So, why aren't they looking at Marla? I just don't believe he was murdered. Nobody would want to hurt Brian. I loved him even with his affair." Her hands shook and she felt the same way she did as a seven year-old trying to convince her mother she hadn't raided the cookies. But, she *had* raided the cookies. The only thing she knew for sure was that she hadn't killed Brian. Briefly she wondered if she were going crazy. Maybe she had killed him and had some kind of amnesia about it. *That IS crazy, Mona.*

"Seems like this is small potatoes for the CBI. Why would they get involved instead of the police?"

"I'm just giving you a heads up, Mona. It's possible someone from Hawk wanted it looked into. It would have to be someone with a little clout. Maybe Travis' boss, the sheriff? I don't know, but looking at what they have, I'd say you have about three or four weeks before this thing heats up. We're lucky that we had the holidays to slow things down. It takes their minds off the law."

"Why can't they let my husband rest in peace? If he's up there looking down, he's probably crying right now." Mona was feeling sorry for herself, but even more, she was worried sick about the girls. She'd have to tell them but she'd wait as long as possible before doing it. She didn't want to worry them more than necessary. She hung up and paced around the kitchen. She could lose everything. She could lose her girls, the farm. It was unthinkable. She'd have to get to the bottom of this quickly.

She had to talk to someone. She knew she should get a lawyer but she also knew how expensive they were. A defense attorney could bankrupt her. She decided to wait to see if she needed one. She might have to resort to a public defender if it got to that. She would have asked Travis to come over, but didn't want him getting any romantic ideas or wrong ideas about her motives. Instead, she decided to talk with John.

She rang the dinner bell, feeling guilty that she hadn't prepared any food. She'd offer John a sandwich and coffee. She's sure that was better than the pork and beans he usually heated up in his bunkhouse on the gas burner.

They sat eating their sandwiches and munching on chips. She tried being completely open with him.

"John, I'm in trouble here," she started. "Tell me what you've heard."

"Mona, I've seen the looks when I go to town. The way they look and whisper. But, I'll be damned if I know what it's about. Thought maybe they think there's something going on between you and me." John blushed under his weathered skin.

"They think Brian was murdered. And, worse, they think I might have done it." Mona wondered if she was telling John too much. What if it was him? She'd never know unless she tried to get his confidence. If it wasn't him, maybe he could help her figure out who it was.

"My God. It's worse than I thought. He was found in the field, wasn't he? How could you have killed him? Wouldn't you have done it in the house?"

"They think I took a stun gun out there and disabled him. They think he drowned that day. They're saying that way it doesn't matter that I'm smaller than he was, all I had to do was to turn him over."

"My God." John took a big gulp of coffee. His Levi's had holes in them and his boots were almost worn out.

They heard a scratch at the door and John got up to let Bo in. The dog looked at Mona and wagged happily. She tossed him the remains of her sandwich.

"So, I need your help." Mona knew she was taking a big risk. What if John was involved? He had a grievance with Brian over his land. John had gone to Denver that day, but he could have done it before he left. She made a note to verify John's story about going to Denver. He could kill her too and at least they'd know she didn't murder her husband.

"Shoot."

"I'm not sure I like your choice of words. But, here's what we know. The insurance company thinks someone killed Brian. They think he was murdered that day. He drowned in the ditch because he had been shocked unconscious. Now, the CBI thinks he was murdered. So, it's almost certain that he was killed by someone."

"By the fence, maybe?"

"By the fence and also by a stun gun. That's what they were looking for in your bunkhouse that day."

"Wait a minute. They don't think that I could've done it?"

"You're one of the people who had motive to kill Brian."

"Wait just a minute," John said. He stood up quickly out of his chair. "I never killed nobody in my life and don't expect to either." He paced the kitchen, his cowboy boots clunking on the floor. Bo paced with him in an empathy dance for the man who had taken Brian's place.

"John, relax. I'm a suspect too. In fact, I'm probably the prime suspect. But, believe me, I didn't do it."

"Well, then," he said. "I guess you and me are in the same club."

"I guess so. So, I need your help." Mona knew she was taking a big risk. What if John had been involved, even if helping someone else? Besides, Travis never really said that John was a suspect. Maybe they suspected Mona all along.

"What can I do?" he asked. "I'll do anything. I don't want to lose my life's work."

"You mean the land. Don't worry about that John. Nobody is going to take that away. Provided you are telling me the truth and you had nothing to do with his death."

"I was in Denver that day," he said.

"The trouble is you'll need to prove that in case they start looking at you for his death. You see, if I prove that I didn't kill Brian, then they might think you did. You had motive. Brian didn't want to give you any land."

"Mona, you know I wouldn't hurt a fly," he said. John looked stricken. "Besides, only you and me knew about the land."

"Wanda knew. That means everybody in the county knows."

"God."

"You'll need to get receipts or anything that would prove you were in Denver when he died. Credit card receipts, anything."

"Sometimes it doesn't pay to be an invisible man," he said. "I'm not the kind of fella people remember who he is. I don't know if anyone would remember seeing me."

"I know the feeling," Mona said. "I've always been that way myself."

John sat back down and Mona poured more coffee into his cup. He was so wiry and thin that she felt he needed to eat more. She pulled a Sara Lee Cheesecake out of the freezer and put two slices in the microwave to thaw.

"How can I help?" John asked. "I want to clear my name. Before I do, I have to tell you something I'm not sure you know about me. I'm not sure how much your parents told you about my situation."

"Not much. You were always a mystery to me. I assumed you were to take the place of my dead brother."

"Nobody could take his place in their eyes. That wasn't the idea. They needed help at the time. I needed a place to stay and a steady way to eat every day. They took me in when I was just twenty years old. We came to a kind of understanding over the years."

John got up to take his cheesecake plate to the sink and rinse it. Mona noticed the telltale ring of his chew on his back pocket. Thank God he didn't chew in the house.

John, I thought you were younger than that when you came. Eighteen or so. My parents always said you were turned out at seventeen."

"That's what you don't know about me." John sat down again. He had become very nervous. He touched the pocket that contained the chew, but didn't draw it out. "I was in prison at seventeen. It was a juvenile facility. For robbery. Nobody got hurt. Except me. I was desperate, didn't have money to eat. I robbed the Loaf-N-Jug in Vail. Stupidest thing I ever done. Cops were there before I could even ask for the money. Got put into a juvenile facility and that's why I only had to stay until I turned twenty-one."

"How did my parents come to hire you?" John's story wasn't a surprise to her. She knew that he'd been in jail. Her parents hadn't told her, but in Hawk County nothing was a secret for long.

"I went from farm to farm soon as they released me. I told people up-front that I was a felon. Wanted them to know what they was getting into. Your parents were the only ones who trusted me. I was your brother's only friend."

Mona teared up. "I didn't know. I'm so glad they were such a good judge of character."

"You trust me?"

"If my parents trusted you, I do."

Mona looked at John for facial reaction. The truth was she didn't trust him completely. What was stopping her from trusting him?

"Thank you, ma'am."

"Can you get together receipts or anything that would prove where you were that day?"

"Mona, I pay cash, same as you pay me."

"Mona had some qualms about income tax. She doubted John ever filed. Besides, they only paid him ten or twelve grand a year. Of course his room and board was free.

Still, he probably hadn't gotten a raise in a decade, maybe two decades.

"There was the CB call from Mr. Gilkinsen. Remember I told you that day I came back? That's how I knew to come back. I didn't buy the livestock, if you remember."

"We can give Mr. Gilkinsen's name to the police, but only if they ask. We're not volunteering anything. We may have to get lawyers, and if that happens, I'll get one for you. I don't think I'd want to take a chance on the public defender."

"God, this is serious."

"Yes, it is very serious. Is there anything that you know that might help? Do you know anyone who had it in for Brian?"

"I know you know about Marla. I doubt she could do anything like that."

Mona felt a stab of jealousy. She pushed it away. "Does she have any male friends that might have been jealous of her relationship with Brian?"

"No. Don't think she had many friends. Her boyfriends were mostly skiers that came to Vail and left after ski season. She liked the skier type; that was the word. Thought they was rich is what I heard. Ski bums don't usually have a lot of money."

"Do you know how she met Brian?"

"Probably down at the pub where he sometimes went."

"Pub? He never was a big drinker."

"I know," said John. "Kind of a health nut. Could've gone ahead and eaten those hamburgers and fries."

"Yes, I guess that's right."

"What about Mark Eckland?" asked Mona. "Could he have hurt Brian for any reason?"

"Mark? I wouldn't know. Didn't like me much. I wasn't educated enough for him. Or, rich enough. I steered clear whenever he was around. Steered clear of his wife too. She had a way of making me feel about two feet tall. Brian

165

liked Mark though. I thought he and Brian was like this."
John put his two crossed fingers out in front of Mona.

"Anybody else? What about Wanda."

"Old Wanda? I doubt it. She's crazy and strong as an ox for her age, but why would she hurt Brian? I'll try to think if I know of anyone else. I feel like I need to come up with a murderer, or I'll be it."

"I know the feeling," Mona said. "But, let's don't look at it that way. Let's talk about something else."

"You want to talk about the weather?"

Mona laughed. "No, I've been thinking about the radiation rumors. I know they've been around for a long time. Decades. But, do you think any of that harmed my parents or the ranch?"

John got quiet and hesitated. "All I know is what I see. I've seen too many animal miscarriages and stillborn animals. It ain't normal. I'm no vet, but it don't seem right."

"But, that's probably true of all the ranches around here, don't you think?"

"Not what I've heard from the other ranch-hands. Far as I can tell, we get three times the number. Lots of cases of thyroid cancer too. That's the most common cancer caused by radiation. I read that after I started reading up at the library." Mona learned something else about John. He went to the library. She didn't think he owned a computer.

Mona felt a chill. They had well water. What if there was some chemical. Radiation. She had enough worry without worrying about that. Maybe she'd have water brought in for drinking and cooking.

"Do you have any theories about why?"

"No ma'am. I noticed it happens more in years when I let the herds graze near the dump."

"The dump?"

"You parents and then Brian used a couple acres for burying trash and stuff. Didn't want to pay the county dump fees."

"Where is this?"

"It's up the mountain on the grazing land. Almost the Southeast corner of the ranch. You know, up where the old abandoned cabin is."

Mona had almost forgotten about the cabin. It was a crude log structure that stood on the grazing land. It did have a log floor and a stone fireplace. There was an outhouse. Even though it was on the ranch property, nobody ever monitored it unless they were going up there for some reason. She'd heard of a few hikers that used it in an emergency—a snowstorm or something. Mona hadn't been there for years.

"Maybe it's the toxic chemicals from the dump. I'm not even sure that's legal, John."

"They didn't ask me for help with that decision."

"John, I'm going to show you some papers and I want you to tell me if you've seen them before."

"Okay."

Mona went to Brian's office and took the logs out of their hiding place. She took them to John.

"No, ma'am. Never seen these. Looks like lots of numbers. Accounting books?"

"Yes, I think that's what they are."

"I'm not involved in accounting or anything. Never have been. Is this like that Enron deal?"

Mona laughed. "I don't think so. So you know what these numbers could be?" Mona pointed to some puzzling numbers that occurred in each group of log pages.

John inspected them carefully. He looked as if a light came on in his head. "Well, yes. These look like land coordinates. They did a set for me when they surveyed the land for my house."

"Really? I hadn't thought of that. I've never seen coordinates before. I was thinking maybe they were bank numbers of some kind."

"No, see here, these numbers?"

"Well, can you tell where these are?"

"No, but I can see if the surveyor can come out and show you."

"That would be great," Mona said. But will it? Mona could almost hear her mother chiding, "Mona when will you learn some things are better left alone?"

Chapter 20

Monday, Heartbreak Ranch

Marla would not go away. She called Mona again and asked her to come over, saying she desperately wanted to talk.

Mona reacted to Marla's urgent tone no less anxiously than anyone else in Hawk. There was something about being beckoned by a beautiful woman that neither men nor women could resist going. Mona wanted to hate her, to like her, to witness her.

Mona knew she would go, even while protesting.

"I can't do that, Marla. I can't be seen with you. The way people around here gossip." Mona imagined Brian saying that very thing to Marla, only for very different reasons.

"Please, I'm begging you." Marla's voice had the insistent quality of a woman who usually got her way. Mona could imagine Marla tossing her thick red hair, her pretty eyes blazing. Far be it for Mona to be Marla's first denial.

Mona hated the way she most likely sounded cowardly and pretentious to Marla, like some high-school cheerleader who didn't want to be seen with the unpopular girl. Or worse. All the while she felt overwhelming jealously about Marla. Not envy. Jealousy.

She never wanted to think of herself that way. She knew for certain that she and Marla could never be friends, and she also knew with certainty that she may have to be friendly with her, possibly for the rest of their lives if

Marla's son turned out to be step-brother to her daughters. She also knew that whoever liked Mona in this small community already liked her, and those that thought ill of her already thought the worst.

"Nobody will know you're here. What if I come over there? It's harder on me because I have to get my boy ready to go out and all. Nathan is prone to getting sick and I don't want to drag him out. I think he has his dad's immune system."

Mona let the remark pass. Brian got lots of colds but in the last couple of years he seemed to disappear when he got sick. He would tell her that he was shopping or looking for farm supplies. Could it be that when Brian felt sick he went to Marla's for comfort? Mona realized she tended toward lack of empathy for sick people. She knew she withheld comfort and sympathy. Like her mother.

"Just tell me what you want, Marla. We can discuss this over the phone."

Mona didn't want the hangover of angst and jealousy that seemed to follow her visits with Marla. It started her obsessing all over again about Brian and Marla and what they did together. She didn't need any images in her brain.

What if that sweet little boy was Brian's child? Would he want her to accept him? Probably, knowing Brian. She had gone back in her mind trying to remember if Brian had seemed proud or anxious the way a new father would be. She knew he went off by himself and he had plenty of time to do have an affair since he didn't work nine to five. She'd given him time to become a father again. Without her. Mona never had cause to doubt him and never had doubted him. She knew he had supreme trust in her.

"I don't want to do this over the phone," said Marla. "But, I guess I don't have a choice if that's how you want to be. I need money from you, Mona. From Brian. I think I deserve it because Brian would have wanted it to go for his son. Pure and simple. He promised to always take care of us and I'm cashing in on that promise. I'm in a desperate place here and Nathan and me need money to eat."

Mona felt the unmistakable tug on her heartstrings. Could it be maternal instinct? Tears stung her eyes. Still, the excuses came. Why should she be responsible for a woman who had an affair with her husband? How did she know Marla wasn't lying about her relationship with Brian?

"Marla . . ."

"I know what you're going to say. That I'm after Brian's money, that I'm taking advantage of his relationship with me. I know you guys are wealthy. But, I've got something more than that."

"Like what?"

Mona let the "wealthy" remark slide. Marla had no idea what Brian had told Marla about their financial situation. Money had been a delicate issue with him. If anything, he probably showered Marla with inexpensive gifts and let her believe he had lots of money.

"I've got some papers here that Brian told me to keep for him. They're important and he wouldn't want them falling into the wrong hands, if you know what I mean."

Stunned, Mona said, "I don't know what you're talking about. What could you possibly have that I don't know about?

"Oh, I think there's lots you didn't know about. You didn't know about me and Brian. Or, Nathan. You didn't even know your husband had another whole family."

"Marla, it remains to be seen whether Nathan is Brian's child."

Mona's conscience nagged at her. She shouldn't punish a child for the parent's sins. She should leave the little boy out of it.

"Do you have some kind of proof of paternity or something? Is that why you called me? Because, if it is, you can mail it to me and I'll have my lawyer deal with it."

"That's not why I called. Besides, I heard you don't even have a lawyer yet."

Who could have told Marla that? Mona went through the possibilities. Wanda? John? Was it possible John was seeing Marla? Mona couldn't see it in her mind's eye. And when she did "see" it, the result was a laughing fit. What about Travis? Mona doubted Wanda had talked to Marla, so it had to be John or Travis. Given Marla's reputation, as much as Mona hated to rely on reputations, John or Travis could both fall victim to Marla's charms.

"I'm hoping we can do this without lawyers," continued Marla. "They just take the money for themselves anyhow. We might as well agree on an amount of money and let it stay between us. No muss, no fuss."

"Marla, what are we talking about here? You're saying what you have doesn't have to do with your son? Because if it does, I don't care if it becomes public. I couldn't be any more humiliated than I already am. Besides, I don't believe in keeping everything secret. Can you honestly tell me this has nothing to do with your son?" Mona still found it hard to call the boy by his name. *Nathan. Nathan.*

"No, not yet, anyway. If you won't give me money for Nathan, maybe you'll give me money for this. It's some information that could get you in big trouble. It has to do with the BLM and your husband. You know, the Bureau of Land Management." Marla struggled to get the words out, and it sounded like she was reading from a piece of paper.

A thrill of shock went through Mona. It wasn't what she expected. She had been caught up in the little romance between Brian and Marla. Was it possible that Marla was more involved with the ranch than Mona realized? A new emotion trumped the jealousy and grief Mona bore. Fear. She could actually lose the ranch.

"What could my husband have to do with the BLM?" Another wave of fear overcame Mona. Her breathing quickened and her hands began shaking. Could it be that Marla knew more about what's going on than she did?

"I have some papers that will explain it all. But, I don't want to put them through the mail. Can you pick them up?"

"Yes, but I don't want to meet you at your house. Someone will notice my car. Can we meet someplace else?"

"The diner? That's neutral ground. You can buy me and Nathan lunch."

Mona thought about this for a second. That would be worse gossip fodder than going to Marla's house. They'd be on public display at the diner, which had become the hub of activity and information for Hawk County. Besides, Mona knew she wouldn't be hungry. Then again, Marla and her son might be. She'd buy her a meal some other time. It just wasn't worth it.

"How about someplace even more neutral. I could meet you behind the post office. You know that little park?"

"Yeah, I take Nathan there to play sometimes. There's a secluded spot right by the swings. We can meet there."

"Tonight?"

"Not tonight, I'm working," said Marla. "I got somebody to watch Nathan for me."

"Where are you working?"

"There's a night club in Vail," she said.

Mona didn't ask what she would be doing. She hoped for Nathan's sake that it was a waitress job and not a dancing job. The evil jealousy crept over her again.

"Tomorrow night, then."

"Ten o'clock," said Marla.

"Okay, then. Ten o'clock at the park behind the post office. I'll be there. Oh, you didn't ask what you want for this information."

"Ten grand ought to do it."

"Ten thousand dollars? How do I know this information is worth anything? Besides, all I can spare right now is five."

Mona had second thoughts the minute she opened her mouth. Five thousand would pay one of the books and essentials for a semester. It was no small amount of money to her. She decided to agree to meet her and then back out if something seemed off. Of course, this whole thing seemed off to Mona. What was she getting herself into?

"Five, then," said Marla. "That would at least last a couple of months. Cash would be better if you can do it. I don't want to wait to get a check cleared. Besides, paper trails are no good."

Chapter 21

Tuesday, Heartbreak Ranch

By six o'clock, Mona was sorry that she set the meeting time with Marla for late at night. What had she been thinking? She was sometimes in bed by nine o'clock. Why was she so worried about how she looked for her "Marla Meeting?" For God's sake, what did it matter what Marla thought of her? Brian was gone. She wasn't competing with anyone for her husband. Adolescent jealousy never quite goes away.

Marla didn't exactly work her looks to her advantage. She could have married the richest guy in the county or the state with her looks. Why had she resorted to being a waitress and working in nightclubs? Marla no doubt had low self-esteem; at least that would probably be the general consensus. What would it take to get Marla out of her head? She should be using her energy remembering Brian, bringing something positive from his death. She should be obsessing about her children, not about some woman who had slept with her husband.

She called Wanda, asked if she could come over and talk. To Mona's relief, Wanda was delighted.

"I'll put a couple pot-pies in the oven," she said. "Come on over. I could use the company."

Soon, Mona found herself sitting in Wanda's warm kitchen, eating homemade chicken pot-pie and drinking tea. Wanda provided the womb of comfort that Mona needed. Wanda had put a shot of brandy in her tea, to Mona's objection—and appreciation. She'd be a basket case by ten o'clock but she'd be sober by then. Enough to drive safely.

"You feeling the loss?" asked Wanda. Wanda's haunted look reminded Mona that her elder neighbor knew all about grief and its comings and goings.

"Brian? Sure. It's constant, a constant ache in my chest. But, something else is bothering me."

"Out with it, then." Wanda ate heartily and Mona wondered how the bird-thin woman stayed that way. Thin crepe skin covered her sinewy arms. Sunspots covered the crepe, typical for ranchers and farmers. Wanda no longer grew crops or harvested anything other than hay, but there were the animals to care for. John occasionally went over to help Wanda with repairs or heaving-lifting.

As if clairvoyant, Wanda said, "hope you're not wasting any time worrying about me. I've lived a good long time and I'm doing just fine by myself."

"It's Marla Rodgers."

"That woman again. That slut," Wanda said.

Wanda's outburst shocked Mona and it must have showed on her face. She put her cup down.

"Sorry," Wanda said. "At my age you get so say whatever you think. But, she is, you have to admit. How can one redhead cause so much havoc?"

"I don't know," agreed Mona. "I'm meeting her tonight. In the park behind the post office."

"Why, in God's name would you do that?"

"She's got some information for me. Some papers from Brian."

"Why doesn't she mail them?" asked Wanda. "It really isn't a good idea. What if she wants to hurt you? This idea smells like five day-old fish."

"She wants money. Seems she's in a dire situation. Besides, it was my idea to meet her there. She wouldn't be planning anything. I doubt she's smart enough."

"You can't give that woman any money," Wanda said. "It would be wrong. You have to know that. She'd only want more. Besides, if it got out it could be taken wrong. Don't get me wrong, my lips are sealed. But, you ask me, don't give that woman one red cent."

"I have to get the papers from her. And, I keep feeling if I pay her off, she'll leave me alone." Mona felt she was revealing too much, but couldn't stop herself. She had to tell someone and she wasn't sure Travis did not have some kind of relationship with Marla.

"You know how that goes, at least in those television movies. At least, let me go with you. How do you know she doesn't have copies?"

"No, I'll be alright. I have to get the papers from her. I'll be fine. And, I'll ask her about copies. Since I don't know what it is, it might not make any difference. I'd have to think of it as a donation for her son. I'll take my cell and call Travis if anything seems wrong."

Mona thanked Wanda and went home at seven. Thanks to the brandy in her tea, Mona took a two-hour nap on her sofa. She woke at nine o'clock and got up and showered. She primped in front of her dresser mirror like she was going on a date. All the while, she chastised herself for being so stupid. What the hell difference did it make what she looked like? Who was she dressing for?

Mona got to the park ten minutes early and anxiously waited for a car to pull up. She felt some fear. What if Marla had arranged to have Mona beaten or threatened? At eleven, Marla still hadn't shown up. She had been stood up. Somehow the anger from that eased the grief and jealousy that ate at her insides. Funny how some emotions trumped others. She dialed Marla's number and got no answer. She tried two more times. Was it possible she had changed her mind or forgotten? Mona decided to go home and call Marla the next day. Who knew, maybe she had gone on a date at the last minute. It wouldn't be the first time Marla chose a man over another engagement. Disgusted and angry, Mona drove away from the park. By the time Mona left the park, snow had started coming down faster, threatening to become a full-on snowstorm.

Chapter 22

Tuesday night, at the park

Mona fumed as she drove from the park. She'd been stood up by a woman she'd fretted about for days. Powdery snow swirled in front of her headlights. For the first time, Mona wondered if the documents Marla wanted to give Mona even existed. What if the documents were pictures of Brian and Marla together? She felt used. Worse, she felt obsessed.

Anger filled Mona. She decided to drive by Marla's house to see if she was home. She wouldn't stop; she'd just drive by. Mona felt like a teenager again engulfed in the torment of unrequited love. Now a stalker, she envisioned seeing Marla through her living room window chatting happily on the phone to one of her many boyfriends. Mona couldn't imagine Marla staying home alone at night being a good mom. There had to be more to her than that. Random thoughts of revenge flooded Mona. She could have Travis keep a close eye on her.

As she drove, Mona thought of more ways she could harm Marla. Who did Marla think she was?

She could call Social Services to have them check in on Marla and her son. When had she become so judgmental and angry? She could help spread the vicious rumors about Marla. When had she become so obsessed with another woman? She had probably thought more often about Marla during the last few months than her husband ever had. She should be grieving for Brian and not acting like a jealous school girl. She took some deep breaths and tried to drive out the negative impulses that had consumed her. By the time she'd driven five more minutes, Mona realized she needed to grow up, worry about her daughters and Heartbreak Ranch instead of her own insecurities. Still, she was close enough to Marla's house not to turn back.

As Mona drove by the white clapboard house, she saw lights on inside. She drove around the block again to calm her pounding heart.

The white houses, all the same, occupied the entire block. The bungalows, with their pillared front porches and downward-sloping eaves had been popular in Colorado and throughout the West at the turn of the last century. They were open and simple with two stories or one and a half stories. They wasted no space and every material used in them was quality.

Trees along the street alternated from blue-green evergreens to shimmering Aspen trees with their ghostly white trunks showing through the dark night. A few cottonwoods stood majestically over the bungalows. Mona had forgotten how beautiful and calm this small town was. And yet in this serene setting, her heart pounded with dread and fear.

Damn it, she thought. Marla is home and she just decided not to show. She dialed Marla's number. No answer after ten rings. She decided against ringing her doorbell. It was clear that Marla had stood her up. Tears stung her eyes. How many ways would she let this woman humiliate her? Chances are she didn't have anything for Mona. But why would she specifically bring up the BLM? She felt goose bumps creep over her skin. She felt the need to retreat.

***

On the way home, Mona became aware of car lights in her rear-view mirror. The lights got closer and closer and she was afraid the car would ram her. Her Jeep Cherokee had a lot of power and she could probably outrun most cars. She remembered Brian insisting on a V-8 engine. She was aware of the Jeep's instability because of its height and she didn't want to cause an accident, especially since the weather had turned bad. She kept to the speed limit. Could it be Marla trying to catch up to her? Maybe Marla had fallen asleep or had trouble getting a baby-sitter. Mona let up on the accelerator. If it was Marla and she wanted to talk, Mona would pull over and they'd talk.

The car rammed her back fender. She couldn't see the vehicle past the blinding headlights. They seemed high. It could be a truck, thought Mona. The bumps felt substantial. If this was Marla, she was trying to run her off the road. The force of the hit caused Mona to momentarily lose control of the Jeep. She got her hands back on the wheel and stabilized the car. She felt thankful for the snow tires Brian had put on the Jeep, and she hoped it was enough. The blanket of snow on top of the icy highway gave the car some grip. Still, she couldn't decide whether to pull over or drive faster.

Mona struggled to see a face just past the headlights in her rear view mirror. She needed to see if the driver was a man or a woman. If the driver looked like Marla, she'd stop. She shook all over, not just her hands. Her heart drummed violently in her chest. What was the lunatic trying to do? Thoughts of carjacking went through her head. She shouldn't stop the car. She knew that much. Carjacking was almost unheard of on Colorado's Western slope, but not impossible. She sped up even more. She knew she had pushed the Jeep's top speed.

It was futile; the headlights blinded her. As the vehicle behind her bounced up and down she could catch a glimpse of its form. Whatever the vehicle was, it had bad shocks. She saw only a dark shadow, genderless, faceless. Mona sped up, trying to lose the threatening vehicle. What should she do? There were no turnoffs and if there were they would lead to an isolated area.

She looked at the speedometer. Eighty. She didn't want to get into a situation where her Jeep had to take sharp corners. She could see it all now: woman overturns Jeep on country road; woman killed driving at high speed. It would look like a suicide. In some ways death seemed an easier option right now. *Except for the girls.* The girls were saving her right now. Still, the thought of death sometimes seemed like a refuge. Was this what real depression felt like?

Maybe Brian would meet her there on that safe "other side." There was something else that shoved the dark thought from her mind. Her shy side trumped her death wish. She didn't need to call any more attention to herself. She didn't want to be a tragic paragraph in the newspaper. She didn't want her and Brian's lives to both end in tragedy. She didn't want the girls to be orphans at their still-young age.

Again, the car behind her bumped the SUV and caused it to swerve. She thought of calling Travis, but he'd think she was becoming a walking disaster. Besides, the cell was out of arms reach, inside her purse. She'd probably crash trying to find the damn thing. A new headline: woman dies reaching for fallen cell phone.

She tried to lose the truck. It could be a bunch of kids playing chicken or something, but they usually chose someone they knew. Country kids were easily bored and sometimes got into more mischief than they would in the city. Besides, Mona only saw one shadow in the car. If there were more, they had hidden out of view.

Mona pulled onto I-70, trying to get off the county road that she knew had many potholes. She almost lost it on the turn-off onto I-70; her SUV swerved and fish-tailed. She decided to continue her drive east to Vail if the car continued to trail her. It wouldn't help to draw someone back to the ranch with her. Even if John were there, she didn't want whomever this was to know where she lived. She knew where the Vail police station was. The Jeep could do the sloping high-altitude climb to Vail better than many vehicles would.

Maybe she could lose the car if she drove a little faster. She sped up what little more the Jeep would allow. The car stuck to her like glue, threatening to bump her if she slowed down slightly. The car must have had a bigger engine than its old chassis implied. The car did bump her again at the higher speed, almost causing her to lose control of the car. The driver seemed to have done this before.

Mona again reached for her cell, but her purse was just out of reach. Her hands shook and her heart thumped in her chest. She risked losing control if she took her eyes from the road. Halfway to Vail, Mona felt a full-blown panic coming on. This country was isolated. There were only occasional cars and a few big-rigs that blew by so fast they probably didn't even see her. She blinked her lights at one of the big trucks to see if the driver would turn around and help her. One of them blinked his lights back at her and leaned hard on his horn in greeting. The big-rig slowed but didn't turn around. Truckers struggled to drive over any pass and they usually didn't want to stop unless they had to. They could never gain momentum again and they had schedules to keep. All the while, the vehicle behind her stuck to her like she was towing it.

Mona slowed to see if the car would pass her. She pressed the horn. Maybe it would scare him. Mona felt a forward jolt and heard a thump. He had hit her, hard this time. He was not going to stop until he ran her off the road. But, slowing served a different purpose. She could see the vehicle. It wasn't a car as Mona originally thought. It looked like a pickup truck. An *old* pickup truck. Maybe decades old. Dark in color. Mona saw a gun rack with a shotgun in the back window of the truck. That was not a good sign.

She struggled to identify the driver's silhouette. Could Marla be doing this? Mona doubted it, but maybe a friend or someone defending her honor? Nobody else knew Mona would be out. Except Wanda. Maybe Wanda had told someone. Mark Eckland? She concentrated on flat surface of I-70. She comforted herself with the thought that this was relatively flat right now. A coating of white snow had started accumulating on the pavement, but Mona had faith in her snow tires. Vail was on the west side of Vail Pass, and there would be no pass to go over until she reached the far side of Vail. She intended to stop at the Vail police station.

Mona felt another bump. Whoever this was, he was trying to kill her or scare the hell out of her. The aggression of the bumps gave Mona the impression this was a man, not a woman. She didn't know many women who would do physical stunts like this. She looked at the gas gage. Noting that the tank was full, Mona felt relieved she had recently filled the gas tank. She felt for the cell again. It was no use, grabbing it would mean certain accident. The way the drive of the truck tracked the turns of the road, Mona had the thought that this person knew the highway well.

Mona started coming up on Vail. Soon, she was outrunning the truck. The adrenaline, the job her body had undertaken to save her life, made her feel alive. She knew at this moment what the "will to live" was and knew for a fact that she didn't want to die. She didn't want to leave this earth even if it meant possibly seeing Brian again.

Finally, Mona saw the police station. She'd been there before visiting a friend who worked there. She pulled into the lot quickly, causing her SUV to swerve and fishtail. She pulled up to the front door so fast that she feared she'd drive right through it.

At the police station, it was clear they weren't going to give Mona much time. She was a "down-valley" girl and not a wealthy tourist. She asked for her friend but was told she had retired.

She'd have to come back tomorrow and file a report, he said. Besides, everyone in three counties had an old pickup truck with a gun rack in back. Without a license plate number it was hopeless. She wasn't sure if it was the same one she saw leaving her ranch the day of the break-in, but she had a pretty good hunch. Not enough for anyone to go on, she knew. Feeling foolish, she decided to go home. Mona told them not to bother calling, but she did call Travis for an escort home.

"I'm sorry, Travis. You're going to think I'm going nuts. Maybe I am. They say people go nuts when they lose a spouse."

"I like it when you think of me, Mona. You know you can call any time. I watched on the way up here to Vail and didn't see anything. No trucks like you described. A couple rigs, and a few SUVs."

"I didn't think you would see him," she said. "Can you follow me home? I'll be okay from there."

Nothing happened on the way home. The truck did not reappear. Mona almost wished it would. Had she imagined the whole thing? She wondered sometimes if Brian's death was pushing her over the edge of sanity. It wasn't only his death, but what she hadn't known about his life that drove her nuts. She longed for one single hour with him to ask him questions. She thought of her near meeting with Marla and felt almost happy it hadn't happened. It was time to let the whole matter go. The last thing Mona wanted to do was discuss Marla with Travis. She knew that accusing Marla of tailing her and trying to bump her off the road was not going to elicit any sympathy. Most people would think she had made the whole thing up. They might even think that she was trying to point to Marla as Brian's killer. She wouldn't tell anyone else about this incident.

***

By the time they got back to Heartbreak Ranch, it was one o'clock in the morning. Travis came into the farmhouse with her. They both felt wound up, so Mona put on the teakettle and they sat and talked. Mona poured a shot of whiskey in her and Travis declined, saying he had to drive. Mona had noticed that John's truck was gone.

"Could it have been John following you?"

"No, John's truck is much newer. He's got a larger Ford to pick up hay bales and feed bags. One thing John splurged on was a new truck a few years back. Besides, John wouldn't do something like that."

"Well, the one thing we're sure is it wasn't me," Travis said.

Mona looked at him.

"Oh, come on. You can't believe I'd do something like that?"

"Not really, Travis. Not after all you've done. I'm just mystified who could be doing this to me. It's like someone's trying to drive me away."

"Well, Mona, you've been under lots of stress to say the least."

"Do you think I imagined the whole thing?" She was sure he heard the anger and nerves in her voice.

"I don't know what to think. I'm just being honest here. And, what were you doing out this time of night? Not that it's any of my business or anything."

Not wanting to get into the whole thing about meeting Marla, she chose to be vague. The urge to talk about Marla and Brian started to overcome Mona but she caught herself. The only thing worse than obsessing in private was confessing obsession to other people.

"I just wanted to go for a drive. I missed Brian." Mona knew tears were running down her face, but she never had been the sobbing kind. The tears would have to find their own way out.

"I'm sorry. I know how hard this is for you." Travis reached out and touched her hand and looked at her with his boyishly handsome face.

"Thanks, Travis. You're such a good friend. You've literally saved my life."

"Just remember that," he said. "Where is that ranch hand of yours anyway?"

"He goes into town every now and then."

"Up valley? Or does he stay in Hawk?"

"If he's not at the diner or the Hawk Bar, then he's gone up valley to Vail where there's more action."

"It isn't natural for a single man his age."

"Look at you," she said. "You're single."

Travis blushed. "I suppose I am. I don't spend much time in bars and strip joints, if that's what you mean. I would like to have more of a life, though."

Mona changed the subject. This one made her uncomfortable. The subject of strip joints left an opening to discuss Marla.

"You still want to know why I went out this time of night."

"I don't think it's any of my business," Travis said. "I would like to know if you want to tell me."

"Maybe sometime soon. Let's just eat pie and drink tea." Mona poured another good shot of whiskey in hers. Her hands still shook from the adrenaline. She held the warm cup with two hands.

Chapter 23

Wednesday morning, Heartbreak Ranch

Mona heard Bo's distant insistent bark and John's shout from the bunkhouse to quiet him. She wondered if John knew that she could hear his reprimands to Bo. Some days when the wind was quiet and especially when snow was on the ground, the wind carried the sound of John singing *Amazing Grace* in a strong unsophisticated voice. He could carry a tune. The thin Rocky Mountain air seemed to carry sound an astounding distance, as if notes could sneak between the wider-spaced oxygen molecules across the snow at nine thousand feet above sea level.

Mona knew this day could prove stressful. She had woken reluctantly in a sleep-deprived stupor. Dread washed over her as soon as she woke. Foggy images of Brian and Marla haunted the dreams. Other images featured her two daughters as they were away at school. She jumped out of bed so quickly after noticing the time on the alarm clock that her head spun with dizziness.

Mona threw on a sweatshirt with a faded orange Denver Bronco logo and jeans, tossed back some mouthwash and spat it into the sink promising to brush her teeth later, and padded downstairs in bare feet. She feared she probably looked like a woman twenty years older than her true age. She had hardly thought about her blond hair, which usually took care of itself, falling just to her shoulders in a straight bob. This strategy worked for her when she was younger, but the mirror told her she might have to put forth more effort.

She usually put on makeup later in the day; a touch of taupe eye shadow and brown-black mascara, maybe some lipstick to give her pale lips some color. She had taken to wearing sunscreen in SPF15 to keep away the "Wanda look," but noticed with brief glances at her reflection, that most days she looked as white as a sheet of paper. Still, it didn't matter.

Bo continued to bark from the bunkhouse and John continued to try to hush him. It was nearly ten, an unusually late hour for Mona to rising. She hadn't gone to sleep until nearly four in the morning despite resorting to an ironic double-shot of brandy in her herbal tea. Lately she needed extreme physical exhaustion to bring her to the edge of sleep.

John had probably finished with the chores long ago and was making his mid-morning coffee. Mona loved the spontaneous part of ranch life.

The doorbell and knocking perturbed her. She ambled to the door, hoping it wasn't important.

"Travis!" Mona let him in, embarrassed about her appearance.

"Did I wake you?"

"Is it that obvious? I had trouble sleeping last night. Want coffee?" She noticed the huskiness in her voice; she'd hadn't had anyone to practice her voice on in the mornings.

Mona had a brief panic that Travis had come to give her bad news about her daughters. *God, no.*

Travis must have read and interpreted the look on her face. "Don't worry; it's nobody close to you. Everybody's fine. Near everybody, anyway. Why is it that I get this reaction from people when they meet me at their door?"

Mona sat on a dining chair before she made it to the kitchen. Her head spun. Lack of sleep, maybe. She felt close to tears.

"You okay?"

"Will be. I'm worn down, I guess. Lately I think everything's an emergency. I startle at every little noise. Come on in the kitchen. I'll make some coffee. I've got some coffee cake." Mona was aware that her voice cracked when she talked, a trait she hated about herself but could do little to change. Thank God the girls were okay.

"Sounds good." Travis walked into the kitchen, his Tony Lama boots thunking on the red stone. He put his hat on the table in the breakfast nook.

He must have noticed her looking at his boots.

"Sorry. Am I supposed to take them off?"

"No."

"Just checking."

"What's the bad news?" she asked as she put the pot on.

"It's Marla Rodgers. She was found dead this morning. Thelma Atkins had her son for the night, brought him home, found her dead."

Mona felt the adrenaline surge through her. Any second, her hands would begin shaking and she'd probably be unable to pour the coffee.

"Dead! My God. Was it suicide?" The shock woke Mona from any sleepiness leftover from her hard night.

"What would make you ask that?" Travis looked at her suspiciously. Mona looked away, knowing what he was thinking.

Mona felt dizzy again. She sat at the table. Her heart pounded in her chest and her hands shook.

"You all right? You look pale."

"It's just unexpected. She's so young."

"Yes, she was," Travis said. He sounded angry.

"What happened to her?" Mona asked.

"That's what I came here to find out if you know."

"Why would I know? Why don't you tell me how she died? I'm shocked at this, to tell you the truth. How did she die?"

"Looked like a bad knock over the head with a cinder brick. Looks like whoever did it came in through the back patio door and caught her off guard. There's a bunch of cinder bricks just piled up back there."

"My God," Mona said. "Who would do such a thing?"

"That's just it, Mona. There's talk it might be you. I volunteered to come out here and get a statement from you so you don't have to go to the Glenwood Police station. That's the nearest in Hawk county. But, here's what I know. The CBI who is working on Brian's case is going to link the two deaths. Because, you know, Brian and Marla were linked. So to speak."

"My God, Travis. I could never do such a thing. You know yourself that I drove to the Vail Police Station last night."

"I know. But, that in itself is suspicious. I checked with them and they didn't even make a record that you were there—never took an official statement from you. I didn't say I thought you did it. Now, just let me turn on this tape recorder and get a preliminary statement to save you a trip in. They're dusting Marla's place, going over it with a fine-tooth comb as we speak."

"God, Travis." Mona held her throbbing head in her hands.

"So far they don't have anything important enough to bring you in. There's talk that because it wasn't a gun, it could have been a woman. Women hate to use guns, for the most part. They tend to be attracted to pharmaceuticals and drowning as vehicles for murder and suicide. Or knocks on the head."

Mona decided to ignore Travis' opinion about murder weapons and gender. "What about the son? What happens to him?"

"He's being sent to the Grandma's house in Denver. Seems she's willing to take him."

"Before we go any further, I have to say this. I can't keep secrets from you."

"Go ahead." Travis signed, as if expecting bad news.

"I was supposed to meet Marla last night at the park behind the post office. She had something for me. Some files or something that Brian had."

"Files? What kind of files?"

"I don't know. But, that's not all. She wanted money for them."

"She was extorting money from you?"

"Not in so many words. She was selling me information that might interest me."

"God, Mona. You know what that is?"

"Blackmail?"

"Motive. It gives you motive and opportunity. This is trouble. But, I'm glad you told me. Wanda already told me, so if you hadn't said anything, I'd be real worried."

"There's more." Mona wrestled in her mind on how much to tell Travis. He might as well know it all, she decided. "When she didn't show up at the park, I drove by her house. I don't know if anyone saw my car."

"As a matter of fact, one of the neighbors described your car. It drove by between ten and eleven last night. She couldn't tell the color of the car, but said it was some kind of late model Jeep. I believe that description fits your car. Plus, they said the woman—they were sure it was a woman—was looking toward the house."

"You believe me, don't you? I could not do anything like that, no matter how upset I was. There is just no way."

"The thing is that everybody says that, but people do these things. I've never met a perp who didn't say they were innocent. I'm never surprised anymore about the things people can do. I can tell you that I believe you though. I don't think you have a mean bone in your body. I can't give you special treatment though. If the facts show that you had anything to do with this, then I can't help you."

"Did you just call me a *perp*?"

"Sorry, but I did. You know I love you to death, Mona. No pun intended."

"Thanks, Trav. I don't expect anything more than a shoulder to cry on from you. You've helped me enough."

"We're not done here, Mona. I've got to turn on the tape recorder and you can repeat to me what you told me. I think it's better to get the whole story down. That is, unless you want a lawyer before you say anything. It's your right.

You can include the reason you drove to Vail if you want, but I have to tell you, it looks like you were going to turn yourself in. Like I said—you might want a lawyer."

"God, Travis. The lawyer business again. Do you know how much a good lawyer costs? They make it look so damned easy on television, don't they?"

"They sure do. Unless you're a celebrity it's going to cost a fortune. It could even cost you your ranch. But, a lawyer could keep you out of prison. That would be worth it."

"I'm not willing to bet Heartbreak Ranch yet, Travis. There's got to be a way to solve this. Any lawyer I could afford probably wouldn't do much better than we could do ourselves. I've worked with enough lawyers in my life."

"I know. We'll figure this out. But, in the meantime, I'm going to call in the police from Glenwood to help with this. Vail police may not want to deal with this. I'm too close to you to do this by myself. They'll interrogate you, but I want to make sure they don't pressure you into saying anything you don't want to say."

They waited an hour for the police to show up.

When they did, they took photos of Mona, of her hands, of her jeep, of almost everything.

"This is to protect you, to show that you didn't have any damage to yourself as if you were involved in an altercation of any kind," said one of them, a woman.

It took them two hours to complete their interview with Mona.

"I noticed you didn't read my rights," Mona said. She regretted it immediately.

"No need, Mona. You're not under arrest. We're doing this for future use, remember," Travis said.

"You should expect a visit from some investigators. If they continue suspecting you, they'll ask you a lot of the same questions I did. They might take finger prints," said the male police officer.

"Should I get a lawyer? I'm still weighing that in my mind. What would you do if you were me?" Mona certainly didn't want her propensity for cost saving to send her to prison.

"You haven't been charged with anything. I'd wait and see. Sometimes getting a lawyer too soon makes you look guilty. I didn't want to tell you that until we interviewed you. And, like you say, you might not be able to afford the best anyway. It's likely to do more harm than good at this point. Be careful who you talk to. I'd be careful about what I say. Don't volunteer too much information." Travis touched her hand lightly.

"You said the boy is okay, is that right?"

"Yes, like I said, he's gone to stay with his grandma in Denver. I'm going to meet her at the station today. He's down there is custody of Child Services. There's something else."

"What?" Mona asked. What more could there be?

"The grandma is interested in establishing paternity for the boy. If he is . . ."

"Brian's?"

"Yes, if he is Brian's, the grandmother would like child support."

"I'll be glad to have a DNA test. It would put my mind at ease either way. I'll pay support for him. I'm sure the girls would accept it. They'd be shocked, but so was I. What do you think, Travis? Do you think he is Brian's son?"

"I can't honestly answer that, Mona. Let's don't get ahead of ourselves. I have some papers for you to fill out to get this started with the DNA test. They say they can do the test for Brian if you have some of his hair or a toothbrush. The hair would work better, though."

"I have his hairbrush. It's still on the dresser. Haven't had the heart to put it away."

"See if you can find a toothbrush. If there is any saliva still on it they may be able to extract his DNA. Hair only works if there are follicles attached, so if you have a brush that has his hair in it, I'll take that. If you also used the hairbrush, it could confuse the matter."

Mona went to see what she could find; was she doing the right thing? What if she simply ignored the matter? Could they still try for support money? She'd always wonder if the boy were his. But, she wanted to think of the boy. What kind of life would he have without his mother and father? She found the hairbrush and a toothbrush, and brought it back down to Travis.

"You know how much you mean to me, don't you Mona?"

"I think I do. Your friendship means the world to me, but that's all it can be for now."

Mona didn't want Travis to think she was flirting or trying to trap him into a relationship. She was not ready for that and neither were her daughters.

"One more thing before I go. Do you know where John was last night?"

"John? I think he went to the pub."

"He might be asked to establish that. We don't know that he doesn't have something to do with this."

Mona nodded. She couldn't imagine John doing anything like that, but who knows how people's minds work. He was such a loner. Loners do strange things. It was odd that he didn't have a girlfriend, hadn't had one forever as far as Mona could tell. She would let the investigators pursue it, though. If he did do it, then he was a threat to her too.

After Travis left, Mona made sure the deadbolt was locked.

Mona did a few chores, checked on the animals. John had been doing a wonderful job keeping the ranch going. The animals were well cared for. She waved at him as he came in from checking the pastures and fences, as he did nearly every day. Every once in a while he would find a stranded animal, although that was more common in the spring when calves or lambs became separated from their mothers. Sometimes an ill animal would go off by itself, an instinct to find a secluded place to either die or get well.

Could this hardworking caring man be involved in a murder? In two murders?

Chapter 24

Wednesday, Wanda's Ranch

"Glad you stopped by," Wanda said. Mona believed the old woman. Walking into her house was like entering a safe place. She had opened the door before Mona had even rung the doorbell. Wanda turned and walked into her great room where she had started a fire in the stone fireplace. Mona could see the ghost of a young woman in her. It reminded Mona of the movie that Michelle Pfeiffer had been in. What was that movie? *Lady Hawke*? In the movie the heroine would turn by night into a hawk and by day back into a beautiful woman. There was that time, at dusk, Mona thought, where you could catch glimpses of both the hawk and the beautiful woman.

"I just needed a shoulder," Mona said.

"I don't doubt it, young lady," Wanda said. "Not with all that's going on. Want a glass of beer or something? Nothing wrong with a beer now and again."

"No. I'd better not." Mona wondered if the old woman had a drinking problem as much as she pushed alcohol on Mona. Then again, it was her business.

"Well, you don't mind if I do? I can make you a cup of tea."

Mona sat sipping her tea while Wanda drank her Coors right out of the bottle.

"I have to come out and ask," Wanda said. "Did you kill that woman? It's all over town that you did."

Shocked, Mona replied, "Of course not." Mona realized how defensive she sounded. And how blunt Wanda could be.

"Didn't think you could do something like that. Like I thought, there's only one person in this room ever killed someone."

Mona felt sorry for Wanda. "Wanda, don't," was all she could get out.

"Oh, I know. I must sound like I'm feeling sorry for myself. You're the only one who knows."

"And, I'll keep it that way. But, believe me, I never harmed that woman. I feel so sorry for that little boy."

"Lots of women in the county hate that woman. I suspect most are jealous of her, but jealousy's hate in another form. Nothing causes so much alarm as a pretty and loose woman in a small town."

"This is a damned hard life, being a ranch wife," Wanda said. "Nothing glamorous about this life. Wears you out and wears you down. By the end of your life you look like an old saddlebag that's hanging out there in the barn. What's that saying 'rode hard and put away wet'?"

Mona touched her face and felt thankful for the SPF15 she had slapped on it before she left her house

"Believe me; city life isn't much more glamorous. Maybe if you've got lots of money," Mona said. "Life would be easier with unlimited funds."

"I think lots of people used to get away with murder all the time," Wanda said. "Sometimes it was people nobody cared about. A retarded baby that was born and buried behind the barn. A used-up wife that wasn't any good to her husband anymore and dumped in the river. A young girl has a baby by herself and nobody ever knows about it. Hell, I bet people still get away with it if it's somebody nobody knows."

"Are you talking real people here?" Mona asked. "People I might know?"

"I'm not saying nothing," Wanda said. It was clear the beer had gone to her head.

197

"Why don't we talk about something else," Mona said. She needed the company but no more scary truths and secrets.

***

Thursday morning Travis stopped by Heartbreak to check on Mona and to tell her that only two sets of clear prints were found at Marla's place. Mark Eckland's and Isabel Eckland's.

"Of course, they could have gone over for tea as far as we know," Travis said. "Doesn't mean much unless they were on the murder weapon, which in this case was a cinder brick. And, there were no prints on it. This is going to be a tough one. There were no papers of any kind, no envelope you're your name on it or anything. Of course, they'll be considering that maybe you went there to take it. Maybe you have whatever it was. They don't have a way to connect Marla's murder with Brian's. Course, they don't tell me everything, but I've got ways of overhearing and reading things."

"Thanks for keeping me informed." Mona felt hurt by his comment about her taking anything from Marla's house, but she felt comforted to know that nobody could have seen her that night at Marla's house, because she hadn't gone in. If she had, maybe she would have ended up murdered too.

"You don't let me down, now. I trust you, Mona that you're innocent here. I don't think you would've told me you drove by Marla's house if you weren't."

Mona wondered for the first time since Brian died just how innocent she was. Why were these things happening all around her?

Chapter 25

Thursday morning, Heartbreak Ranch

The surveyor came to go over his findings with Mona. Mona stood outside on the porch waiting for him, not sure exactly when he'd arrive. She rubbed the arms of her cashmere sweater. The crisp freeze of January had leeched all moisture out of the already dry Colorado air. Mona scratched at her dry arms through the sweater and reminded herself to slap on lotion later.

"Your husband stopped me down at your entrance sign. Wanted to know what I was doing here. You didn't tell him? He must have been off the property the day I came out to survey."

Mona felt a shock go through her and pictured Brian, tall and strong and standing down by the HBR sign. It took her a full minute to understand his mistake.

"What's the matter?" he asked. "You feel okay?"

"My husband's dead," she said. She was aware of the rude abruptness of her comment but she still had not stopped her hands from shaking.

"Oh, God, I'm sorry." He looked stricken.

"It was probably John, my ranch-hand you saw. He's been with us for years. Don't worry about it, it happens all the time. The mistakes, I mean."

Lately, Mona found herself blurting out the fact of Brian's death and watching in wonderment as the recipient of her outburst cringed. She worried she felt too much power in the reaction she got. It really wasn't fair, she realized, but maybe it was the anger built up inside her. *My husband's dead, you idiot. My problems are much worse than your petty ones. It's worse than that; some people think I killed him.*

"I see. I should learn to mind my own business. I just like to have everything out in the open. One time, a wife had me survey the land because she wanted the best half when she got divorced. Turns out the husband didn't even know about it. I didn't think this was the case, since you wanted me to find this one parcel. My name's Groggins, by the way. Jim Groggins. You can call me Jim if you'd like." Jim Groggins evidently expressed his discomfort with rambling stories.

He kept looking at the house, pointing with his chin like a dog would do when wanting to go someplace.

"Come in. Let's get coffee. And, relax, I'm not so bad once you get used to me."

"That'd be great," he said. "I need to use the little boy's room after that long drive from Denver. And, by the way, I don't think you're bad at all." He looked at her a little sideways and lingering, like men used to look at her. She smoothed her hair.

When they got settled in the breakfast nook, he took out his notes and neatly penciled drawings.

"Your husband called me a few months ago and sent me some diagrams, wanted me to survey the property. That's why I called and asked if I could come. I did hear about your husband, so sorry for the mistake. I thought maybe I'd gotten wrong news. Shame that was." Groggins shook his head from side to side.

"It's okay. I thought since Brian wanted you to come, then you should finish what you started."

He moved in a slow deliberate way, kind of like a sloth, Mona thought. She felt relief at getting back the original drawings. She had felt regret at letting them out of her sight.

"These drawings all point to different places in a five acre region of your land. They point to precise areas and points of time. See here? You've heard of longitude and latitude, of course."

"Yes, I see." The more Mona looked at the drawings, the more she recognized the handwriting. Her father's. She never realized her father had such skill with surveying. There also seemed to be some math involved, judging by the numbers on the documents. It wasn't too shabby for her dad; a man with only a high school education. He had obviously spent some meticulous care with them.

"It's fascinating, really. This spot here. It's almost like some buried treasure is out there. You have any idea what it might be?" Mr. Groggins had a twinkle in his eye, kind of like the "lottery twinkle." She'd seen it in Brian's eyes hundreds of times. Something about the promise of finding buried treasured brought out the little boy in him.

"No, none at all. Except that it might have something to do with the Bureau of Land Management."

"Yes, I noticed some little notes here referencing the BLM. But, I've never seen anything like this before. But, you asked me to survey it, and that's all I did. I didn't do any digging or anything like that."

He looked to Mona like he'd love to do the digging himself. She imagined his job was normally boring and routine. His fantasy was probably about digging and hitting pay dirt.

"Did you mark it so I could find it?"

"Sure did. Little orange stakes and flags. I suppose I should tell your ranch-hand I did it so he doesn't remove them." Mr. Higgins's eyes again revealed a hidden emotion. Envy? Fear that John would dig up the prize, whatever that might be?

"Could you take me out there?" Mona asked. Not waiting for an answer, Mona put on the tall rubber boots, her heavy coat, and a pair of gloves she kept in the mudroom by the kitchen door.

They walked about twenty minutes, so it was clear the area was near the edge of the property to the Southeast. Mona hardly ever went up there, but knew that it was near the shared BLM range property that bordered her ranch with two others. They had an out-building there, the small cabin with a fireplace and not much else that was once used by ranch-hands when they checked on livestock in the winter. She knew it was up there. Her parents had forbidden her and her brother from going up there, but they'd been a few times anyway.

The BLM sometimes leased grazing land, which would allow any livestock as well as deer and elk and other wildlife to graze freely. Brian always said it was a practice leftover from the free-range era where any herd was legally able to graze anywhere, but as ranchers bought up the land it became a source of contention.

Mr. Groggins strode ahead quietly and with the determination of a foot soldier. He didn't talk much, which made Mona nervous. They kicked up a flock of Canadian geese that had come in for the winter. The sight always thrilled her, as she could hear their sturdy wings whistle in the air above them. She always thought it was good luck when they flew directly over her.

"It's beautiful up here," Mr. Groggins said. "Just beautiful. You're lucky."

Sometimes it took a stranger's eyes to remind her of how lucky she was. She looked around at the cold isolation of her land in winter, the raw beauty even with winter-stripped trees and a covering of snow and ice. What was she doing following a virtual stranger into an isolated area? She didn't see John anywhere. Even her dog, who had switched loyalties to John almost completely, was not within earshot. She had seen John leave in his truck; he had probably taken Bo with him. She hadn't brought a cell phone or anything. Feeling stupid for breaking one of the most basic rules she had told her girls; never go anywhere with someone you don't know, she turned to start back.

"What's the matter?" Mr. Groggins called to her. "We're almost there. Do I make you uncomfortable? I'm perfectly safe, you don't need to worry."

"No," she lied. "I just get uncomfortable that Brian died on the ranch."

"I wasn't sure how he died, Ms. Morgan. I'm awfully sorry. It's a shame. Hope it wasn't a farm accident."

"No. Heart attack," she lied again.

"Oh, sorry. It's just I hear so much about farm accidents, and he must have been young, since you're young yourself. Of course, for all I knew, he was older than you. I never met him in person, only talked over the phone."

"Don't worry. No need to tiptoe around me. I'm just not that sensitive." She remembered her father always telling her and her mother to "grow a backbone." Maybe she'd finally grown one.

Curiosity overcame her sudden anxiety and she turned and pressed on. Besides, she was at the age where she felt braver being alone with men. Youth brought vulnerability to women along with its attention. Mr. Groggins had shown a shadow of interest in her, but she quickly realized he was interested not in her, but in the mystery of her property.

Once they got to their destination, there wasn't much to see. Bare frosted earth covered the entire area. A large mound of bare earth rose from the more flat earth around it. It was as if a large grave resided there. It was immense. Probably stretches to about four or five acres, Groggins told her. It was like something had been buried there. What? Bodies? Mona shuddered. That couldn't be. She couldn't see her father as a serial killer. She remembered the story of the California vineyard owner who had killed migrant workers and buried them on his land. Impossible. Her father had been a gentle, if put-upon soul, who was never bent towards anger or revenge. Besides, why would he take the time to document such a spot so carefully? If it was John, it was doubtful her father would be involved. He had loved John like a son. But, her father would go out on a limb like that for John, nor for her for that matter.

"What do you suppose it is?" Groggins asked her. She pranced around nervously on the bare soil.

"I don't really know," she answered. She was afraid to know, was more like it.

"Well, could be anything, really. But, if your dad took all the trouble to map it to those documents, you can bet whatever turns up, it's bound to be valuable. Could be something like old bomb shelters, but I don't see any openings." Groggins seemed excited by the prospect.

"You're an optimist, Mr. Groggins. What if it's something terrible?"

"Well, you don't expect something bad, do you? Maybe it's gold or something? In my experience, people only take time to document things that may be valuable to them."

"Have you ever found gold buried on somebody's land?"

"Never got the chance. Guess I'm a ten-year-old boy at heart." Mr. Groggins let out a healthy laugh and Mona was no longer the least bit afraid of him. He looked harmless; more like an accountant than a surveyor.

"You want to help me dig down a little ways?" Mona asked.

"Sure. I'll have to go back to the truck and get a shovel."

"Why don't I stay here and wait. There's another in the garage. We can both dig." She regretted not asking him to get her cell phone while he was at it. Then she regretted not bringing shovels to begin with.

Mona paced the field while she waited for him. She almost changed her mind. What if they unearthed something that would implicate her father in something illegal?

Soon, he returned with two shovels. She chose a spot that seemed to be marked on the diagrams as important. Judging by his heavy breathing, he must have sprinted part of the way.

They dug down about four feet and were about to give up when they hit something hard. They dug more around it. It was a heavy barrel or tank. Mr. Groggins hit it a few times with his shovel.

"It's full of something."

Again, Mona had a bad recollection of a man who had buried bodies in barrels on his property. If Mr. Groggins was an optimist, she was surely the opposite.

"Want to bring one up and open it? "he asked.

"No, I don't think so. What if it is toxic?"

"Like toxic waste or something?" he asked.

"Yeah. I think I'll get the BLM guy out here and find out from him what it might be. He seemed to know a lot about my husband's dealings. And, my dad's before that."

Mr. Groggins seemed determined, but Mona guided him to his truck. She told him to send his bill to her.

***

After the surveyor left, Mona went back to the ranch house and called Mark Eckland and left a message with Isabel to have Mark call him. When Isabel pressed her about what she wanted, Mona told her about having the land surveyed and about finding barrels on the land. She wanted to know if he knew anything.

By two o'clock, Mark called her from his cell. He was driving somewhere in his truck.

"Those barrels are waste, that's all. Your parents allowed the BLM to bury them on your land. I wouldn't dig them up, they might be toxic. Besides, what's on top is probably more dangerous, uranium tailings."

"What's in them?"

"Just some waste from some tests that were done up at Roulison."

"My God. Are you saying there is nuclear waste on my land?" She knew about Roulison and had always had a curiosity about it. Who would come up with an idea to wring oil from oil shale using nuclear blasts? It had always seemed like something a young man would do just because he wanted to play with explosives.

"Don't get your dander up. It's not harmful."

"How do you know it's not harmful? My God, we've got a drinking well. The animals. My God, our drinking water." Mona was terrified. "How long's it been there?"

"For a long time. A few decades, I'd say," Mark said. "Probably as long as you've been on earth, and they're still radioactive. If I were you, I'd forget about it. You don't want to get the county in an uproar."

From Mark's cold tone, Mona decided to drop it with him. She'd decide how to go forward from here, but wouldn't include him.

"Okay, if you say so."

"Now, promise me you'll drop this. We don't need a public scandal," Mark said. "You can trust me. If you don't want the barrels on your property, I'll have them moved. You just have to give me some time. If you call anyone, they'll probably seize your land. Your land and everyone else's in this county will become worthless. You don't want your property seized, do you?"

"Why would they do that?" Mona felt that her business experience served her well in this discussion. She had met plenty of men who said inaccurate things with authority in their voices. It didn't make what they said true. There were always options.

"Because, those barrels are government property."

"I just don't understand what's gone on here," Mona said.

"You don't need to understand it, Mona. Why do you think Brian never talked to you about it? You just don't need to know. Believe me, you don't want your parent's name brought into this. Do you want to ruin their memory that way?"

"Okay, if you say so," Mona said. Mark made it sound like he and her parents had been involved in a cover-up of some kind. Why wouldn't Brian have said something to her? Had she been married to a complete stranger? First she finds out he had an affair and possibly a child she didn't know about, and now this? She decided she had better play along with Mark. She was certain he would not help her.

Chapter 26

Thursday, Heartbreak Ranch

It was only five o'clock and John sat at the kitchen table, waiting to have an early dinner with her. She had used her nervous energy to cook, baking a shepherd's pie complete with homemade mashed potatoes, and wasn't in the mood to eat alone. She vowed not to make cooking for John a habit. Eventually she'd have to venture out and meet people. *People? How about concentrating on your girls? On the ranch?* Bo sat contritely at John's feet, as if to signal Mona that he was no longer her dog.

What if John had killed her husband? What if he wanted to get her out of the way too? Maybe she was too trusting. Was there any way he could claim the property that he had lived on for so long? Maybe he would have a claim to the entire estate. Mona's mind reviewed her estate situation. She didn't have a formal will. Bad, she knew. But, by law, everything would fall to her two girls. But did that put them in danger? She would talk to a lawyer.

"You okay, Mona? You seem quiet." John's words rang ironic to Mona. He was the ever-quiet man calling her quiet.

She jumped at the sound of his voice. "Just thinking," she said.

The phone rang, causing another startle reaction in both Mona and John.

"Mona, this is Travis. Just wanted to tell you that John's been eliminated as a suspect."

"Really?" Mona couldn't help looking at John. From his look back, she could tell he knew the conversation included him. Mona turned her back to John.

"He was in Denver like he said when Brian was killed. He bought gas near the stockyard in Denver that day and the clerk remembered him. And, there's a CB radio operator who says he talked to him while he was almost in Denver. There's no way he could have killed Brian, driven to Denver, and driven home."

"That's good to know."

"Wait, is he there with you? You sound like he might be."

"Yes."

"Good, God. What if it had been him that did the killing?"

"I was just thinking that. Just as you called. But, it doesn't matter now, does it?"

"Damn it, Mona. I just wish you'd be more careful. That's all."

"I will. I promise." Mona hung up the phone.

Mona put a shepherd's pie and a cup of coffee in front of John. She had spiked his coffee and her tea with a jigger of brandy, with his nod of the head taken as agreement. Mona felt thankful for his humble quiet personality. She felt no need for excessive talking or posturing around him. He was what he was and she could be herself around him.

John ate quietly and politely until Mona decided to break the cozy silence that had settled over the room. It got any more quiet she'd have to put on music.

"That was Travis," she said. "He said you'd been eliminated as a suspect."

John put down his fork. "Of course I was eliminated. There's no way I could ever do anything like that. Me and Brian, we had our differences, but we settled them like men. We might have come to fists over the land, but that's about it. I'm a patient man, Mona. I would wait my entire life for the land that's coming to me. I don't need to kill nobody for it. It wouldn't be worth it. I'll just wait on it."

"Well, you're not going to have to wait. You let me know anything you need to get that house built. I'll be glad when they get this all cleared up and find what really happened to Brian. Do you have any ideas about that?"

"I wouldn't want to cast 'spersions on anyone. But, the only people he hung out with besides you were the Eckland's, Wanda occasionally, and . . ."

Mona knew immediately that he was about to say Marla's name. "Marla. I'm not too sensitive about her." Her lie surprised her.

"Well, yeah. I never saw her around here though. So, unless someone was protecting her and came out here, I just don't know. I go into town a lot though. Since I wasn't here that day. I know you didn't do it, though. You couldn't have."

"Well, you know they still doubt me. I was in the vicinity at the time. I drove by her house—I admit that. I had opportunity and from what they see, I had a motive. I could have killed Brian in a jealous rage. I could have killed Marla for revenge." Mona looked at John for a reaction. She got nothing from John. He still suspected her. If he didn't he would say so.

They ate quietly for a while. Mona ruminated on the fact that Skye did have a stun gun. Again she suspected John. John had access to the house. He could have gotten Skye's stun gun. Mona just couldn't see him going to all that trouble. Plus, now he'd been eliminated. It couldn't have been him. He would have simply hit Brian over the head with a shovel. It was more his style.

"Anyway, you can trust me." John broke the silence just as Mona was thinking of putting on music.

"I know that John. I'm sorry if it ever seemed like I doubted you. We've got to trust each other. We're into this land together now." Mona forced all suspicious thoughts about John from her head. He had been officially cleared. Of course, that made her seem more of a suspect in their eyes. Maybe the CB guy was his friend.

"Thank you ma'am. And thanks for letting me stay on."

"What I pay you amounts to peanuts, John. But you've got a home here. And, you've got your land. By the way, I'll continue paying the property tax on it, even though you'll get a separate statement since we turned it over to you. That should help a little. I'm sorry I can't pay you more. I may need to count on you to keep the ranch up if anything happens to me."

"Don't say that. You're going to be alright. This will all blow over. And, don't think about the money. I don't have many needs. I earn enough for food and a pair of Levi's every year. Every few years I need a new pair of boots. I live real simple. The land to build my place is all I need."

"What about a wife and family, John. Haven't you wanted that?"

Mona detected a blush under John's weathered face.

"No ma'am. I never thought I'd make a good family man. If I want to see a woman, I go into town."

It was more information than Mona needed. It did bring to mind more questions. Was it Marla? When men 'went into town,' how did they know where to find these women?

"I didn't mean to pry into your personal life."

"I just don't want you to think I'm one of those men that hates women. I like women. Respect them."

"I didn't think that, John. Just don't want you to be lonely, that's all."

"Well, I don't want you to be lonely either."

Mona remembered that she too was alone now. She certainly didn't want people thinking she was lonely. She had her children. She'd fill up her life with their love.

When John left, Mona hugged him. She felt him pull back awkwardly, and Mona thought she'd never try hugging him again. "Thanks for joining me for dinner. Every once in a while, it's good to sit down with someone and eat."

"For me too, ma'am. I'm not such a good cook. I cook beans and cornbread, that's about it," he said.

***

The next day brought another early visit from Travis. They sat in the breakfast nook and drank coffee. Travis had brought doughnuts from the Hawk Diner. They tasted homemade. Mona had given up her "city-slicker" ideas about calories and metabolisms and ideal body-fat ratio. Still, the increased effort of country living had slimmed her down.

"Mona, they're still looking at you for Marla's death. I thought I'd better tell you. Seems you're the only one with motive to kill her."

"I knew it must be looking bad right now for me. I can hardly believe that. I couldn't do anything like that. I can't believe what evidence they would have."

"Your fingerprints at Marla's house. On a cup that was in her kitchen sink."

Mona thought of the day she was at Marla's. The woman must not do dishes very often, she thought. That was a while ago.

"I've got an explanation for that," Mona said. "I went to visit her, to see her son. I took them cookies for thanking them for being at Brian's funeral. I did that for several of the local women. We had coffee and that was it."

"You probably shouldn't tell me too much," Travis said. "And, your landline phone records indicate you called her several times that night. Maybe trying to make sure she was home or something."

"Travis, I told you the story. She wanted me to meet her. When she didn't show, I called her house."

"It just doesn't look good, that's all I'm saying. You can explain it to me, but it'll sound completely different when you're on the witness stand testifying."

Mona was so nervous after Travis left that she spent an hour or so looking up lawyers in Denver. It looked like she might need one, despite her efforts to avoid it. She decided to heed his advice and not talk until she talked with a lawyer. She might say something that sounded bad that she couldn't take back. Hell, maybe she already had. Then, she decided to inspect Brian's office again. There had to be something there, something she was missing, something whoever had broken in was looking for and didn't get.

Mona went back to the cubbyhole where she'd found the logbooks. She took them out again and inspected the space. She tapped on the walls, which were lined with cedar panels. One sounded a little hollow. After some work, she discovered that one of the panels came out. She hit pay dirt. Her heart leapt at the sight of a hidden cubby. Treasure?

Chapter 27

Friday, Heartbreak Ranch

The cubbyhole yielded three old canvas bags of cash. The bags were dirty and worn, as if they'd been around a long time, and had brass rings through which a thin rope strung the rings together. Mona put the bags aside to count later, then retrieved a safe-deposit box key and additional papers mostly dealing with the BLM and radioactive waste. Mona found another logbook. This one had entries in Brian's handwriting. Ever the organized person, Brian had logged any money that he had taken, presumably from the bags of money that were also stored in the cubbyhole. The money Brian had taken from the bags was over fifty thousand, according to Brian's notes. Where had the money come from and why hadn't Brian talked with her about it? Brian, what the hell was going on?

The sight of the money and records brought both excitement and fear to her.

"That's how we paid for this house renovation. And college for the girls. Now it makes sense." Mona's voice echoed from the angled ceiling. "I'm talking to nobody." Are you happy Brian? Did I know you at all?

At the time they decided on the expensive remodel, it hadn't made sense to her that they could afford it, even with the savings they had used. Brian had wanted only the best materials for the kitchen. He had insisted on expensive hardwood for the wainscoting, not pine. The counters had to be real Colorado slab granite. They had not borrowed any money to do the renovations, and Mona had wondered about it at the time. Brian always claimed he was using his severance from his corporate job, but it never added up to Mona and their bank accounts never depleted.

She also understood why paying for college had become a non-issue. Mona had worried so much over where they would come up with the money, that Brian had taken on the whole task. The fact that they hadn't yet had to get student loans for the girls now made sense. My God, where had the money come from? She remembered the doubts she'd had last year that came to her like recurring toothaches.

Had Marla had gotten any of the money. Mona doubted it unless it was a very small amount. She felt selfish thinking about it; it was Brian's money too. Maybe her son was his son. But, they were married and financial decisions should have been between the two of them. Mona had always considered herself an intelligent educated woman who knew much about money. She had allowed herself to go into denial about where the money had come from. She'd let Brian take over managing the money because she trusted him completely and those chores had to be divided somehow. Truthfully, she felt only relief each time Brian came up with money to pay for something.

Mona sat and counted the money. There was about eighty thousand dollars in cash. So, there must have been a hundred thousand and thirty before Brian's withdrawals. Depending how you looked at it, it was either a fortune or a moderate amount of money. It was amazing how quickly a small fortune seemed like not enough to cover the bills. If it had been her parent's life savings, it was hard earned money. It was nearly impossible as far as Mona could discern. Ranchers just didn't make that much from their land; they were lucky to keep their horses in hay. Mona puzzled over the money and the log. Something seemed familiar about the log entries. The numbers on the left hand side of each withdrawal.

Brian had penned in the entry "10A" to the left of a withdrawal that looked like the amount of the girl's college tuition for the first semester of college. Sure enough, there was a similar entry labeled "10C" for the same amount. "C" for college. Mona got out her daughter's tuition records from her desk downstairs. The amounts matched. Brian had told her that he had gotten a small grant for the girls, but he never told her the amount. Something about Government Farm Workers of America. It hadn't made much sense to her at the time, but she had decided not to question freedom from money worries. She had even tried looking up the organization on the Internet and had given up after a couple of tries. Maybe she hadn't wanted to know the source of their good fortune.

Astounded, Mona started from the front of the log. The first entry was "84A." These initial withdrawals were for relatively small amounts of money; one thousand or less. They were also further apart. There were only two withdrawals in the first year. The year "93A" showed a marked increase. Mona calculated. Where was she in 1993? She looked at the amounts. There were six withdrawals for "94." If these numbers represented years, then four of these would have been for her own college tuition, room and board for Colorado State University. At the time, CSU was on a quarterly system instead of semesters and so her tuition was due every three months.

Mona had a flash of enlightenment. That was how her parents had afforded a college education for her. They had even paid for special classes like ballet and art. They continued paying after she got pregnant, married Brian, and wanted to continue with college. She had felt rich in comparison with her college friends, most who were going to CSU because they qualified for cheaper in-state tuition. She never questioned where the money had come from. At the time, her local friends had chided her. Where had her parents gotten the money for college when most of them were scrapping to keep their farms and ranches going? Most of the locals needed their kids at home to help on the ranch until they got married. Some kids paid for college by showing sheep or steers in the National Western Stock show and selling their animals. Even after they got married, many were needed to help with harvest or sheep shearing.

It got down to her young age. Mona had only cared that she got to go to college. Brian had gone to college too, but as far as she knew, he paid his own tuition. It seemed from the beginning that Brian was mysterious about money. On top of that, Brian had to go home most weekends to help with his parent's farm. Mona hadn't wondered about it at the time, hadn't needed to know where the money came from. Of course, she never asked for a car or clothes. Farm kids didn't ask so much back then, and besides, it was chic to wear worn-out jeans and gauzy shirts. Her memory of college was four years of parties, dating Brian, blue-grass festivals, the annual Pig Roast in which a whole pig was buried and cooked over coals, punctuated by learning. She had been so happy back then, going to college, becoming a mother, being a married woman on campus.

She hadn't gone home too much back then. Her parents were still coldly detached from her since her brother's death in the accident. She got the feeling they were glad she was gone. They only had to try to relate to her when she was home. She hadn't known their financial effort for her.

They were like statues sometimes, and sometimes more like rocks. It was as if all life had been sucked from them when their son was killed. She couldn't fill the void that was left by that and she sometimes wished that it were she who had gotten killed instead of her brother. He was forever canonized in death even though she knew he hadn't chosen it.

Could the money have something to do with her brother's death? Could it have anything to do with Mark Eckland and his experience in Viet Nam? Mark was clearly over sixty-five years old now. Surely they didn't get a settlement of any kind from her brother's death in an automobile accident. Mona doubted her parents had carried life insurance on her or her brother. There didn't seem to be a connection, although Mona always divided life into the time before her brother was killed and after. It seemed she always tried to link everything in her life to that one event.

More likely, it seemed related to the BLM and to Mark Eckland. Yet, Mona was reluctant to call Mark and ask him. Maybe it had been he who broke into Brian's office that day and was looking for the money.

Mona found it ironic that Brian would continue her Dad's bookkeeping methods. Why had he not told her about what he found? Didn't he think it concerned her? It seemed she had been married to a total stranger.

In the end, Mona put the money back in the cubbyhole but kept the safe deposit key and directions to the bank, which was in Denver. She'd go there in the morning and clear out the safe deposit box. The money, which had initially excited Mona, had lost its luster. She felt in her heart that it wasn't hers, that it hadn't even belonged to her parents. Otherwise, wouldn't Brian have said something? She remembered seeing Brian huddled with her father, talking in low tones or going over a paper. They always hushed when she entered the room, but it was no different than when she was a child. She had been secretly pleased that Brian and her dad got along so well. It was as if she had provided her parents with a substitute for their dead son. But, they had John for that, didn't they?

Mona made a point to tell John she'd be driving to Denver the next day. He asked her couldn't he go for her? But, she didn't think she should involve John. Not just yet anyway.

"John, did Dad or Brian talk much to you about finances?"

"Money, you mean?"

"Yes. Money. About how much the ranch brought in, that kind of thing?"

"No, ma'am. I don't suppose they figured I was educated enough. Why? Do you want me to help with something? I always thought I was good with numbers." Mona doubted it; he probably had a ninth grade education at most. Then she reminded herself that an education doesn't replace a natural talent for something like numbers.

"Not just yet. Just watch the place tomorrow. I'll be back by five or earlier."

"You just call me if you need me. I keep my cell phone on."

Mona had to chuckle at the thought of a cowboy carrying a cell phone. Technology was wonderful.

***

Mona enjoyed the drive to Denver the next day. It was a clear day with no threat of snow. She always loved driving through Vail with its immense lodges and Nordic looking ski chalets, the long serpentine ski runs lining the mountain, dotted with skiers and snowboarders. She loved the long winding climb up Vail pass, and even loved how her ears became stuffed up as she climbed up over ten thousand feet.

By ten in the morning she was at the Silverado Bank. She'd forgotten that it was Saturday, and so the bank had limited personnel. She waited thirty minutes for someone to open the box. By ten after ten she was staring into the open safe deposit box. She had to present Brian's death certificate and the probate papers to get the key to the box. Her hands shook so much she was embarrassed to sign for the key. The box had been changed to Brian's name from her parent's. He had been having the bill for the box sent to a PO Box at a Mail and More store in Denver. So, Mona had one more place to go that day.

The safe deposit box contained her uncle's war medals. Seeing them made her cry; a Purple Heart and a Bronze Star.

His discharge papers were in there too, along with a photo of her parents receiving his medals from two uniformed officers. She strained to see the faded picture. One of the uniformed men receiving medals alongside her uncle looked a lot like Mark Eckland. She heard the stories about how her uncle died and how Mark was injured in the same battle and had tried to save him. She stuffed the photo and discharge papers into the large tote she had brought with her. She'd take everything that could give her any clue into was had happened to Brian.

The box also yielded several Certificates of Deposit. Five of them, to be exact, for the total amount of five hundred thousand dollars. So the hundred thousand in the cubbyhole was just spending money? Where in God's name had that kind of money come from? It wasn't millions, but it was a lot for her parents to have saved. She'd never seen a listing of her parents' assets. If they had that much, why would Brian keep it from her? Was he planning to leave her and take the money with him? Or, was his silence meant to protect the money? If someone else wanted the money or if it really belonged to someone else, that would be a reason for Brian to keep it quiet. Damn it, if he were here, she could ask him. Now, what if nobody knew the answers?

Mona decided to take the contents, close the box, and hide the CDs in another safe deposit box in her own name. Then, she drove to the Mail and More Store, showed the owner Brian's death certificate, and opened the box. She told the clerk to cancel the box, since Brian had died. She opened the mailbox. It was half full. There were a couple bills for the safe deposit box, a few junk letters, and about ten from Marla. These brought tears to Mona's eyes. She shredded them and deposited them in the trash can outside the store. On the way home, she regretted the action. What if Marla's letters gave her some clue as to what was going on with Brian? It was done, though, and Mona had to believe it was for the best.

Chapter 28

Monday, Heartbreak Ranch

Brian's death and the mystery surrounding it had taken a dark turn. She had to act, and act fast.

Mona had the house and ground around it tested for radioactivity and the house tested for radon gas.

To her relief, it was within normal range. Colorado had a slightly higher radioactivity level anyway because of the uranium content of the clay soil, and Heartbreak Ranch was in normal range. Of course, the dump site had much higher readings, so Mona would have to have the clean-up done. Some of the pastures had much higher levels, which could explain the miscarriages and malformations in some of the animals. The affected areas were mostly pasture and alfalfa fields. Mona took out the map the surveyor had left with her and carefully marked the radiation levels on the map. She'd have John fence those areas off from the livestock.

Upset and not sure how much of this information to tell the girls, Mona decided to talk to John about it, then Wanda.

"It makes sense," said John. "You don't just find two-headed lambs and calves being born for nothing. The livestock grazed on that area for years before your Dad finally quit using it for pasture. Ever since then, the livestock's been more normal. To tell you the truth, I never go over there. Always thought it was poison. Arsenic in the water or something like that. But, arsenic's more likely to kill the animals outright."

Mona then went over to Wanda's house.

"I've been expecting this conversation," Wanda said. "It's Mark Eckland. He came to me over thirty years ago with an offer I couldn't refuse. Only I did refuse. He's treated me fairly despite the whole thing, but many times I've regretted my decision. Could've used the money. Just look how it helped your parents. My God, I couldn't afford to send my daughter to college. She might still be talking to me if I'd had a little more money to help her. I'm sure she doesn't know how much my land is worth now. A good sight more than it was thirty or forty years ago."

"What are we talking about, Wanda?" Mona sipped on the small glass of brandy that Wanda had poured for her. Wanda had already finished hers.

"That God-awful plutonium or uranium, whatever is buried in your parent's pasture. In your pasture, I mean."

"What are you talking about? Why would there be radioactive material buried on my property?" Although she knew it in her heart and from talking to Mark Eckland, she had hoped it wasn't true that her parents had been involved. Mona felt alarm rise in her. What had she exposed her children to?

"Money. It all gets down to money. You know yourself, that money's everything. I don't know the whole story, but Mark Eckland was involved in coordinating some of the clean-up of those tests they did down at Rulison. What a mess that was." Wanda had opened up and spilling the entire story. Mona had no doubt that her memory was impeccable.

"The way Mark explained it was he got so much money to move the mess out. He could save money and pay a yearly fee for storage if we'd agree. He said the storage facilities charged so much it was like rape. The contract was for millions to clean up the mess the government left. It was all top-secret. Nobody was to know, but we didn't know *how* top-secret it was until your Dad decided he wanted the stuff off his land. It was after those lambs, poor little things, were born with all kinds of problems. Some of the ewes couldn't carry a lamb past a couple of months. Your Mom started reading about radioactivity and cancer and it scared the hell out of her."

"Why would they agree to something like that?" Why had Wanda kept this a secret from her?

"They were so broke up after your brother got killed in that accident. They couldn't handle losing the ranch too. You know the money problems with owning a ranch. All your wealth is in the land itself. And, the land you want to pass down to your kids. The only way out is to lease or mortgage your land. The route they took was easier than a mortgage. It was a way to save the ranch without giving it away to the banks."

"God, I never knew."

"They didn't want you to know. I'll be damned if my husband wasn't the one to get the cancer from it. Him and your Dad got it. Maybe I would have had an easier life with the money."

"Wanda, they never spent most of it. They squirreled it away in a bank deposit. I might never have found it."

"Well, mark my word, they spent enough of it to keep the ranch going. They spent to send you away to school."

"But, why my parents? What about the other ranchers?"

"Your parents weren't the only ones. There's about five other ranches in the area with the stuff buried on it, including the old Morgan farm---Brian's family. Thank God I didn't. Think what it'll do to the resale value of the place. Course, nobody's supposed to know."

"My God," Mona said. "What did my parents do? What did Brian do to us?"

On the way home, Mona alternately fretted and panicked. How much would it cost to clean up the mess on her property? Would she have to destroy her livestock? Could they take the ranch?

Chapter 29

Monday, Heartbreak Ranch

Panic filled Mona. What if they'd think she really killed her husband and then his lover?

The reality of it, no, the "unreality" of it smothered her. How do you prove yourself innocent when someone decides you've got the best motive to kill someone? For the first time, she wondered if she could actually go to prison, and the thought sent cold chills from the bottoms of her feet to her head. She had been so worried about how much this was going to cost; money for a lawyer, lost time, lost trust. She never actually thought she could be accused of murder.

Prison. She hadn't even discussed this possibility with the girls. In fact, they didn't know that she was considered a suspect. It was a good thing she was low-profile enough to have stayed out of the papers—for the most part— except for articles about Brian's murder. She had Travis to thank for that, as he had refused questions from the Glenwood Springs papers. She started trembling when she thought of having to tell them that anyone suspected her of anything so vile. Not to mention that lawyers would probably bankrupt her. That was something new to her, the reality that she was caught in middle-class limbo, with too much money for a public defender and not enough for the best defense lawyer.

She was fast becoming the most likely suspect. She certainly had the strongest motive. She knew she didn't have anything to do with her husband's death. Nor did she have anything to do with Marla's ugly death. Ultimately, she could be framed for not only Brian's death but for Marla's as well. She hadn't done it. Not unless she was completely insane and didn't remember any of it. Anything was possible. A year ago she'd never have imagined herself in this situation.

She always told Brian the only way she could kill someone was in protection of the girls. She wasn't positive she could do that either. She'd have to have a weapon in her hand at the time. The thing that bothered her, that seemed to tie the two deaths together, was the old pickup truck that she'd seen on her property and trying to run her off the road weeks ago. Who drove the truck? If she knew that, she might know who the killer was.

Mona decided not to tell John where she was going and dodged a phone call from Travis. Better he stayed back from this. He could lose his job--or worse. She set out early on Monday to find the mysterious pickup truck. Besides, she was not sure how much to trust Travis.

***

Mona must have driven two hundred miles that day and saw parts of Hawk County she hadn't known existed. She saw rundown and ramshackle parts of Hawk that she never had wanted to see. On one rancher's property she thought she saw marijuana plants growing in the fields farthest away from BLM grazing land. Mona saw beautiful snow and ice covered vistas, beautiful expansive fields with clusters of evergreen trees. She saw cattle of all breeds and even a couple of mule deer that had come down from the high-country to feed. She must have seen hundreds of rabbits and even a fox.

What she didn't see was an old pickup truck.

If the pickup truck was from Vail or farther up Vail Pass, there was no way she'd find it. She gave herself this one day to find the truck. She told herself she wouldn't become obsessed with it, wouldn't let it eat her up as Brian used to say. Maybe the truck had nothing to do with either death. It reminded her of an old pickup truck her dad had. Maybe she was pulling up an old memory.

She saw any number of broken down vehicles as she made her way through the maze of country roads. Many of the roads were washed out from the last spring rains, or were snowed in, even with the lack of snow this winter produced. Many times during the day she got out of her Jeep to open a gate onto someone's property. Many times she read on a sign: PRIVATE PROPERTY STAY OUT. Other signs warned: MEAN DOGS. She persisted despite this. Border Collies were common in the county and were generally not mean and nobody kept mean dogs because they didn't want their livestock attacked.

Most people in the county knew her and would wonder what she was doing on their land, but if she encountered a rancher or ranch-hand, she would say she was driving to relieve stress. In recent years Hawk County started having more problems with packs of dogs that were the result of "city people" dumping their unwanted pets in the high-country.

She pondered her "just out for a stress-reducing drive" answer to the local ranchers. Mona knew this answer would either rankle or amuse whatever rough-edged cowboy or rancher she encountered. This would prove true for both men and women.

"Stress is one of those made-up things like chronic fatigue and panic attacks," Wanda had said once. While Mona knew that there were such things as stress and chronic fatigue and panic attacks, and had probably suffered from at least two out of the three at some point, she knew not to argue with a crusty old Colorado rancher. These were tough people who fought with every fiber of their being to keep their ranches going. They did this day after day until one day they died. There was no vacation, no retirement plan, and no retirement celebration.

She also suspected many of them suffered from depression and even panic attacks at times, but they were simply too tough to acknowledge any such thing. They lived and died with their inconveniences and pain. Granted, sometimes they had a little help with a bottle of brandy or whiskey.

Mona encountered a few surprises during her drive. Mr. Buchanan was trying to grow grapes. His Southeast forty was devoted to what appeared to be two-year-old grape vines that in spring would unfurl their green leaves and produce blossoms. Mona laughed a little at that; a sixty-year old Colorado rancher growing grapes. He probably made his own wine and had a dream of bottling and selling it. He'd probably not get very far without someone's professional advice. Several ranchers down-valley from Hawk had sold their land to California and Texas yuppies who wanted to grow grapes and open wineries. It turns out that Colorado soil and climate was good for growing wine grapes, although frost was more common than in California and trying more often than not led to heartbreak. She knew from her stint in the business world how hard it would be to literally grow a business from the ground up. Many of the successful wineries Hawk County had seen recently were backed by big money from the West Coast or Texas. She had to give the guy credit for trying. You never knew.

Mona also found out that the Bennett ranch had started growing Black Angus cattle and that the Smith family had built a brand new barn. Mona wondered whether she should do these drive-arounds more often. She almost started enjoying the drive despite the rutted roads and dusty coating covering her and her car.

But, for most of the afternoon, Mona didn't see one old pickup truck. Then, about two o'clock, as she was about to head home, she saw it. It was in some pasture land about ten miles from the Eckland ranch and just north of the Smith's ranch. Mona thought it might be government land. It wasn't fenced in, which was one sign that it was open range.

Mona stopped, but left her SUV running, just in case she needed to get out quickly. She looked around before getting out of her car. She was one hundred percent certain that this was the truck. There were no plates on it. It looked to be an early sixties model Ford pickup truck. There was a gun rack in the back window, but no rifle. Maybe she had imagined the rifle when she saw it from the highway, but she didn't think so.

Mona got her cell phone and called Travis.

"Can you get somebody to come and look at this pickup truck? Maybe it has fingerprints or some other evidence. I'm pretty sure this is the one."

"Will do. It just looks suspicious that you're the one that found it, Mona." Travis fretted about her going off on her own to investigate, but Mona suspected he was embarrassed about his own lack of ability to find it. Or, had he even tried? At this point, she saw no other option. The boys at CBI weren't about to believe her. She doubted they'd even try. Even to Mona it seemed like a Hail Mary to clear herself.

"It's north of the Smith place," she said. "I'll wait here until you get here. The keys are in the thing, but you might want to bring a tow truck. Do you need a search warrant?"

"I'll file for one. They might just dust it where it is," Travis said. "We'll take care of it. I don't think you should touch it or anything."

Mona spent the rest of the day back at Heartbreak, waiting and worrying. She busied herself checking on the animals. John had been doing a great job of keeping the animals cared for.

Mona waited and listened to the wind whistle through the stands of Blue Spruce. Whatever was dumped and buried out in Mona's property nagged at her. She even started having nightmares about it. In her dreams, gooey green and black stuff seeped up out of the ground and threatened the ranch house. When Travis arrived, he instructed Mona to leave the scene. He didn't want to put her name in the report. He'd say that he had found the truck and it would tie in with the report that she had filed in Vail the night the truck had chased her.

Chapter 30

Tuesday, Mark Eckland's place

Mona was there at the Eckland's at seven o'clock. No call ahead. No warning that she'd be there. Element of surprise. She'd be early enough for them to be up by most standards, but too early for Mark to have left for work. Mark Eckland seemed to be a man past the age to retire from a government job; he certainly was old enough. In contrast to the local ranchers and farmers, he seemed to answer to nobody, not even the weather. Not even God, thought Mona, as she was certain that he was responsible for Brian's death.

As for Marla, she was not sure. Her death could have been unrelated to the mess that Mona was involved in. Was it some big cosmic coincidence? Brian had always said that there were no coincidences, that when we thought there were, those events were destiny. It was ironic to Mona that she was the pragmatic one of the family, the unromantic cynical one. Maybe that was why Brian needed Marla. Had she been more spontaneous, more fun than Mona? She could let the thought of Brian and Marla tear her up inside and devour her.

Mona felt no fear ringing the Eckland's doorbell. It took two rings of the bell for Isabel Eckland to answer.

"Oh, it's you," she said. Isabel Eckland patted her hair into place. She had on her makeup already, making Mona wonder if she slept in it. She had on jeans, probably size four or smaller and a western style shirt, which was not tucked in. Mona had probably caught Isabel at her worst, which could be comparable to most people's best days. Her nails were perfectly manicured, and Mona stared at the tiny diamond-like jewel imbedded on the ring fingernail of her right hand. The fingernail diamond could not compete with the ostentatious rock on Isabel's left ring finger.

"Can I help you?" she asked. "Mark's getting ready for work."

"I know, that's why I wanted to talk with him. I've got some important business to discuss with him. I believe it concerns his job."

"Come in," she said. She guided Mona into the Great Room, but didn't offer her coffee or anything. That was all right with Mona. She had been up early and had two cups before she left home.

"Mona!" Mark was shocked to see her. Was that disapproval on his face? Fear?

"Can we talk? Alone?" Mona looked at Isabel, who rolled her eyes and walked towards the kitchen.

"I'll be in here if you need anything," she said as she left. She pointed to an overstuffed club chair and motioned for Mona to sit. Evidently, Isabel was a quiet woman in the mornings.

"I'll get right to the point," she said. "I want to know the truth about the radioactive waste buried on my land."

Mark looked at her, obviously not wanting to deal with it. He wiped his brow, which needed it now because he was breaking out in a sweat.

"I believe that what you did, what you made my parents do, wasn't legal, that it wasn't authorized by the BLM. Don't tell me you don't know about this. I've gotten word from other people."

"Who? Crazy Wanda? She imagines things."

"We're not talking about Wanda. It doesn't matter how I found out, but I want to know what it is."

"Why don't you tell me what you think it is," he suggested.

"I think it's some kind of embezzling scheme. Or Ponzi scheme." Mona struggled to remember what a "Ponzi scheme" was.

Mark became quiet. His expression indicated that he was thinking. She didn't want to give him too much time to make up a story.

"I've got documentation. If anything happens to me people will know who did it."

"What could happen to you?" he asked with a snicker. His expression changed, as if a light-bulb went on.

"Let's talk about this, Mona. Your parents agreed years ago to be part of a top-secret operation."

"Oh, come on," she said. "Are you saying they were working for the government? The CIA?"

"Yes, in a manner of speaking. You'll never find record of it, it was so top-secret."

"So, tell me what that was. What did they do that was so top-secret?"

"Let's get a drink and go into the den and talk," Mark said."

"I'm going too," Isabel said, who had returned from the kitchen with cinnamon rolls.

"All right," Mark said. "This will be no surprise to you."

The Eckland's den had a rich feel to it. Expensive-looking wood wrapped the walls with a warm feel. The rock gas fireplace, which Isabel had switched on, only added to the feel. Mark poured each of them a small glass of brandy. Mona had no intention of drinking hers, but the rich oaky smell beckoned to her and she sipped at it. If she hadn't been so full of adrenaline, she could slip into a restful nap in this cozy room in the cozy chair she'd been instructed to sit in. Isabel had chosen a matching chaise for herself, while Mark sat in what Mona assumed was "his chair." She put a cinnamon roll on one of the small porcelain plates that Isabel had set on the coffee-table. She ate it in four bites, but noticed that Isabel didn't take one.

Isabel didn't relax into the chaise, but instead sat daintily on the edge of it and glared at her husband, and Mona knew that she had supreme control in their house.

"To start with," Mark started, "We all know things were different forty years ago. There was the war. The war that took your uncle." Mark looked at Mona for reaction.

"Yes," she said. She felt an unexpected stab of pain at the mention of her uncle. Nobody spoke of him. Ever.

"Then after your brother Bob died in that accident, your parents were devastated."

"I know that. But, what does that have to do with any of this?"

"I was over there with your uncle in Viet Nam. I tried to save him, did save some lives and got some medals. I joined, didn't get drafted. I was a college kid. My parents saved every penny to send me to college so I'd get deferred for the draft. I don't suppose that would work these days, with everybody going to college. But I went and joined up anyway." He wore regret on his rugged features. Was he going to go through his entire life's story?

Isabel had slugged down her drink and got up to pour herself another. She looked like a woman who had heard this all before. She waved the bottle at Mark, who nodded for a refill. Drinking first thing in the morning. No judgement.

"It all gets down to money," Mark said. "I got out of Viet Nam, finished college, jumped ahead of the line because of my service went to work for the agency."

"The BLM?" asked Mona.

"Yes. Anyway, that brings us to Rulison?"

"The atomic testing?"

"Yes. 'Project Plowshare', was what we called it. The government's name for an effort to use nuclear weapons for peacetime purposes. Some kind of biblical reference about "beating their swords into plowshares." It was supposed to shake loose natural gas and create a lot of jobs. It was an atomic bomb unleashed a mile and a half down inside the earth. The site was chosen for its remote nature and the promise of the natural gas."

"This bomb, just how big?" asked Isabel. She evidently hadn't heard this part of the story before, a fact that astounded Mona. She and Brian had shared everything. At least, she had thought they had.

"Twice as big as Hiroshima. It was a forty kiloton bomb, if that means anything to you."

"My God," Mona said.

"Remember it was underground. It was 1969. In September. Rulison was a ghost town at the time. The government saw it as "god-forsaken land." Not heavily populated—like New York City. Couldn't grow much except a few sheep there. Mining had pretty much failed or played out. Nobody wanted to live there. Nobody who really mattered to the government, that is. You have to remember they're sitting out there on the East coast. There are millions of them and not so many of us. Less collateral damage."

"Do I detect some bitterness?" asked Mona.

"Some. Same as most people as they get older, I suspect. You know yourself that you begin to see things differently as you get older. Things that don't seem dangerous when you're twenty suddenly become fatal."

"Didn't anyone want to stop the testing?"

"Of course, they did. They were long-haired hippies and they were mostly ignored. They were thought of the same way we think of animal rights activists. The BLM didn't have the entire jurisdiction over the thing anyway. It was the DOE, the Department of Energy that had hold of the strings. Keep in mind, I was just going into college when all this went on. They managed to get the courts to fight the thing but it was delayed all the way to the Supreme Court. By the time the Supreme Court was listening, the bomb was in the ground. It went off on September 10th. People seemed to think it was a cause for celebration. That's how deluded they all were. Made picnic lunches and waited for the blast."

"My God," Mona said. She looked at Isabel, who had gone a little pale. Isabel, some fifteen years younger than her husband, had probably not even thought about it.

"They set off three more tests in 1973, but those got lots less press. Seems people were pleased the Vietnam was winding down and they weren't so concerned with a little thirty kiloton test."

"That's what we get for leaving things up to the men," Isabel said. "They boil it down to blowing things to hell up."

Mona smiled knowingly at Isabel.

"Let me get through this," Mark said.

"I think I remember Mom talking about the blast," Mona said. "She was at home and said it was like an earthquake."

"Yes, I remember too," Isabel said.

"Yes, so do I," Mark said. "We heard that if you wanted to see it, you could put a little pie tin of water on the ground and look for the ripples. By the time the thing passed there was no water in our pie tin. The hell of the thing was it didn't do a thing for the economy or for energy for that matter. The natural gas shook loose all right, but came up in unexpected places, like people's water wells. That brings us to the clean-up."

"The clean-up? My God." Mona realized then what must have happened.

"Millions of dollars went to the BLM for the clean-up. The site was cleaned up in 1976, most of it anyway, but the waste proves to be a problem. Where can you move it where there won't be people for a couple thousand years? And, who wants to move the stuff?"

"What about where they blasted? Is it still radioactive?"

"There've been studies and more studies. You have to remember that the very departments doing the studies are all doing it for the government. They don't like bad news. There was, of course, some bedrock contamination, some deep-water contamination, and of course, some contamination where the mud and water came to the surface."

"Think of it, farmers' wells, the dirt they raise vegetables on," Isabel said.

"Sometimes I think our government spends a lot of money making messes so they can clean it up," Mona said.

"Anyway, the surface contamination was cleaned up and shipped to Nevada for disposal."

"Most of it?" asked Isabel. "Where's the rest?"

"Some of it's still there. I wouldn't go near the place myself."

"And, the rest?"

"I think you know," Mark said. "I decided to share the wealth, as it were. I used some of the allotted money to offer to some of the ranchers around here."

"My God, why would my parents agree to let you bury

radioactive debris on our land?" asked Mona.

"Money. Same as this 'fracking' that everybody's talking about now. It's no different. It's all about money. You can bet there's going to be toxic waste. They try to minimize it these days, but most of the time it's after the fact—after they've made their money."

"I don't know if I believe money could seduce my parents." She remembered her stoic unassuming parents. Her mother hated vanity and hardly shopped for herself at all.

"It's noble for you to say that. Money is nothing unless you don't have any to take care of what you need to take care of. It was for you, Mona. To send you out of Hawk to get an education. And, to pay property tax," Mark said.

"Me? Are you trying to push this onto me?" Bile rose in Mona's throat.

"Originally they wanted the money for your brother to go to college, to keep him from getting drafted."

"So, if you were in college, you didn't get drafted?"

"Yes, that's how it worked with the Viet Nam war. Not very fair, was it? Especially since back then only the rich sent their kids to college. The rest were pretty much at the mercy of the draft."

"How does Marla fit into this?" asked Isabel.

"She doesn't," Mark said. "Marla was an innocent bystander as far as I could tell. Word is you did it, Mona. She was just an innocent girl. You killed her because she slept with your husband."

"Not so innocent," Isabel said. "I know about your fling with her." A voice tremor marred the impact of Isabel's words.

Shocked, Mona looked at Isabel. Mona was too startled to answer Mark right away. They sat together, Mona and Isabel, bound by the common fact that a beautiful red-haired young woman had seduced both their husbands. Worse, Isabel's husband was old enough to be Marla's grandfather. It was a personal tragedy for both Isabel and Mona. Something to bond over maybe. And yet, they'd never be friends, not even close. Mona didn't bother to tell Isabel that she hadn't killed Marla. It hardly seemed to matter.

Chapter 31

Tuesday, Eckland's Place

Mona tried to steer the subject away from Marla. She wanted to get all the facts. Isabel's hand shook as she waved the crystal bottle at Mona to offer her a drink. Mona shook her head no, although the offer tempted her. She briefly wondered if Isabel would try to poison her.

"Mark, why in God's name would you cook up such a scheme?" Mona asked. "Didn't you already have a good job?"

"Good, yes. Good enough? Not for the way Isabel and I wanted to live. Who wants to live their lives out stuck in a small dying town? Besides, Isabel, you could spend a million a year and still want more. Truth is we both wanted more. Let me tell the rest of the story?" Mark had the desperate look of a man willing to do anything. Isabel rolled her eyes, took a swig from her glass.

Heart beating fast, hands shaking, Mona nodded her head toward Isabel.

"Sure, let's hear it." Isabel had the look of a woman who had lived in denial for a long time. Either that or she knew what was happening and didn't want to speak of it. Isabel had most likely heard more truth than she was ready to handle, but Mona needed to hear it.

Mark continued his story: "We're talking big business, loads of money. There's lots of money in waste of all kinds. Lots of waste. What was left at Rulison was some high-level waste left over from plutonium processing. It was done at Rocky Flats for the Plowshare Project. There was lots more waste from milling uranium ore. Tailings, they're called. You know men—they never clean up after themselves."

"I remember Dad talking about tailings. He said they'd ship it out for fill dirt at some of the construction sites. Of course it was radioactive. I asked him if our house was okay and he said not to worry; our house was old, not one of the fancy new constructions."

"They claimed the radiation was low-level. Anyway, lots of federal agencies shared the task and the money for cleanup. There was the DOE, the Department of Energy. They run the facilities and supervise the cleanup ops by the contractors. The EPA sets the standards and limits for the radioactivity. How much can we stand without getting cancer, that sort of thing? The NRC, Nuclear Regulatory Commission took care of licenses. BLM had to survey land and report back to the other agencies. The DOT, Department of Transportation had to supervise shipments and such."

"Shipments to where?"

"Well, Mona, that was part of the problem. Where do you send waste where people wouldn't raise a stink about it? The government likes to look at remote place, like Yucca Mountain in Nevada. Another God-forsaken place where they figure a little nuclear waste won't hurt. Lack of money is what troubles people. Then they worry about the environment. Problem is, people live in this area that they considered God-forsaken land. You have to remember, most of the men making these decisions live back east where they must think it desolate out here."

"My God. I can't believe this. I knew women should have gotten involved in government a long time ago."

"Amen to that," Isabel said, who was getting more sloshed by the minute. Mona figured she'd be napping soundly by noon. Isabel tipped her glass to Mona.

"So, my parents let you pay them to bury waste on their property? Why would they do it when Wanda refused?"

Mark hesitated to glance her way, drink in hand.

"Yes, she told me."

239

"Because we weren't getting any answers. We got about three hundred million dollars to work with some contractors to get rid of some of the tailings. That's where the fill dirt came into the story. I didn't want to do that, to send fill-dirt to construction sites for people to live in for a few decades. Some of them would certainly get cancer from it. How many? Hard to say and harder to prove. But there's more, Mona. There's more radioactive waste than tailings. There's what they call spent fuel assemblies. They will, for all intents and purposes, always be dangerous. Half-live of millions of years."

"My God, don't tell me," Mona said. She felt a chill go from her head down to her toes.

"Yes, but don't panic. This waste is encased in nine-inch steel drums. They each hold about seventeen tons of waste."

Mona felt her stomach sink with dread. "How many drums are on my property?"

"A couple hundred. I don't remember for sure. Some of the lower level tailings were spread on top."

"Why? Why would you do that?"

"Because there was nobody to take them. Nobody wanted them. I was solving a problem for the government and for the contractors. Not to mention give some needed money to your folks. I was doing your folks a favor. Spreading the cash around and taking care of a problem at the same time. You have to remember; most people around here were ready to lose their ranches back then. There's absolutely no chance of this stuff seeping out. The way it is, it's probably less dangerous than the tailings people have sitting under their houses." How was Mark Eckland making himself look like a hero in this?

"So, you took the money and buried this stuff on Heartbreak Ranch?"

"Took some to pay the contractors to move it. Buried some on my own property."

"Of course. But why keep paying them over the years?"

"To keep quiet. There was enough money to do that." How much had he kept for himself?

"Did they know what was in the containers?" asked Mona.

"Your parents weren't stupid. But, they figured that if the waste stayed in the containers, what harm could it do? There is, of course, more waste. I can't tell you where that is."

"You can't tell me, or won't tell me?" asked Mona.

"Can't. Paid the contractors to take it away. Paid them enough they could retire. I think the two of them are dead now. Cancer of the thyroid, both of them."

"My God. You know, I'm exhausted from this. I can't tell you." Yet, Mona was relieved in a way to know the whole story. She wasn't sure where she'd go from here or how the whole thing was tied to Brian's murder.

Mark was good at reading her facial expressions. "I didn't have a thing to do with Brian's murder," Mark said. "Could have been the government though. CIA."

"Now you're scaring me." It sounded too improbable. She promised Mark and Isabel not to say anything about what he told her. She left for home, shaken but relieved to know the truth.

***

Mona knew she needed more information. Something about Mark didn't ring true—his military service record. Mark Eckland was a liar—had he lied about that too? She found a website online to look up military records. The trouble was she'd need Mark's social security number or service id. She'd never be able to get that. She did have her uncle's, though and she knew her uncle had served with Mark. Her parents kept her uncle's information with the folded flag and medals in a deep glass frame. She dug it out of the closet where she had kept it. It had always been on display when her parents were alive, but had put it away when they both died.

Armed with her uncle's ssn and discharge date, she found his record on a site designed to allow reordering of medals. It showed that he had a Purple Heart in addition to a Gold Star and a Viet Nam campaign medal.

But, how could she look up Mark's records without his Social Security Number? She knew from her previous work with computers that there was usually a way to finesse into data by backing into it. It took a while, but she found a website that would let her look up records if she had a full name and discharge date. She tried her luck with Mark's name and her uncle's discharge date. She put in a range of six months and sure enough, she had pulled up his records. And, this one showed the places where Mark had been at certain times. He had indeed been in Viet Nam, but at the time of her uncle's death he was in Honolulu for rest and rehabilitation. There was no sign of the heroism citation for saving a life. According to the government records, he was entitled to a Viet Nam campaign medal and honorable discharge medal. The site had a link to several stores where it would be possible to buy medals.

So Mark had lied about saving her uncle in Viet Nam. There were so many reasons he would do something like that, but he had certainly capitalized on the lie. It got him in good with her parents.

Excited and mad at the same time, Mona felt she needed to talk to someone. She called John on his cell. He was in the bunkhouse.

"What's wrong Mona?" he asked. Bo had happily trotted along with him and Mona tossed him a piece of bacon from the fridge.

"Sit down for this," she told John. "You hungry?"

"Nah. Ate already. What's this about? The girls okay?"

Mona sat at the other chair in the breakfast nook. "I did some research on Mark Eckland."

"Yeah?"

"He wasn't in Viet Nam when my uncle died. All that stuff about him being a war hero is bull."

"Are you sure? Your parents worshiped the ground he walked on."

"Yeah, I know. But I looked it up online and found out that he was in Hawaii while my uncle died. Mark was nowhere near him."

"Well, I don't figure we can do much about that now," John said.

"I can't tell you the entire story yet," she said, "but he was giving my parents money for helping him out."

John looked at her like she had two heads. "Mona, it wasn't like he took money from them. Or did he?"

"No. It's hard to explain except you were on the right track when you talked about the dying and sick lambs and the weird bare patches of earth."

"I'm not following," he said.

Mona took the next hour to explain it to John, hoping that he didn't know anything about it.

"You know, I've seen him over the years around the property and around your dad. And, around Brian. Never liked him much, but left him alone."

"Are you all right? You look a little pale."

John seemed to be taking the news harder than Mona expected.

"It's not that Mona. I was afraid that you did some digging on me too. I think it's time to come clean."

"Come clean about what?" It was Mona's turn to be caught off guard.

"Just so you don't have to come by it on that computer that causes so many problems, I'm going to tell you myself."

"Go ahead. I'm ready." She braced herself to match the intensity of John's expression.

He took a huge breath.

"The night your brother was killed your brother was driving, not me."

Mona took a minute to let that sink in.

"How can that be? They sent you to prison for vehicular homicide. Sorry, but I looked up your record. Why would you lie about that?"

"To protect him. He was the only friend I had. Practically the only one I ever had. I was never good at making friends. We decided it in the hospital when I saw how broke up your folks were over his being in an accident. I didn't have much of a family and maybe one friend in the world—your brother; we figured they'd just let me skate."

"Yeah. I still don't get it," Mona said.

"We were all sure he'd live and he was supposed to go to college and all and they didn't want a drunken driving arrest on his record. It would have ruined everything. So, your parents and I decided that I'd say I was driving the car."

"So you said you were driving?"

"Yep. That's exactly it," he said. "And then he went and died and ruined his life and changed mine."

There was no use wondering if John were lying or not. John didn't lie about anything as far as Mona could say. She touched his arm.

"Thank you for telling me. It explains a lot. It explains why they were so close you to. Why they left you land. They owed you."

"It wasn't only that they were beholden to me or anything. But, we shared this secret all those years and it was like I let their son live on in their memories the way he was. I never had family to speak of. It was a horrible night and I wish it could be taken back."

"I know," Mona said. "We all do. But thank you so much for telling me."

"I think it should stay between us, though," he said.

"So do I."

Chapter 32

Wednesday, Heartbreak Ranch

The letter warned Mona of "serious consequences" if she persisted in "interfering with government business." Whoever sent it made an attempt to make the letter official. It was sent on government letterhead, BLM letterhead to be exact. Mona didn't buy it for a second. Besides, the letter had a faint perfume smell that triggered a memory.

At first, she thought it was Marla's perfume. Then, she recognized it as Isabel's scent; Chanel No. 5. It was the only scent her mother wore sometimes from a small sample bottle she had gotten. If Isabel had sent the letter, she must have mailed it before Mark's confession about the nuclear waste. What should she do? Whom should she tell?.

Almost positive that Isabel was the culprit, she called the Eckland's house on Tuesday.

"Hello?" Isabel sounded tentative.

"I got your letter," Mona informed her. "And, if I were you, I would not do that again. It is a Federal crime to tamper with the mail. Not to mention impersonating a government official." Mona was not sure at all what the law was, but figured that Isabel would not know either.

"I don't have the faintest idea what you are talking about." Isabel's voice had the relaxed tone of someone who'd had a couple of stiff drinks.

"I'm just warning you not to do it again. I'm saving this letter for evidence."

"You don't scare me," Isabel said. "And, if I were you, I'd start looking closer at home before you accuse me or my husband of Federal crimes."

"Just what are we talking about here?"

"You know what I'm talking about. You and your family and most of the other people around here are just trailer trash as far as I'm concerned." Isabel was on a roll. "Uneducated trailer trash. I don't care what my husband did or didn't do. Your parents were involved. Just remember that."

Mona, stunned into silence, thought about listing her two degrees and Brian's degree for evidence to the contrary. Her parents had lived on the ranch forever. There was never a trailer on the premises that Mona could recall. She hung up the phone without another word. Sometimes it wasn't worth arguing with someone. Your own words could be used against you later.

Mona called Travis.

"I don't know what it is about that woman that makes me so upset," she told him. She left out the part about Isabel calling her and her family trailer trash. It wasn't something she wanted to repeat. She did tell him about the letter and how she smelled Isabel's perfume on it.

"Don't let her get to you, Mona. She's trying to deflect blame onto you. I'm getting more suspicious of those two. They're making too big a fuss right now. I smell fear on them."

"Is there a way I can have this letter examined to prove it came from the Eckland's?"

"I can do you one better than that. Let's get a search warrant."

"Well, I've put the letter in a baggie. I'll give it to you when you come over."

"If I were you, I wouldn't call over there any more. I'd stay clear."

Mona called Skye at school. She planned to call Miranda also, but couldn't get her on the line.

"I just wanted to hear your voice," she said.

"Mom, are you all right? I'm worried that you're roaming the house and grieving. You can actually go crazy with grief. Did you know that? Mr. Rhodes, my psychology professor says psychosis can set in if you don't deal with it."

"I'm not going crazy. I miss your dad like crazy, that's for sure." Mona broke into unexpected tears. It happened occasionally. That, Mona realized, was part of the normal grieving process.

"Thank God you don't have to work. How do people go to work every day when they've got big things like you do going on? I'm not sure you're okay. Miranda and I were talking about taking a semester off to help you. We could help out on the ranch and just be around to help you get over dad."

"Honey, when you lose someone you realize you don't really get over it. You just learn to remember them in their best light and hopefully the pain subsides a little. I don't think I'll ever really get over losing him. The best way you two can help me is to stay in school."

Mona knew that Miranda and Skye were not good at ranch life. They became easily bored with the mundane chores that began with sunrise or before and ended with sunset. They were city girls and probably always would be, although they liked the idea of having ranch roots. There was not much here to offer them. Mona wanted them to have college degrees and a career of their choice.

It took until Friday to get the search warrants and Travis promised to tell her the results. They had let him participate, although the CBI actually did the searches. If the BLM were involved, the case would become a Federal jurisdiction case.

Mona waited nervously all day until Travis finally showed up about four o'clock. Mona put on the teakettle and made some ham and cheese sandwiches since both of them confessed to having skipped lunch. She put the sandwiches on plates and carried them and a bag of potato chips to the breakfast nook.

"This is good, Mona. Thanks. It really hits the spot." Some days, the way Travis looked at her made her think of high school and of seductive looks from boys.

Mona chewed her sandwich, which threatened to stick in her throat. Her appetite for food ebbed and flowed these days.

"Well, what happened today?"

"It's real tedious. I've never seen such a detailed investigation before. Makes me rethink how I've done them in the past. They took swabs of lots of things. Bagged a lot of things like clothes and stuff and carried them off. They took blood samples and hair samples from Mark and Isabel. They were both fit to be tied, let me tell you."

"I bet. I'll never get invited to a party at their house."

"Yeah. We can both kiss the Spring Eckland Barbeque goodbye."

"I was never invited, so that doesn't matter. What else?" Mona asked.

"We have to wait for the results. You know how that goes. One little interesting tidbit. They took out a bag of clothes that Isabel had hidden in a scrap bin with some torn or damaged clothes. They had labels that said Prada. The woman tech remarked on that. Does that word ring a bell?"

"Prada? Very expensive. I've never owned a piece myself."

"What is a Prada?" he asked.

"It's a designer label. One blouse would be hundreds. A purse or shoes, very expensive. I don't get it myself. I don't really like it that much."

"Good God. Anyway, they were laughing about how she couldn't bear to throw out a Prada dress or skirt. Probably couldn't take it to the local cleaners. Seems it had spots of blood on it. As they were taking it out, Isabel said something to Mark about getting her period."

Mona almost choked on the last bit. Most women would put stain remover on it right away, not hide it in with the scrap clothing..

"That's so odd, but I can see Isabel not wanting to throw it away if it is a real Prada. Maybe she stowed it there until she could deal with the problem," Mona said.

They finished their meal, had a second cup of tea, and Travis left. He promised to keep her informed on what was found.

Soon after Travis left, John paid her a visit. It was as if John had waited for Travis to leave.

"You know, it's okay to come in the house when Travis is here. I don't want you to feel that you can't." Mona wasn't sure that was entirely true. Did she really want John sitting in on her conversations with Travis?

"Yes, ma'am. I try to make myself invisible sometimes. I was wondering if there's something going on that I can help with?"

Mona made a spur-of-the-moment decision to tell John about the extent of the nuclear waste buried in their fields. She had practically told him anyway, but had minimized it as simply "radioactive tailings."

"Do you 'spose we'll get cancer from it?" asked John. The fear in his eyes reflected the fear in Mona's soul. She didn't know. Nobody knew.

"Probably not, unless the outside of the containers were contaminated—or broken. Mark didn't think so. But, we'll have to have someone come and remove them and test the area.

"Sounds like a mess. It means that Marla probably did have some kind of related papers."

"It sure does, John."

John sat up and talked with Mona until about eleven o'clock and then went back to the bunkhouse.

Mona fell asleep almost immediately, a rarity for her these days. She fell into a deep dream full of rich dreams.

Chapter 33

Friday night, Heartbreak Ranch

Mona struggled to open her eyes, strained to listen. Distant barking—Bo. Someone was outside. She threw on some comfortable old jeans and pulled the old shotgun from the closet. Mona pulled down the box of shells that Brian always kept with the boxes at the top of the closet. She never left the thing loaded. She wasn't about to put in another panicked call to Travis.

She put one shell in the chamber but left the rifle uncocked. Making sure she was awake and lucid, she unlocked her front door and went toward the bunkhouse, Bo's barking becoming more urgent. Maybe she had let her imagination get the best of her. The night air cooled her skin. She shivered. The squish of snow mixed with mud beneath the cowboy boots she had pulled on irritated her. She would have to clean them. She shifted her stride to walk on the patches of snow instead. Bo's barking persisted. Sure now that something was wrong—John would have quieted Bo— she walked faster toward the bunkhouse. She needed to concentrate—not make any mistakes.

Halfway to the bunkhouse she stopped and called to John. "You okay, John?" She heard a quaver in her voice. Her mother's voice had the same quaver that betrayed her otherwise stoic demeanor.

Mona listened. Bo's barking became even more urgent. Mona could now hear his paws bumping against the inside of John's bunkhouse door. She hurried her steps. She again called John's name.

As Mona neared the bunkhouse she sensed something really wrong. She again regretted not having her phone. Now she'd have to run to the house to call 911. She reached the door and knocked and called to John. Bo's barking became almost a keening. Mona struggled to open the door. John seldom locked it. Brian had told her that. She had barely paid attention to that fact, but now it had become important.

She struggled with the door for a few minutes and then decided to break the window with the shotgun. The shotgun had come in handy after all.

Smoke hit her in the face as she broke the glass and poured out the broken pane.

"John!" Mona knew she had to get him out. Fearing fire, she knocked the rest of the panes from the window. She struggled to lift herself through the window. She was not as athletic as she used to be. She had to drop the shotgun to free her hands. Nobody was inside with John. Bo jumped to greet her as she dropped to the other side.

The aroma of fireplace smoke pervaded the room. Had his chimney backed up? She knew that he cleaned the fireplace once a year, along with hers.

She struggled to find the light switch by the front door. She flicked the lights on and saw John lying on the floor. She ran to him and tried to drag him. It was no use, she wasn't strong enough to drag the almost two hundred pound man across the wood floorboards. Bo continued to bark from outside the bunkhouse, now irritating Mona.

"I hear you Bo. If you could help I'd let you."

As if understanding her, Bo came in, pulled on John's sleeve with his teeth. Mona ran to the door and flung it open. Smoke poured out. Mona coughed and choked. Fearing she would lose consciousness, she decided to run to the house and dial 911. She couldn't waste time trying to find John's cell phone.

"Stay with him Bo."

Mona could hardly punch the three numbers into the phone, her hands shook so badly. Her knees knocked together.

The call accomplished, she ran back to John and Bo, this time bringing her cell with her. The room had cleared enough for Mona to breathe, but smoke still poured into the room from the chimney. She went to the fireplace.

"Well no wonder," Mona said. "There's something stuffed up into the chimney." She tried again to drag John, but only managed about a foot before the fire engine arrived.

"My God, Mona but you've had the problems lately." Monte Jarvis, the chief of the volunteer fire department evidently had heard about her plight through the very efficient Hawk County grape vine.

"Yes, I have. I think we need Travis back out here," Mona said.

"Why, Mona, you don't have to go to all this trouble to get Travis McClain out here. He'd come if you'd just whistle." The other two volunteers chuckled. Evidently, everybody knew her business, or at least thought they did.

They took John to the hospital and even gave Bo a little oxygen before they took John away. Travis came out and help Mona unclog the fireplace.

"Mona, you realize somebody did this."

"Why would they hurt John?"

"Why would they hurt Brian?" Travis asked. "What's this?" Travis pointed to a piece of paper on the John's rustic table along with a cold cup of coffee.

"It looks like a letter."

"It's a note. It says here he's confessing to killing Brian and Marla. Love Triangle, he says."

"I don't buy it," Mona said. "For one thing, John doesn't have a typewriter," Mona said.

"I was hoping you'd say that. Who uses a typewriter anymore, anyway?" asked Travis.

"Somebody who hasn't been in the work force for a while," Mona said.

"I'm thinking Isabel Eckland," Travis said.

"I was hoping you were," Mona said.

"Of course, you could have set her up," Travis said. He stared intently at Mona.

"I hope you don't believe that," Mona said.

"You know I have a soft spot in my heart for you Mona. Let's keep this note to ourselves for a while, how's that?"

"Thank you. It's one less thing we need to explain."

Chapter 34

Thursday, Heartbreak Ranch

John sat at Mona's table in the breakfast nook, refused again to go the hospital. John's hand trembled as he lifted his coffee cup, and swayed a little in his chair. He seemed unaware, and he would never admit to a physical weakness or nervousness. Mona's stomach turned. She hadn't eaten.

"Anybody want eggs?" she asked. Eggs and toast might settle her empty stomach.

She got nods of agreement from Travis and John. Bo showed up by her side and begged so she told him, sure, he'd get some too. She pulled some hickory bacon and a dozen eggs from the fridge. She had a loaf of hearty French bread. Since it was a week old but still good, she'd make French toast too. She loved having someone to cook for.

"Whoever this damn fool is, is crazy. Crazy like a fox. Chances are, he's after you too. Fool will kill us all. My damn head is killing me."

Mona had never heard John so negative, nor say quite so much at one sitting, but considering he had almost died, she figured he was entitled to be at least a little bitter. John reached down and scratched Bo's ears. The dog had not left his side since John had come home.

"We'll get the person responsible for this," Travis said.

"And, how do I know it's not you?" John asked him. His voice had a gravelly angry note, abrasive like a bad chord on a violin.

"What's that supposed to mean?" Travis asked. "I'm trying to help."

Did John really suspect Travis? Did he suspect her? Travis would have little motivation to get rid of John, but what about her? After all, if she got rid of him, she wouldn't have to forfeit part of her land. What he didn't realize was that the small amount of land that she had given to John was almost nothing to her. In fact, she was glad someone else would be responsible for it. And that he'd stay and help her run Heartbreak Ranch.

"You can trust me John. I know it's hard for you to trust anyone right now, but you can trust me. It'll come with time."

"You can trust me too," Travis said. "Although you can't really tell someone to trust you. That said, you can trust me."

They talked, ate breakfast, and talked some more, ate some more. John seemed agitated and said he was not a bit tired. When would he be tired enough to lay down on her sofa and sleep? He couldn't go back into his bunkhouse until it aired out. He seemed oddly energized. It might have had something to do with the oxygen and I.V. drip they'd given him in the ambulance. Mona had felt the kick of extra oxygen whenever going to sea level. For a couple of days you feel like you can climb Mt. Everest. Mona figured after he did a few chores, he'd crash in the afternoon and need some sleep.

By mid-day Travis hadn't made any signs of leaving her house, and part of her wanted John to go to sleep on her sofa so she'd have a quiet house. The conversation between John and Travis had begun to deteriorate. Mona realized neither trusted the other and they were both reluctant to leave Mona alone. She wanted to tell Travis to leave, but she had to admit to her own fear. If he wanted to stay, let him stay. She decided to let them duke it out on their own. Her days of being the mediator were gone. At least, she wished they were. Old habits die hard.

Since they were still in her house at one o'clock, Mona took some Coors out of the fridge for the guys, since she figured they wouldn't want iced tea. Maybe it would make John feel like taking a nap. She poured herself an iced tea and put a squirt of concentrated lemon juice in it, fresh lemons being a little rare in Colorado this time of year. She sliced some ham and made ham and cheese sandwiches and pulled out the never-ending bag of potato chips. Having gone through the French bread, she used a new fresh loaf that she had on hand.

"You don't have to go to the bother," said John. "I can open a can of beans back at my place."

"You're not supposed to go back for a couple of days while it airs out from the smoke. Did you forget they told you that? Besides, they said you could have some residual effects from the carbon monoxide. You almost died, for God's sake. Give yourself a rest. You can sleep in my guest room or on my sofa. Your choice. Beans, for God's sake!"

***

Mona put sandwiches in front of both of them and decided to eat hers standing at the kitchen island. She didn't want to get drawn into their argument.

"I've got to go check the livestock," John said. The cows are out in the shelter but someone's got to give them hay and oats and break up the water. The sheep need new water and feed. I should have moved them from the barn when all this happened."

"I'm going to check on them today. I've done it before.

"I'll put some blankets on the living room sofa. I'll check on the ewes before I go to bed. Just take your boots off at the door when you come in, that's all I ask." Late winter meant they'd have pregnant ewes, due in early spring, and John checked on them every day to make sure none looked sick or in distress.

Travis glanced at her. His eyes warned her of danger, but Mona refused to become frightened of John.

The guys ate in silence for a few minutes. Mona wondered if she should have made them two. Travis got up and made himself another.

"You want another, John?"

"Sure," he said. He tossed Bo the remnants of the first.

"Mona, how can you be sure you can trust this guy?" Travis spoke quietly and pointed the knife at John. "He's had as much opportunity as anybody to do all this killing. Besides, nobody keeps track of his comings and goings." Travis looked visibly upset.

"Don't go getting your hackles up," said John. "I was cleared with one of those alibis." John evidently overheard anyway, in spite of Travis' attempt to soften his voice.

"Anyone can get a trucker friend to say they talked with you at a certain time," Travis said. It wouldn't be the first time someone covered for a friend. There's no real way to track it like there is with a cell phone."

"I may not have many friends," said John, "but the ones I do have don't lie."

"Well, I'm telling you, it's not me either," Travis said. "I just happen to care about this lady here and her girls. I always have."

Mona felt her eyes well with tears. It hit her at the oddest times. She certainly didn't want to cry in front of two sparring men. It wasn't like they were fighting over her, but it made her feel silly all the same.

"If it means anything, I don't think either one of you could have done such terrible things. God knows who could, but I know it's got something to do with Mark Eckland."

The landline phone rang and Travis started to reach for it. Mona didn't want him answering her phone. What would the girls think? She asked Travis to hand her the portable that was on the island.

"Mark?"

"Speak of the devil," said John.

Mona put her fingers to her lips to quiet him.

"Yes, I'm alone." She looked at Travis and shrugged. "You want to come over? I guess that would be okay. You need me to do anything?"

She hung up the phone and explained to John and Travis that Mark Eckland wanted to come over and talk. He didn't say about what.

"That's not a good idea," Travis said. "But it's a good thing we're here."

"No, I want to talk with him alone. He won't talk openly with you two here. Besides, I gave him the impression I was alone."

"We're going to hide somewhere. Where's the best place, and don't argue with me," Travis said.

Mona stowed them in the pantry off the kitchen, which was really like a small room with shelves lined up against all four walls. There was plenty of room inside for two or three grown people. It had a light that pulled on with a string. Mona always kept it spotlessly clean, and had put a small braided rug in there. It wasn't an unpleasant place to spend a little time, but Mona had second thoughts about putting two suspicious men in there. She put Bo outside and hoped that he wouldn't bark. He was smart and obedient, so she told him to be quiet and not bark. But, if she left him inside, he'd certainly point out the pantry to Mark.

Mona never understood why, but the pantry could lock from the inside. Maybe her parents had used it as a safe place. She never knew the logic, but had always been afraid the girls would lock themselves in. Brian had never gotten around to taking off the lock. Now, though, she told them to lock the door from the inside. She didn't want Mark opening it for some reason.

Mark arrived in record time; he must have been driving when he called her.

"Mark, come in," she said as she met him at the door. She waved him into the kitchen so that Travis and John could hear.

"There," she said and pointed at the kitchen table. "You want coffee?"

"Don't go offering me any food or drink. I'm not here to be sociable." Mark's eyes were cold slits.

"Why are you here?" Mona's pulse sped up and she was glad she had two men in her pantry. A chill went up her spine. Bo continued to bark from outside the kitchen door.

"I'm here warning you to back off. I want you to leave me and my family alone."

"Or?"

"Or, there will be consequences and I don't just mean financial. You and your daughter's will not be safe here. Do you understand me?" He started edging toward Mona, pushing her against the kitchen island.

"You should go back to the city. There's nothing for you here anymore. You got money. Go back and live your life. You know yourself that Brian was the only reason you came back here. I'm even willing to buy this property to take it off your hands. I'll give you better than market value."

"You think my parents would want you buying this property? It's been in the family for a hundred years. Why would I sell now?"

"I just don't feel comfortable with a single woman working this ranch."

"Why would you worry about it? Why do I care if you are *comfortable*? You've got your own troubles."

"What troubles do I have, except you?" Mark asked.

"Why are you so worried? What have you done? Did you kill Brian?" Knowing that two men were hiding in her pantry gave her courage to say more than she probably should. She could imagine what Travis and John were thinking. They were probably silently willing her to keep her mouth shut.

"You have no idea the bigger consequences of this, Mona," Mark said. "I could kill you, leave a note and make it look like suicide. You have a choice to make. Leave or die."

"Did you kill my husband?" Tears fell down her face.

"If I did, he deserved it. You realize he cheated on you big-time, probably even fathered a child with the whore he cheated with."

"If you're innocent, you don't have anything to worry about," she said. "You can turn around now and I won't say a word."

"It doesn't matter if I'm innocent or not, you're judged by word of mouth around here. You're out to ruin my reputation and my wife's and I won't stand for it. I could lose my job, my pension, my savings, and my life's work. Just because of you. I won't have it." He reached into his jacket pocket and for a minute Mona thought he was going to pull a gun and shoot her.

"Wait!" she called. John and Travis came out of the pantry quickly and Mona was afraid they'd be shot or that Travis would pull his ever-present gun. John rushed him as Travis lagged behind. Travis was soon on top of them both as they struggled to the floor. Mona heard a popping sound and John and Travis got up off of Mark.

"He's okay. Just stunned."

"Stunned?" Mona looked at Mark, who lay immobile on the floor. A stun gun lay on the floor beside him.

"He had it on him Mona. It got him before it got us," Travis said.

Within the hour, Travis had police come down from Glenwood to take him in. He didn't want to risk doing it himself. They bagged the stun gun and cuffed Mark and took him away in a squad car. Mona was afraid the stun gun might have killed Mark. He was an old man and he lay still for a long time before the police were able to get him up walking. It hadn't occurred to Mona to call an ambulance.

Travis, John, and Mona talked almost all night after the Glenwood police took Mark off. The adrenaline kept them all going, even with a couple pots of coffee with brandy.

Mona worried about the girls and the three of them talked about it. She needed to really talk with them about

Marla and her son and Brian. She worried they didn't have enough to charge Mark Eckland with Brian's murder. What would she do then? She'd have to leave Hawk. Leave Heartbreak Ranch.

"I'm going to sit them both down and have a long honest talk. Especially if it turns out they have a half-brother. They'll need to know," Travis said.

The thought of it turned Mona's stomach, but at least she could think of it now. She could imagine herself and her daughters opening their arms to a baby brother.

"Well, I'm going home. Stayed up long enough. I've got to get to work in a few hours," Travis said.

"Me too," said John.

Travis left and Mona gave John blankets for the sofa.

The next morning when Mona got up at seven, John was already up and out. Nothing kept him down for too long. He had made a pot of coffee and it looked like he made a ham and egg sandwich.

Travis called at eight.

"Mona, are you okay this morning?"

"I'm fine. I've got a headache from not getting enough sleep."

"Yeah, me too. Of course, I had a few beers yesterday too. That might have a little to do with it."

"You're forgetting you had a little brush with death," she said.

"I don't linger long in bed Mona."

Mona felt a little perturbed that Travis had called. She needed a day or two Travis-free days.

"Mona, I'm not stalking you or anything."

"I was just thinking it's a bit like stalking. Really, I can take care of myself."

"I care about you. You know that. And, I've got a world of patience. Besides, the forensic report is in. I've got news."

"Tell me."

"The blood on Isabel's clothes matched Marla's."

"My God. Do you mean Isabel killed Marla?"

"That's the way the evidence points. There's more. Mark Eckland's prints were all over the battery charger and tools that were in that old truck. Of course, he might say that he used it to repair fences, but the fact remains that the charger was souped up. And, he left it abandoned—why would anybody do that? Nobody in their right mind would want to supercharge an electric fence. He must have revved it up enough to kill Brian—that fence combined with the stun gun killed him, or at least knocked him out and he drowned. Mark probably watched him die."

"My God. I was right about those two."

"Thank God there's no children. They'd be orphans right now with the two of them up on charges."

"Why would Isabel kill Marla?"

"Mark had a long-time affair with Marla. Everybody knows it. There's more."

"There's more? I'm so relieved right now I could cry. But, I've got so many questions," Mona said.

"We found a bunch of documents in the Eckland's basement. There were beside a shredder, so I don't know how much of it was shredded. They had Marla's prints on it, so the CBI thinks that Marla had possession of them at one time."

"It's probably what Marla was going to give me. What do they say? Of course, if you had gotten them, that would have let the cat out of the bag about Mark." Mona felt a stab of sorrow because she wasn't sure if Mark had given Marla the documents or if Brian had.

"Most of it is classified. We'll never really know. You don't think the government will let all that out, do you?"

"Is there a chance the government set this all up to cover-up?"

"That's already what Mark's saying, but I doubt it. Mark did most of the covering up for them. The documents must have something about your parent's property, or Brian would not have been so interested in them."

"But, that doesn't explain why Mark would kill Brian? It *was* Mark who killed my husband, wasn't it?"

"We think so, Mona. Brian probably wanted to end the deception. Maybe Mark didn't want to pay Brian any more. Maybe Marla talked him into coming clean. I've got no idea. Unless Mark talks, we'll never know why. We think we have enough forensics to link Mark with Brian's death, especially if the stun-gun marks match up."

"There's something else I have to know Travis."

"What's that?"

"Were you and Marla having an affair? Seems everyone else was."

"Nah," he said without hesitation. "I guarantee it. Don't like redheads especially. Why would you think it though?"

"Just something Marla said to me in passing. That she knew I hadn't lawyered up yet. Only you and John probably knew that."

"It was me who let that cat out of the bag. I ran into her in the diner one day and she asked me who your lawyer was. I was stupid enough to blurt out that you didn't have one. I knew my mistake right away. Can't believe she actually used it against me though," said Travis.

Chapter 35

Two months later, Heartbreak Ranch

When the DNA came in, Mark and Isabel could no longer deny that they had been responsible for both murders. Mark killed Brian and Isabel killed Marla. Would Isabel have killed Marla anyway, without the evidence that she had against Mark? They'd probably never know. The DNA enhanced the other physical and circumstantial evidence, which included the receipts for stun guns found at Mark Eckland's house. Some of the receipts had the serial numbers on them, one for the stun gun that Wanda had and one for the gun owned by Mona's daughter. Mark had given one to Travis, which Travis in turn had given to Wanda. Whether Mark bought the stun guns as part of a plot to kill Brian, Mona would also never know. It wouldn't really matter. The result remained the same. She was now a widow and her children didn't have a living father, while Mark had destroyed his entire family.

The gloves, Brian's gloves—Mona had them both now. Nobody had asked how the glove had gotten off Brian's hand. Maybe he'd taken it off himself and laid it over the fence like a potholder to grab onto it. Mona wouldn't know, but knew that she would probably burn the gloves along with a few of Brian's other things. She didn't want to see them and be reminded of where they had ended up.

***

The Glenwood and Grand Junction papers put the story on their front page, and Mona had to scramble to explain the whole situation to the girls. It seemed Mark had a lot of business and political clout in two counties, and his involvement in a murder and a BLM scandal shocked the normally quiet area.

Word was that Mark became hysterical when he learned that Isabel had killed Marla because of his affair with her. Not only that, the CBI labs had done DNA testing, which matched Mark with Marla's son. Mona felt gratitude to the boy's grandmother, as she wasn't required by law to give her permission for her grandson's DNA testing. She had to admit an immense relief that Brian was not the boy's father, although she felt sorry for the boy. It did not change the fact that Brian could have been his father and that he had betrayed Mona.

If only Brian had not become involved with Mark. If only he had discussed with her so that they could make a decision together. If only Marla hadn't come into Brian's life. If only the government had not thought of the Western part of the country as a vast wasteland and a testing place for nuclear weapons and tools.

Her "if only" thoughts could go on forever and Mona had to deliberately decide not to think about it. She vowed to look to the present and to the future and not dwell too deeply on the past. She could obsess forever about Brian and Marla and about her parent's inability to really be honest with her. She didn't want to take away from her relationship with Skye and Miranda. She knew Brian loved her and always had. She knew she loved him and they built a life together. That is what she chose to remember.

***

John started building his new house. He worked alone for the most part, but he had blueprints provided by an architect in town who volunteered to work with him free of charge. All he had to do was agree to let the house appear in a Colorado architect review magazine. It seemed like a fair exchange and so John accepted the offer. It was to be a modern log home. Mona had not had any idea that John wanted any house larger than the bunkhouse he currently slept in. You never knew about someone's dreams, she realized.

One day, John showed up at her kitchen door with a Shetland sheepdog pup for Mona. She named the dog Queenie, since Mona and the girls would pamper her. John explained that he had found three pups on his bunkhouse doorstep one day and figured one of the neighbors thought Bo was the father. It was possible, but unlikely, since Bo was hardly ever left the ranch.

"Always felt bad about Bo coming with me," he said.

***

A few months later, after the BLM had come to clean up her property and cart away the offensive waste containers, Mona and the girls could start to heal in earnest. Mona turned to her financial problems. She contemplated an idea Travis had about the two of them starting a private eye business. Maybe they were good at rooting at the truth.

She got her life insurance settlement, of course, since she had not caused Brian's death, but she agreed to turn over a portion of the remaining BLM money to the government. They'd decide how much she could keep based on the fact that government property had indeed resided on her property. She hoped the money she gave back would go for something good but she felt that it would disappear like smoke into the BLM machine. The life insurance would be enough to help keep the ranch going and pay tuition for the girls.

She sent ten thousand dollars to Marla's mother for her grandson, because she knew that woman had a long hard road ahead of her.

Mona had to agree to testify at both Mark's and Isabel's trials. Mark's trial of course, would literally be a

Federal case since he had defrauded the government and misused his power as an agent of the government.

An auction was held to sell off Mark and Isabel's property and belongings to help pay for the legal fees. Mona drove by the day of the auction and saw a huge crowd. She drove right past and home to Heartbreak Ranch. The auction made her think of the HBR wrought iron sign she and the girls had found at a similar auction. She felt now that the *Heart Break Ranch* sign protected them in some way, that the events that had unfolded had happened for a reason. She wasn't a bit sorry that they had come back to Hawk. This was their home.

She had grown up on this land and it was Brian who brought her back home.

END

Afterword

This novel is based on a true story of the way uranium tailings and nuclear waste was disposed of in the seventies.

The Manhattan Project. Operation Plowshare. These were code words for U.S. government sponsored programs to harness the energy embedded in the shale that exists in the United States in mostly western states.

The history of nuclear testing began early on the morning of 16 July 1945 at a desert test site in Alamogordo, New Mexico when the United States exploded its first atomic bomb.

Colorado became involved between 1942 and 1945 when the state's uranium ore supply was required by the "Manhattan Project."

By 1946, almost three million pounds of uranium oxide were taken from areas in western Colorado (and caused booming growth for some of the smaller Colorado towns.) While first used for the creation of possible nuclear weapons (The Manhattan Project, for example), it later evolved into attempting to use nuclear energy to loosen oil from oil shale. This has evolved into today's "Fracking."

Nuclear waste is classified into several categories; high-level waste from spent nuclear reactor fuel and liquid and soled waste from plutonium production, waste from contaminated tools and clothing, low-level hazardous waste from medical and other consumer uses, and uranium mill tailings. The mill tailings are left over from extracting uranium from ore.[1]

The actual nuclear testing that forms the basis for part of this story happened in Western Colorado in 1969 as part

---

[1] National Geographic, July 2002. Page 14.

of a 3-part nuclear "test" program sponsored by the Atomic Energy Commission. This program was called *Project Plowshare*. This project led to a The forty-kiloton Rulison test was detonated 6 miles west of Grand Valley, Colorado (near this book's fictional Hawk County), on September 10, 1969. Its purpose was to release natural gas reserves locked tightly in the sandstone and shale Mesa Verde formation. The estimated cost for the Rulison project was 6.5 million dollars, funded primarily by a Texas oil company. Four such tests were carried out. The second nuclear stimulation project, Rulison, faced opposition in Colorado. Environmental groups filed suits opposing the project. In the Project Rulison test, a single nuclear device of forty kilotons was detonated Sept. 10, 1969, near the town of Rifle, Colorado. Engineers detonated two smaller thirty kiloton bombs in different areas, although these bombs received much less publicity.[2]

In 1971, around 5000 homeowners in Grand Junction, Colorado, were notified that their houses might be built on uranium tailings, which was given away as "fill-dirt."

[2] High Country News, He Felt The Earth Move, Chester Mcqueary, December 12, 1994
[3] New York Times, Dear Sir: Your House Is Built On Radioactive Uranium Waste, H. Peter Metzger, October 31, 1971

About the Author

S.M. Arthur grew up on a ranch in Colorado where she learned to love nature, wildlife and the West. She now resides in Denver with her husband and near her two grown daughters. She earned B.S. and M.A. degrees from the University of Colorado, and worked in the corporate world.

She enjoys nature, keeping up with environmental issues, books, travel, and writing about reading and reading about writing.

For more information: www.its-a-mystery-to-me.com

www.ingramcontent.com/pod-product-compliance
Lightning Source LLC
Chambersburg PA
CBHW071500110726
47908CB00003B/680